BODY
AND
SOUL

Praise for Andrew's previous books

Candescent Blooms (Salt Publishing)

"Marvellous"

– The Telegraph

The Greens (Snowbooks)

"An evocative, emotional read"

– Kaaron Warren

Frequencies of Existence (NewCon Press)

"Andrew Hook is an undisputed superstar of strange fiction"
– Neil Williamson

BODY AND SOUL

ANDREW HOOK

Elsewhen Press

CONTENTS

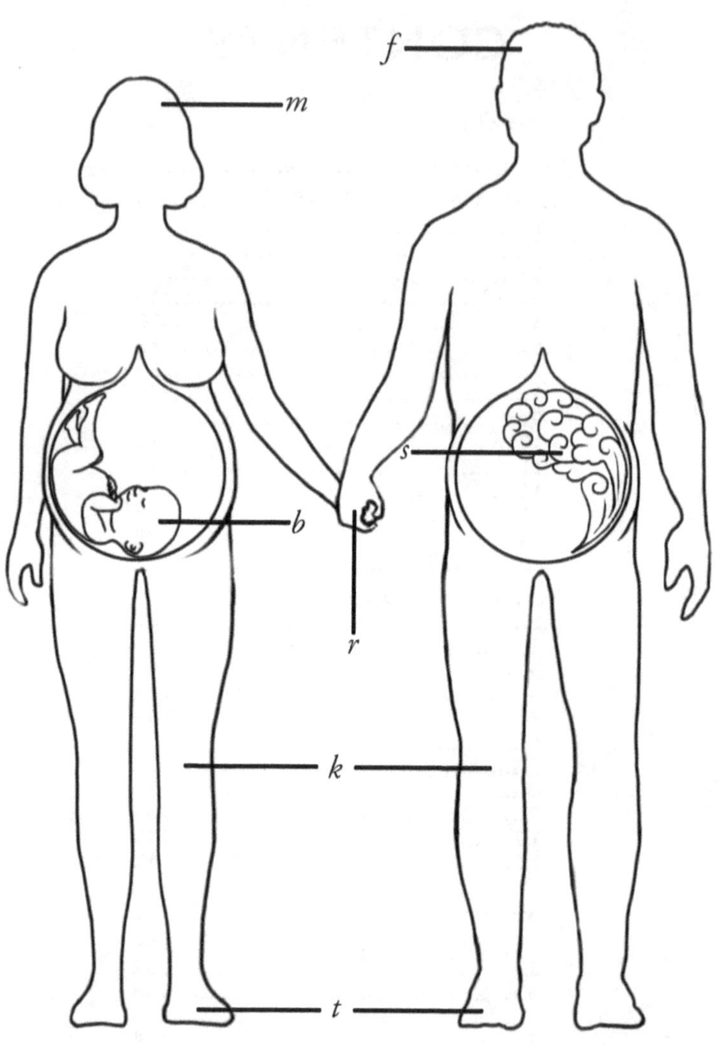

Found diagram with annotations, period unknown

For my late father, who gave me my soul.

vii

PROLOGUE

Calvin ran.

Stones kicked up by his rough sandals described arcs in his wake, as though symbols of speed. His right palm sweated where it clutched the hoe, the polished wood slipping in his hand and hindering his progress. Dry wind fluttered his clothing, accentuated tears. Inside his chest, something thundered; wanted out. It wasn't his heart, although that too was pounding: with exertion, trepidation, excitement.

The vegetable garden was some way from his shack. Too far, perhaps. He hoped Moss could forgive. As he crested a ridge it came into view, blotted the landscape. They had come to the shack some time ago, made it theirs; boarded the fallen sides with remnants of wood, salvaged some clear plastic that halted the rain whilst providing a view of the stars, divided the interior into three for eating, sleeping, and toileting.

It wasn't much. But they didn't need much. No one had much. No one he knew. Not much was there to be had.

He slipped on the moist moorland, his sandal going one way, his foot another. Something twisted in his ankle, a sharp pain ran faster than he did. He pushed on. Smoke from the dampened down fire, untended since the previous night, smudged sharply drawn clouds above their abode. He couldn't see Moss. Knew she must be inside. Hoped Dell was with her. Knew he had to be, too.

The pain in his ankle intensified the closer he reached the shack, as though some opposable force was pressing him away. He faltered, slipped again, cursed. The motion inside him heightened: a palpable feeling of presence. It spurred him. A final effort. *The* final effort. Nothing else was required and everything else was essential. Breath came ragged from his mouth in gasps that he could almost visualise. He dreaded to think he might see it.

Whatever pain circled his ankle he knew Moss was having it worse. Her swollen stomach had pressed hard for days, the interior movement fascinating yet alien. But something had to give. He hadn't known today was the day, still didn't know – but the spiralling inside his own body was an obvious indication of labour. And he had to be with Moss. Now. Right now. Or all would be lost.

The wind keened around his ears. He shut out the noise, didn't want to hear anything carried on the breeze. A pain in the side of his stomach began as a dull ache, then became stronger. Maybe a stitch, maybe not. There were only a few hundred yards to go. He could make it, he knew he could. Then suddenly he expanded, with both feet mid-air he floated; just for a tenth of a second, but as his foot touched ground again he knew it was over. Something exploded inside him, a wrenching suction of air. He dropped the hoe. Then his distended stomach abated, deflated; almost simultaneously he heard the cry of the baby, brought on that wind which now made his mouth dry.

He paused a short distance from the door of the shack, breathing heavily. Despair pricked like a triangle inside him, hurting his sides, his throat. He couldn't go further. He couldn't face Moss. He should never have gone to the garden this morning, he should have stayed and kept by her side.

The shack door swung open. Dell came into view, sweat running over her forehead, clutching a bundle in her arms. The midwife glanced up at him – her expression unreadable.

"You better go inside," she said, her voice hoarse. "You don't want to see this."

Calvin turned his face away. He didn't know what he felt: shame, rage, incompetence. But more than this, more than not wanting Dell to see how he felt, he didn't want to see the child; not even a half-glimpse. The pain was too great.

He nodded. Shuffled into the shack. In the bedroom Moss lay on one side, facing the wall. He opened his mouth but found no words for her.

The shack door closed behind him. The cries of the baby could be heard through the thin walls but then there was a sudden crack which shook one side of the building; silence. The faint residue of the soul inside him shifted out of his pores like wisps of smoke; a smoke mimicked as Dell stoked the remains of the fire, until the heat intensified, until it consumed.

Calvin dropped to his knees by the bed. Couldn't help but watch as the fleeting tendrils dispersed into air. Cracks in the walls sucked them into daylight. He breathed out – realised he had been holding his breath. Moss remained still, but Calvin's body began to shake with the sobbing. It would be some time, he knew, before they'd dare to try again.

CINNAMON KISSES

1

Calvin couldn't remember his birth, but this wasn't unusual. Not many could.

The settlement in which he was raised held fifteen families, ten children. On Heart, as far as Calvin knew, the extent of his settlement was common. Occasionally traders would visit. If the elders allowed, they would let them tell tales of their travels, the children initially rapt with attention although gradually becoming bored. Knowing what was beyond things you knew wasn't something that interested them: did it matter? What mattered was the family, community, the harvest. Things you could see.

Things that you couldn't see might well not exist.

Yet Calvin, apart from the other children, *did* find satisfaction in the stories. If not from the tales themselves, then from the tellers. Once, when they thought he was sleeping, Calvin overheard his parents wonder if he might become a traveller himself: spoken in whispers, not only to avoid him hearing but to extinguish the thought. Yet the whisper became a seed, sustained 'til it grew. So much so that when he sat amongst the other children, listening to stories, he became convinced he heard them differently. As though they spoke to him simply, alone.

In the group of ten only two remembered births: the amalgamation of body and soul. Calvin accepted this at face value, even if both Levi and Citroen were adept at extemporisation. Off the cuff remarks stuck, became truth. Both perceived their births as light – the coincidence of flesh and the ethereal – with a noise like two metallic saucepans banged together. Calvin wanted to hide his interest, yet his curiosity rubbernecked. Even if it didn't matter – considering he was already born – there was a thirst for knowledge that mirrored his feelings for the travelling tales.

This is Calvin on the cusp of maturity: curious, wilful, dedicated, observant, a worrier. Standing three quarters of a man tall, hair blond and wild, eyes blue. Fingernails bitten down to skin. Skin around fingernails close to misshapen lumps. Always a question. Always a *Why?*

There was commotion at the edge of the settlement. Calvin looked up from his sister's crib. A man was in view. There was rarely trouble, but the elders formed a barrier in front of the shacks, their arms linked in a sign of solidarity as well as strength. The man walked on. His hair was unkempt, his clothes ragged; but then no more so than most of them. Behind him he pulled a red plastic wagon on wheels. One of the wheels had broken, and the wagon lolled a rambling stance, threatening to spill contents that were piled haphazardly, a difficult column.

Calvin's eyes were drawn to the items on the wagon. Given the distance, their exact nature wasn't discernible; but he knew they were artefacts and that they would interest him. He also knew it was unlikely any of the elders would trade.

They weren't suspicious, but they were poor. The most they could spare in food and drink would be given to the traveller in exchange for a tale. Story or fact: these were interchangeable. From the settlement's point of view, anything outside the radius of a day's walk wouldn't affect them. Curiosity might be satisfied, but nothing more.

The elders broke ranks to allow the traveller into their midst. In the centre of the settlement a fire raged. Cloth sacks encircled the flames. The children were rounded up, beckoned to sit. Calvin caught Citroen's eye: yet the glimmer in his wasn't reflected. He sat on one of the sacks, watched the traveller negotiate the story. Items from the red wagon were spread out on the ground. None of their uses were apparent to Calvin, and in no time at all they were back on the wagon. Despite the elders lack of interest, Calvin's only increased. He wondered if he might catch the traveller later, at the outskirts of the settlement, before he went on his way.

The traveller was tall. Taller than most. When he grinned it was clear his teeth were rotten: black holes in a universal smile. His arms extended from a jacket that was too small for him, as though they had been wrenched through with unnecessary force. In contrast, the ends of his trousers splayed over his shoes, were scuffed and grubby with dirt. He turned once, arms extended, taking in all of the adults and each of the children.

"My name is Book," he said. "Let me tell you a story."

Calvin was once told that many moons ago the population of Heart had more than one given name.

Families were more personal than universal. Identifiers were required to establish a link. As the population thinned so did the need for identity. When your immediate parentage was known, you didn't need a tag for remembrance. Calvin believed there might be other reasons to blur families, but couldn't be sure. It was one of those things that he filed away for later, in a memory that couldn't be trusted.

So there was no surprise in him that the traveller was called Book, or that his name was apt as a teller of tales. Names were mutable, could be changed without question. If Book wanted to be Book then he simply had to call himself Book. Not that Calvin had seen many books: those that he'd witnessed were artefacts on trolleys, tied to the sides of ponies, or slung in a backpack over a traveller's shoulder. Picture books were curiosities. Those without pictures were unintelligible.

Stories, though; stories were key.

Book squatted to his knees, his jacket touching the ground. Calvin watched him through the flicker of the fire. His shoes were thick and black, suitable for long distance walking. Calvin knew that travellers were loners, they didn't crave community or desire association through numbers. One day, Calvin was sure, he would father a child; but travellers held no such interest. There were rumours that travellers couldn't harbour souls: either through their loneliness or a medical reason. Calvin tended to believe that they were travellers by choice, not ostracism. He knew his own tug for travel came from curiosity, and didn't find this at odds with the pull of evolution.

Book opened his hands, palms outward.

"One evening," he said, "I came across a settlement not five moons from here. The inhabitants were bad: like fruit left to rot. They had no sense of purpose, no desire for betterment. Females were shared by males were shared by females were shared by males. Their progeny, when it was birthed, could not be attributed to any set of parents. Consequently many of their babies were destroyed."

He stood suddenly, the story gaining stature. The fire appeared to leap with him.

"Many bones I saw; few graves. Those who weren't killed were bundled in corners of dilapidated shacks, excluded drafts, whilst smoky wisps cast chill air before they dissipated. The inhabitants of the settlement seemed to regard them only with curiosity. *There was no human connection.* Perhaps this is to be expected: certainly if the anomaly was not intended. However here, here my children, it was deliberate. A cautionary tale, perhaps. A tale of woe."

Book squatted again. He whispered: "Those babies who did receive body and soul will still be corrupted through the corruption of parentage. Believe me this: we have no right to upset the equilibrium."

Calvin considered the message, knew it was true. The immediacy of the bond between mother and father was intense. Once birthed, the child belonged to the community, but it was the responsibility of the birth parents to present the child whole. If the community were corrupted, then so was the continuity of existence. Calvin had heard enough stories about Heart to understand that this was a factor in The Fall. He didn't doubt the truth in the traveller's words. There was no need to.

One of the elders placed a hand on the traveller's shoulder. Food had been prepared. The story was brief, but essential. Within Calvin an urge erupted to see such a community; perhaps, youth on his side, he might convert them. Yet good intentions weren't the sole arbiter of that urge, and he knew it. A corkscrew twist ran through his insides: a frisson of fear and confrontation. There was more to the life that he lived: this was fact. He wanted to view it.

Citroen leant into him, his dark curly hair brushing Calvin's cheek: "Can you imagine our life if we had been born into that settlement?"

Calvin turned, disliking the proximity. "You can remember your birth, I can't. You know more than me what it would be like."

"Absence," Citroen mouthed. "Eternal nothingness."

"Death?"

"Yes, death. Whether the child lives or not the result would be the same. No understanding. No anything."

Calvin knew the score, had tried to get his head around the concept of a body without a soul, a soul without a body, but despite the stories, despite the education, it remained nebulous. Direct experience held the only capacity for understanding, yet in this instance direct experience held *no* understanding. No understanding *was* the experience.

These stories abounded within the few children in the settlement. All speculation. They were joined by other questions: why was it so cold at night, so warm during the day? How did the moon above them change shape? Why were animals constructed differently from people? Did they require the confluence of body and soul? What caused the colour of the ground to change, year in year out? How might snow fall as rain? Or rain as snow? How did water disappear when it didn't simply sink into soil, such as that which ran stagnant on the roof of their shack after heavy downpours.

Questions begat questions begat questions. Outside of the settlement, it appeared travellers might know the answers, yet outside of the stories the travellers were unapproachable.

"Get up." Calvin realised he was daydreaming. Citroen was pulling on his arm. "It's getting late." He pointed at the sun, the edge of which touched the surface of Heart. "The traveller is already asleep."

Calvin rose to his feet. He'd hoped to speak to Book before he turned in, however remote the possibility might have been.

Citroen ran ahead, caught up with Blink and a couple of the others. Only a handful of children were of their age: on the cusp of adulthood. Calvin's sister, Acorn, was newborn, and the youngest in the settlement. Both Blink and Citroen had siblings, also younger. Calvin wondered whether someday he might fall in love with one of them. The possibility was likely, although currently he paid them scant attention. Equally, wondering whether Blink or Citroen might one day have feelings for Acorn bordered disturbing. He pushed all such thoughts out of his mind, and entered the main communal shack where beets were bubbling: the rich odour of the soup permeating the air, the rich colour staining the wooden spoon purple.

Calvin avoided Blink and Citroen as he circled the inside of the shack. They had left a space for him on the bench but he preferred to mingle with the adults. His mother, Sky, was turning the beetroot, ladling it free from the broth and immersing it again, as though a brief gasp of air could improve the taste. Beside her, Queen and Zeal were pairing utensils and cutting bread. Calvin favoured the homely atmosphere: he knew no different, but could imagine it.

"How are you, Calvin?" His mother smiled. Stray blonde hairs escaped her fringe. Her eyes were bright yet tired; a forced sparkle. She ran a hand across her forehead, removed sweat but added a beet-coloured smear.

Calvin smiled back. "I'm fine," he said. Other than the storytelling he had spent the day gardening. Whilst the beets his mother currently cooked were not of his making, the following years would be. That and the other root vegetables he had managed to find purchase within the thick loam of the moorland soil.

He picked up a cloth from the table and wiped his mother's forehead: reverse parent. She ruffled his hair.

"Aren't you going to sit with your friends? Food is almost ready."

He nodded; but dawdled.

"Anything else?" She asked the question, but it was more of a statement; no expectation of an answer.

He shrugged. How could he tell her that he wanted to speak to the traveller, that a small part of him, like the root of a beet, wanted to extend and find nutrients in another part of the soil, of Heart? That he didn't understand his own longing, or the subtle push of dissatisfaction that crept around his body like a template. All life was here. A happy, fulfilled life. Yet...

Yet he turned and sat on the bench next to Citroen and Blink, waited patiently as the food bowls were assigned, ate heartily and hungrily, making small talk of the kind that was expected of him; whilst tempering his inquisitiveness towards the Traveller sound asleep but a few shacks away.

3

Night fell like a closed door.

Calvin crept out of the shack and lay on the ground looking at the stars. They spread above his head like dew-diamonds on a spider's web. In his mind's eye he made connections between them; joined the dots. He created shapes, animals, equipment. Sometimes it appeared that the night sky's pantheon mirrored life on Heart – a monochromatic representation symbolising objects but bereft of soul. Perhaps the sky and the earth needed to co-exist in order to create a serviceable reality. Perhaps he thought too much.

He closed his eyes, shut out the stars. Night cocooned him. Stillness held him. Inside the shack, Citroen's snoring had infiltrated a dream: One of the ponies had gotten loose and Calvin had chased it over the moors, extending his journey beyond his knowledge, until the pony had entered a darkened shack with a metal door. Inside the shack, the sides reverberated with the pony's hooves, as it attempted to force an exit. Calvin woke with the sound in his head, only to find Citroen's mouth by his ear, exhaling loudly.

Citroen had been only one reason why Calvin now found himself outside. The main reason was the pull of the sky. Two nights in seven Calvin would wake and sleep under stars. It wasn't something the elders approved of – dangers were muttered, although never elaborated. For Calvin, it was the expanse. Unlike in daylight, when the focus was on the land and tasks at hand, with the sky only important in terms of seasonable weather, at night it transmuted into a portal – expanding the mind together with the universe. Outside simply looked so much *bigger* at night. And in darkness so did the moorland itself, stretching out into the blackness that engulfed its permanence, obliterating the horizon that fenced them during day time.

If there was a third reason, it didn't manifest itself in Calvin's consciousness until it actually happened: a nearby door opened and Book emerged into the night, his dark clothing establishing his presence like soil under water. A shift in the air confirmed his existence and Calvin sat up, his heart racing in unexpected anticipation.

Book hadn't seen him. Calvin waited whilst he retrieved the wagon with its belongings, the unsteady contents cutting the still night with such a noise that he was surprised no one awakened. It wasn't unknown for travellers to leave overnight. They were private people who didn't appreciate awkward goodbyes even from temporary acquaintances. And with long journeys to travel, the mask of darkness bore sanctuary from harsh sunlight; although how they negotiated moorland in near blackness had often made Calvin curious as he looked at the stars.

Calvin edged his body towards the door of his shack, uncertain as to whether he should approach Book or allow him to leave in peace. But stealth didn't matter, Book had noticed him anyway. As he passed Calvin in shadow he paused for a moment. "Come with me boy." Then he continued on his way outside the settlement.

Calvin stood – took but one quick look around him – then followed.

At the boundary of the settlement, marked by a thin line of stone, Book turned to face him.

"I know why you're here lad. You have the call."

"The call?" Calvin rubbed his eyes. Up close, the traveller's breath was fetid.

"The call of the wild. Of the unclaimed spaces."

Calvin stepped back. "I'm not sure...I'm curious, that's all."

"That's right. Your curiosity is key. Heart will open to you. You just need to allow it."

"I'm not sure I understand."

Book swept his hand backwards towards the settlement. "You know there is more than this. Even if there is not much more. The choice is yours. Either shackle yourself to your current existence or expand your horizon." He lowered his voice. "I'm not saying one is better than the other; but then when I say the choice is yours I'm not being totally honest either."

"No?"

"No. Because the call is inside you. I saw it at the storytelling; I saw your mind create a tangent. You're thinking about this already, aren't you?"

Calvin shuffled his feet. Suddenly he seemed very young, inexperienced. Voicing his thoughts might make a mockery of them. Even if it seemed he found a sympathetic ear.

Book grew impatient. "Hurry boy, I should be off on my way."

"I *am* curious," Calvin repeated. "I have questioned my role in the settlement, queried the traveller's life. I just need more information, that's all. I need to know what's out there beyond stories, beyond snippets."

"Travellers can tell you all they want," Book said, his eyes wide, like a cat's suddenly exposed to the dark, "but the experience has to be yours."

He took a step forwards; now several steps beyond the boundary of the settlement.

"You see," Book said, "it's easy. One foot first, then the other, then repeat."

Calvin felt pressure in his chest, couldn't place it. No one he knew had left the settlement, and from the elders' anecdotes, no one they knew had returned. Even the travellers never came back twice.

"I'm not ready," he said. "I need to know what I might gain before I can choose what to leave."

Book scratched his cheek. "Maybe you'll never be ready, maybe you're too wise." He bent down and sifted through the objects on the wagon. "Here, take this."

The shape was ill-discernible in the dark. It fitted into Calvin's palm, smooth on one side, ridged on the other. Calvin turned it in his fingers: one end ran to a point, the other bowed like a pregnant cow. A hole ran through the middle in a corkscrew fashion. His fingertips appreciated the textures: it felt familiar yet alien simultaneously.

"What is it?"

Book winked. "That's for you to find out." He began to pull on the trolley in order to leave.

"Wait." Calvin stuffed the object into a pocket. "Can you tell me one story? Just for me. Before you go?"

"Why should I?"

"Because I'm asking, because I'm curious." Calvin paused. "Because I have the call."

Book thought for a moment. Nodded. "Deal." He looked about. The dark still held them. "A little further from here though. Too close for comfort."

Calvin held his breath. He had been further than the edge of the settlement, of course, but never in the dark. Then he nodded, and followed Book with his creaking trolley into the reaches of the night.

The darkness engulfed them as though they were descending into a Boggart hole – the night taking on the substance of mud, the openness somehow constricting. Calvin didn't expect to find any imps out on the moors, but like walking with closed eyes the disorientation he felt as they moved away from the camp was unnerving. Book didn't speak; only the trolley broke the silence. Within Calvin's pocket, the artefact's curves and ridges were tantalising. Calvin wondered if the object were a talisman. Some of the elders had mentioned such things; but his understanding was that any magical object had to be imbued with such magic by the magician himself. The object did not hold its own importance, but was assigned it. So unless Book practised the art – rumours of which abounded, but none were substantiated – it was simply an object that held an attraction.

At the point at which they had travelled sufficient distance that they could no longer discern the shacks against the night, Book halted. He beckoned for Calvin to sit. The ground was soft, slightly damp. Calvin knew he had been there before, but it was a different world in the dark. He considered this summarised his feelings towards travelling: experiencing new sights, sounds, people – outside of the comfort zone of familiarity.

Book opened his palms. "What kind of story do you require?"

Calvin hesitated. It was a good question. Heart was vast, their settlement was tiny. Surely all stories could only be like the stars above their heads: infinitesimal in the scheme of things. He wanted something more, something personal. Something, perhaps, that Book had not told before.

He made up his mind.

"Tell me the story of your life."

4

Book looked at Calvin curiously. With the darkness surrounding them it was difficult to discern his expression, but Calvin could guess it.

"All of it? We don't have time."

"No. Not all of it. You understand the parts I want to know."

"A forthright young man. I like it." Book steepled his fingers. "Until the approach of dawn," he said. "No longer."

Calvin smiled. "Then you're already wasting time."

Book shrugged. He pulled his jacket tight around him. Without the proximity of the shacks the ground had gotten colder. Calvin, being younger, didn't notice. Or perhaps it was the glow of the story that warmed him.

Book spoke: "Once I was like you. Uninformed, ill-informed, curious. I'm no longer curious, but I couldn't settle down even if I wanted to. Communities are close-knit. No one likes strangers. You may see me provided with fare for a story, you may see someone buy one of my artefacts, but what you won't see is friendship, acceptance. I'm regarded warily because of my curiosity. In Heart, it doesn't pay to be curious. Because if you are curious, you might discover things that you don't want to know.

"Yesterday evening I related the story of the depraved settlement. I saw you take in the details. You would want to go there, to see this for yourself, wouldn't you?"

Calvin considered this, nodded.

"That's not because you don't believe the story, but you can't just accept it either. You want to know for yourself. You want to see for yourself. Because you are called." Book paused. His breath could be discerned as a semi-transparent white smoke which temporarily coloured the night. "Your story is my story. I recognise you because I know you. Because I know me.

"Many moons ago I was living in a settlement much larger than yours. You see your wooden and metal shacks and you know no different, but there are other places, some colossal, even though the number of inhabitants might not be much greater. Some of these places have shacks that extend skywards almost as far as the eye can see. Those are uninhabited. Most are dangerous. I've witnessed these structures fall; become reclaimed by the earth. No one on Heart would choose to live there, but there they remain. The land leading into these places is hard, made of the same substance – or similar – as some of the shacks. Everything is overgrown. For what purpose these places existed can only be guessed at. But it is from here that most of these artefacts come."

Calvin eyed the wagon but other than the red dulled by the dark the contents weren't discernible. He had ideas: animal shapes fashioned out of wood or other material, books, glittering trinkets that could be wound around fingers, wrists, necks; questionable metallic objects, use unknown, of all sizes and angles; items which could be spun or turned by their own volition; mirrors, scraps of clothing, coloured stone. All useless: apart from those mirrors that still gave reflection. But those were rarely seen. Calvin knew an elder maintained one – had witnessed his own face in it – and in some respects their worth was only under that of food, family, and shelter. Even so, the worth didn't amount to much.

Book continued: "Something has been lost. This much is evident. The way of life was different once on Heart. Better or worse, who can tell? So much time has passed that there is no one around who knows any different. No one that I have met, that is certain. And does it matter? Not to the settlements that I visit. A moribund curiosity is the most I can stir. Apart from some individuals, such as yourself. And then I wonder if I'm doing more damage than good by telling my stories."

"Isn't it good," Calvin interjected, "to know and seek the truth?"

"Truth is, it's a fool's game, lad. For the truth of the past is unknowable. We might piece it together, but for what end? To learn from it? Whatever came before us seems unlikely to come again. I can't imagine how these structures were built; in some cases, what for."

"And yet you still travel, see these places, tell your stories."

"Because I have the calling. There is no choice."

"There is no choice within the settlement either," Calvin mused.

At this, Book raised his head that had been lowered for the latter part of the conversation. "This is correct. You were born, you will live, you will die. You remain within the settlement and all of those things will take place there. Outside of it is where the mystery lies."

"But at a cost."

"That's right. At a cost. It is unlikely you would return to your family even if you knew the way. You would be thrust out to survive purely on the goodwill of other settlements, and believe me, not all of them are kind, or even indifferent. And whilst you may see much, you might come to know nothing. Nothing except that you wished you had remained where you were. It's not much of a life, this life."

And yet, Calvin thought, *it is a life.*

Within the settlement, it was heretical to think of leaving. Yet... Calvin wished he could determine the extent of the 'something else' that sought to pull him away so he might make a proper decision. What he needed to hear from Book was an absolute positive or a corresponding negative. Something noncommittal only troubled him. Leaving now would literally be walking into the dark.

Book stood. Calvin thought he heard his legs creak.

"Can't sit still for long," Book said. "I'll seize up, take root."

"You haven't really told me the story of your life."

Book coughed, spat. "That's because the story would take *your* lifetime. You have your own life to experience, not mine. Don't live in the shadow of others."

The wheels on the wagon squeaked as he pulled on it. Calvin threw him a question, knew the answer.

"Take me with you."

Book turned, smiled. "Travellers travel alone."

Calvin shrugged. "Always?"

"Always."

"Children?"

Book hesitated. The line from the wagon went slack. "We won't meet again." He flicked his eyes towards the darkness. "We won't meet again whether you travel or not. But we might hear of each other. I ask you one thing: keep secrets secret."

"But I don't have any secrets."

"You do: but you don't know them yet. And you will: that's for sure."

Book began to walk. Calvin stood still, watched him go, then turned and made his unsteady way back to the settlement.

It was but a short time 'til sunrise. The air was still, birdless. Not yet did the corolla of the sun burn bright at the edge of the horizon, like the penumbra of a half-opened eye. The shacks reformed themselves as he approached them, reinforcing perspective. He mused over what Book had told him: had more questions than answers. Yet this was a decision that didn't need to be made any time soon. He was still a boy, after all.

He had almost reached the communal area when the shack door opened and Citroen slipped out. He wasn't startled when he saw Calvin, which indicated he knew he was already outside.

"What are you doing?"

Calvin stepped back. "Me? What are *you* doing?"

"Couldn't sleep. Woke and saw you were gone. I know you come out here sometimes. What do you do?"

Calvin shrugged, confident Citroen hadn't known he had been talking to Book. "I sit and think. Look at the stars." He paused. "What do you see when you look at the stars, Citroen."

Citroen didn't even glance upwards. "Shiny things."

Calvin chose his words carefully: "Would you say you saw possibility?"

"Possibility of what?" Citroen's brow furrowed. "I see what I see, shiny things."

I see what I see, thought Calvin. *And what I see is possibility.*

Citroen kicked at the ground under his feet, as though dislodging something from the sole of his shoe. "Listen," he said, "before we went to bed I heard the elders talking about the travellers. They might ban them from the settlement."

Something fluttered inside Calvin's chest. "What for?"

"Says they're a bad influence. The story told yesterday. Dark, wasn't it?"

Calvin nodded. Yes, it had been dark. Abused babies prevented from becoming whole, a society wracked with immorality; but also it had been necessary – to show other ways of living, and to impress how well their own settlement was doing.

Citroen continued: "The elders believe we don't need to be fed such things. *What we don't know, can't hurt us*, one of them said. Truth to be had there, don't you think?"

True there was truth, thought Calvin. Yet truth didn't make it right. "But," he said, "you enjoy the stories, don't you?"

Citroen nodded. "I do, usually. But then, they're also a distraction, aren't they. We could have done more work before nightfall yesterday; only to stop and hear something we didn't need to know. Sometimes the stories are more interesting than others, but we have to stop work before we know which one it will be. I agree with the elders, prevent any travellers from coming and our equilibrium is maintained."

"But we won't know anything," Calvin sputtered; yet even as he said the words he remembered that without travelling he knew nothing anyway.

"We won't know anything about what we don't need to know," Citroen said. "Seriously, other than an occasional interesting story, we're no better or worse from hearing them. And some of the younger children were disturbed by yesterday's story. I think that was why the elders cut it short."

Calvin cast his mind back. Remembered the hand on Book's shoulder. "Was there more?"

Citroen nodded. "Apparently. The elders didn't go into details. I could have asked, but I shouldn't have been listening." He grinned.

Within the grin Calvin saw all that he needed to know. There was a word he had previously heard elders mention in relation to travellers: non-conformist. It was a word he had mulled over many times; held it in his mouth like a pebble, felt it alien there. Within Citroen's smile he felt he finally understood the word. Citroen was conformist, but himself...? If Book were correct, he was non-conformist whether he wanted to be or not.

Rather than argue the point, futilely, he diverted the issue.

"How about the travellers themselves? The more that settlements turn them away, how will they trade, how will they eat?"

But this was a question Citroen had no interest in. He yawned, took a few deep breaths of the morning air, muttered something unintelligible under his breath, and then held the shack door open for both of them to return inside.

As Calvin entered the darkened shack, with all its familiar odours and sounds, he wondered what a homecoming would feel like.

5

"Hey, Calvin. Come here, come over here!"

Calvin looked up from the vegetable garden. The beets needed thinning and he was in the process of harvesting the tender greens that were ready for cooking. Beneath the ground, the red bulbs were bulging, hanging like water droplets in the soil. Several seasons had passed since Calvin had been given sole responsibility for the beets. His harvest of other crops – broccoli, cauliflower and carrots – had also been successful.

His mother had said he had *green fingers*, then laughed as he had looked at his purple-stained hands.

"Calvin!"

Levi was gesticulating at the edge of the settlement. Instinctively Calvin reached inside his pocket and ran his fingers over his artefact. It had been several seasons since Book had visited their community, and Citroen had been right when he had said that a ban on other travellers would take place. On the occasions that it happened, the elders met with them and politely sent them away. Calvin's mother, Sky, had led a couple of those parties, and she reassured him that they pressed bread and other foodstuffs into the traveller's hands before they left. When Calvin insisted on more details, she confirmed some of the travellers had mentioned they'd met similar reception elsewhere.

Storytelling seemed to be a dying art. In recompense, the elders had taken turns to tell stories to the children, but whilst these were never short of entertaining they were repetitive and restricted to anecdotes about the settlement. Calvin's thirst for knowledge, for new experiences, formed within his brain just as the beets formed within the earth. He kept this quiet, but whilst he respected his roots he also knew they needed to find new soil in order to satisfy him.

Levi wasn't a quiet boy. As Calvin rose to his feet he realised it wasn't just himself that Levi's call had raised. Citroen emerged from one of the shacks with a self-satisfied smile on his face. A couple of the elders, Mordent and Tetra, had also been alerted. Levi spotted this and amended his call accordingly: "Hey Calvin. Come and look at this weird-shaped stone."

Calvin ambled over to where Levi stood. The elders had returned to their work, and Citroen, after glancing over and finding nothing of interest, also returned inside the shack. But it wasn't a stone Levi had to show him. As Calvin expected, there was a faint shape on the horizon, visible only from the spot where Levi stood.

"I told you to try and keep this quiet," Calvin hissed.

Levi dug his hands in his pockets. "I wasn't thinking. Didn't think there was anyone about."

Calvin sighed. "Look around you, there's always someone about. We must inhabit the smallest piece of land on Heart!" He tried to keep the exasperation out of his voice. Levi wasn't the brightest kid on the settlement, but in some ways this meant he was one he could trust. Few questions asked. Unlike Citroen, who was becoming more and more adult every day. Calvin associated the word *adult* with the more steadfast elders in the group. Those who had pressurised the others into maintaining the no traveller policy. Calvin's parents, on the other hand, seemed more lenient. It was them he aligned himself with. And when he thought of himself as growing up, it was towards their role model that he aspired.

The figure in the distance was slow in coming forward.

It was getting late in the evening, twilight backlit the sky. Stars were becoming visible like tiny fires just lit. It wasn't dark enough for eyesight to fail, but sufficient to blur the figure like rubbed charcoal on stone. The ground out that way was uneven: hillocks rose and fell, spongy moss cushioned yet deceived, stones underfoot unbalanced and offset. But even so, despite these considerations, the figure seemed to be meandering much more unsteadily than necessary.

Calvin's heart beat faster. This was unusual. It was always exciting to see something unusual, and something unusual had been a long time coming. On two previous occasions Levi – whose work took him to the outer edge of the settlement – had motioned to Calvin that a traveller was in the distance, but on both of those instances the elders had spotted the figure before Calvin could do anything about it. His hopes to greet a traveller before they could be dissuaded by the elders had been dashed. Ideally, he wanted to catch someone now, just before nightfall. To slip away and have a conversation – to glean new information – before the chance was lost. It wasn't that Calvin wished to disobey the elders, but...

"Don't tell the others," he whispered. "And keep your head down."

Levi nodded. Calvin had promised to relay a story should he speak to the traveller. Levi missed the tales too, although he didn't have the calling as Calvin had. Ever since it had been mentioned to him by Book, Calvin realised he could see it in others. So far, other than his mother, Sky, there was no intimation. Levi was curious up to a point, but no further. His mother was simply curious in herself.

Calvin often harboured doubts that his mother was at one with the settlement. Despite the way that she fitted so well into what the elders required – a good cook, housekeeper, listener – Calvin felt that those values were imposed on her rather than being innate. Evidence, other than a sense of unease, was hard to come by, however. If anything, the way she seemed to understand him created a sense of affiliation more than the familial bond. Some nights, looking up at the stars, Calvin wondered if she were the cause of his wayward streak, unlike his father, Royce, who followed the settlement's policies verbatim whether they were disagreeable or not.

The running of the settlement was decided amongst the oldest of the elders, with any disputes carried or waived by a show of hands. It was a fair way to organise life, and Calvin rarely saw any disagreements. Yet sometimes, perhaps due to the pull of youth, he felt sidelined. This estrangement was also evident in Sky: the way she would sometimes tug at the ends of her hair as decisions were discussed, the laughter she exhibited when matters seemed too serious, the wink she occasionally gave Calvin when his father wasn't looking. None of this could be made explicit between them – but it was there, that special something, and it meant Calvin didn't quite feel so alone.

Entering the food hall it was Sky he approached now, darting looks from side to side which were evident to everyone but himself.

"What is it my lad?"

Sky was cutting thick loaves of bread, the serrated edge of the knife dragging through the soft interior in much the same way as Calvin had seen sheep sheared.

"Can you give me a bit?" Calvin was aware his face was flushed.

"Hungry are you?" A smile broke at the corners of Sky's mouth. "You know I'm not supposed to. Shouldn't have any favourites."

"Just a bit," wheedled Calvin, regressing to add pressure; widening his eyes.

Sky surreptitiously broke off a piece of bread and placed it in his pocket.

"Any soup?" Calvin asked.

She bent her head and whispered in his ear. "Now, how am I going to put soup in your pocket so you can take it out onto the moor?"

Calvin gasped. *She knew.* But now was not the time for whys and wherefores. He turned and ran through the shack to the main door. Some of the elders tutted in his wake, but whether that was because they frowned at him gaining the bread or because he was running he couldn't be sure. The only thing he could be sure of was that they didn't know what his mother knew: that he was going to meet the traveller.

Outside the sky had turned as purple as the beets. A wind had sprung up, and a fresh breeze that hinted at hail weaved through Calvin's clothing. The juxtaposition of rain-heavy clouds and the intimation of twilight ground the sky downwards, like a lid closing on a pan. As Calvin left the shack a low flying magpie, black and white like shadow and light, pulled a tangent at his head then settled on the roof of the shack. Normally Calvin would have stopped to regard it. He had an interest in all living things. But this evening other matters were pressing.

Levi remained at the outskirts of the settlement. He stood alone, and had begun to shiver, his thin tunic not suited to the weather, whereas Calvin's jacket that had proven too warm for much of the day was now of benefit to him.

"Is he still there?" Calvin asked, his breath coming hard and fast.

"You can't see him now," Levi said. "But he *is* still there. It's puzzling. He must be able to see the settlement from where he is, but he doesn't seem to make an effort to come to us."

"Maybe he's wary. Maybe he's waiting for dark."

Levi shrugged. Supposition wasn't his forte. "Do I have to wait out here? It's going to pour."

Calvin sighed. "Get back in the shack. If anyone asks where I am, tell them I'm tying back the vegetables because of the coming storm."

Levi nodded. Left.

Calvin watched him go. No one else was outside. At this time of day the settlement was tidying up, preparing for the meal. He scanned the horizon. In the distance a figure hovered, then seemed to fall again. It was all down to perspective. What was clear was that he was wandering. That didn't sit right with Levi's view that he might be waiting for nightfall. If Calvin had been the traveller, he felt he would rest rather than walk backwards and forwards, seemingly in circles.

Nevertheless, his desire for knowledge surpassed any concerns, and with it being evident that Sky in some way supported him, Calvin headed beyond the boundary of the settlement and across the moor.

6

The ground was soft underfoot, peaty. Small mounds and dips hampered his walk. The frisson of approaching rain ran waves of wind towards him, and he leant forwards into the breeze. Flecks of water spotted his jacket; a scouting party for the storm. It crossed his mind that he should be indoors, in the warmth of the shack surrounded by cooking smells and people he knew; it also crossed his mind that he should indeed be ensuring the runner bean and tomato and cucumber plants were securely tied as he had told Levi he was going to do. Neglecting his duties *and* disobeying the elders might invoke some kind of punishment – although whilst this had often been intimated, Calvin knew of no one who had been chastised within his settlement, even though travellers had sometimes told tales of other communities who were less lenient with dissenters. Indeed, there was one traveller who had told the story of how his expulsion from his settlement had occurred via breaking the rules. When pressed, however, he had been vague as to which rules he had infringed.

The figure shifted position. Calvin's view was distorted by his own movement, the uneven ground jogging his vision; but it was clear that there was no evident intent or purpose to the traveller's actions. Calvin furrowed his brow in thought. As the figure maintained in his view whilst the distance closed between them what was also clear was that Calvin must be visible to the traveller. Yet no recognition or any indication that he had been spotted was apparent. The figure moved a few steps, turned, repeated the motion. Briefly Calvin wondered whether the movements were part of a ritual, but rituals, like a talisman, were mostly unknown to him beyond hearsay and random stories. Nevertheless, he clutched his rough and smooth artefact in one hand; it gave him the bluff of surety that he was looking for, despite knowing it was a placebo.

When the figure was no more than twenty strides away the rain, which had been threatening since Calvin left the settlement, fell in sheets. Calvin began to turn up his collar, but it only had the effect of channelling the water down his neck. He dropped his head forwards, avoiding the cold sting of the droplets on his face. Underfoot, the moorland quickly soaked up the water and was soon saturated. Within seconds each step was a squelch. When Calvin looked up again, however, he saw the traveller had not desisted his shambling movements. For him, it was as though the rain wasn't happening.

Closer up, Calvin saw nothing to trouble him. The traveller was male – they almost always were – of a mid-age range. His trousers were ill-fitting, and hung over the ends of his feet; concealing them. Buttons were undone on his shirt and the short jacket he wore wouldn't have prevented much cold from the elements. His chest was a pale white, ribs showed. Yet nothing – even the realisation that he wore no shoes, as one step revealed toes under the trouser bottoms – was untoward as far as travellers were concerned. Without the protection of a settlement, travellers were left to their own devices. If there was one thing that battled Calvin's desire to head onto new experiences it was the lack of home comfort. Although, on reflection, perhaps not one thing, but one of a series of things including friendship, familiarity and family.

Even so, Calvin maintained a short distance between them when he called out, "Hey!"

His words felt swallowed by the rain, which pockmarked the ground like dimples and ran rivulets through the earth like the roots of a beet seeking nutrients in fast motion. "Hey!" he shouted again.

The traveller had turned his face away at Calvin's approach, but there had seemed nothing deliberate in that movement. Neither did his refusal to acknowledge Calvin appear any more deliberate. Calvin stood and waited, water pouring down his face, his eyelashes flicking away drops as he blinked rapidly, clearing his vision. Behind him, the settlement was quiet. Calvin imagined the rapidity of the rain pummelling the buildings' roofs, drumming nature's rhythm into the foundations. The elders would be organising teams to check out possible leaks, they wouldn't be concerned at Calvin's absence. Wouldn't even notice it. And Calvin could rely on Sky and Levi not to give him away.

The traveller wavered in a figure of eight movement, spun unsteadily – through accident rather than design – on the spot, then turned his face towards Calvin.

Calvin stared. The traveller stared.

But Calvin stared with eyes that *saw*, the traveller's eyes were blank; not blind, but without comprehension.

Calvin froze. The figure continued its pirouette. Calvin could only guess at the circumstances, but the likelihood was sure enough. This wasn't a regular traveller. This was someone who had been turned loose from their settlement. Someone who shouldn't be. Someone not permitted to exist. A body without a soul.

He took a step back. Rumours abounded about the nature of

these creatures, and having had no direct experience he could only trust those rumours: they were soul eaters, they craved human flesh, they could not be killed once they reached maturity, they passed their 'infection' by touch, should they find a disembodied soul they would mutate into demons, they were pathetic, they were lowlife, they were dead.

Any or all of these suppositions made Calvin recoil. This was a traveller without a tale to tell, without an experience to impart. Sure, if he were able to vocalise his life it would be an incredible one: a tale of damnation, expulsion, empty hope. But no such tale would be forthcoming, no redemption would be found. As Calvin took steps backwards, the rain filling in the gap between them, he was left to wonder how this entity had survived for so long. For he was also sure that without a companion, the creature couldn't survive in this environment left to its own devices. Unless, of course, there were no sureties. Without knowledge, mystery reigned.

Yet, simultaneously, as the creature's eyes stared without comprehension, Calvin realised that it hadn't even acknowledged his presence, on any level. Maintaining some distance, he tried to speak to it again.

"Hey!"

There was no response, other than that the creature turned away as part of its arc, and continued to meander about the moor.

"Can you hear me, or are you just ignoring me?"

The rain continued to fall like a plastic curtain, blurring the edges of the figure. Calvin noticed its feet sucked at the earth as it moved. There were no verbal responses.

"Do you not understand?" Calvin persisted. "There is someone here with you. I am here!"

Again, there were no indications the creature had even registered his presence. Calvin felt emboldened. Without understanding, there could be no danger. He stepped forwards. Then again. Despite his proximity the creature made no attempt to come nearer or to move away. Up close, his face was expressionless; but it *was* a face, a regular human face. Despite nothing obvious happening in the creature's brain, he existed all the same.

Calvin reached out, touched the hem of the creature's jacket. *No,* he thought to himself, *the traveller's jacket.* With a tug, he pulled the traveller towards him, to face him.

The traveller was marginally taller. Calvin looked up into his eyes. There was *something* there, after all. Nothing that Calvin might suggest was recognition of another human being, but the acceptance found in an animal, an understanding – however brief – that they were not alone in the world.

Rain beat off the traveller's forehead onto Calvin's. In the distance, the sky began to rumble; blackness quickly replacing the purple sunset as the storm took hold and the sun slipped below the horizon. Time was suddenly short. He had to return soon, or he would be missed. Places were set for meals, his would be empty. Sky or Levi couldn't cover for him for too long. He had intended to exchange a brief word with the traveller, to get a quick story or arrange to meet him after dark on the other side of the settlement, but this couldn't happen now. Even so, leaving the traveller alone on the moor wasn't an option either, was it? Now that he knew exactly who he was. It would be like leaving a child alone on the moor – or half a child.

Morality took hold of him. Contact with anyone outside of the settlement was rare and fleeting. The entire expanse of his experience and knowledge came from but a handful of individuals. Ethics were discussed as part of his instruction, but examples were limited to situations he was likely to encounter – or used as warnings as to what to expect should he stray from home. But here, out on the moor, with someone obviously unable to care for themselves, here his morality was stretched.

Yet he also knew, only too well, what would happen should he return with the traveller to the settlement. There was no option then, but to leave him.

It was then that Calvin remembered the bread in his pocket. He pulled it out and broke it in two, shielding it from the rain. With a growing sense of urgency, he pressed the bread into one of the traveller's hands.

Consumed! It was consumed almost before Calvin realised. The chunk moved from hand to face in seconds, the traveller chewing quickly, swallowing faster. He was starved, this was evident. Calvin passed over the remainder of the bread, watched him eat again. Now he wished he had brought more food with him, the bread wouldn't suffice and now the traveller had the taste of it Calvin could detect a palpable change in his demeanour.

"I've no more," he said. "All gone." He spread both hands wide in emphasis.

The traveller unexpectedly made a sudden movement, thrusting his hands into Calvin's pockets. When they emerged, Calvin realised it was clutching his artefact.

"No!"

The wind caught his word, whipped it around the traveller's head, and blew it back towards the settlement.

Calvin reached for the traveller's hand, grasped it and pulled the fingers free. The artefact dropped to the ground where Calvin retrieved it. Its off-white colour plain against the moss.

The traveller reached for Calvin again, again his face expressionless, but his body moving with more purpose than when it had first been viewed.

Calvin turned. He needed to get back to the settlement.

But, he saw, the settlement was coming to him.

A group of elders were leaning into the wind and the rain. They had already covered half the distance, and despite the weather Calvin could see clearly that they were armed with pieces of metal and branches of wood. Tetra led the group. Calvin scanned the others, but there were no women and therefore no Sky. His father, Royce, also seemed to be absent.

The wind and rain took their words and washed all sense out of them. But Calvin knew what they were saying all right: "Get back!"

He moved uncertainly away from the traveller. Morality forced him into making the decision not to compromise the creature. If he were too close, the elders might indeed think he had been attacked, whereas the marginal satiation of hunger had simply turned the traveller to crave more food.

Of course, Calvin also knew that the nature of the traveller would determine his reception, regardless of whether Calvin had seen him first or not.

If, at the back of Calvin's mind, there was a sense of approaching danger, there was no such premonition by the traveller. Having found no further food, he became docile again, and had returned to walking back and forth within a distance that was so precise it might have been determined by the invisible bars of a cage.

Indeed, morality aside, Calvin's thoughts now turned to himself and the punishment that might be meted out for breaking the rules of talking to a traveller.

This, however, was pushed aside as the group of elders reached the pair. Veins bulged on Tetra's neck through exertion against the storm. His face was red, his fingers gripped a downpipe that Calvin recognised came from the stores at the back of the main shack. His eyes were wild, wilder than Calvin had ever seen on anybody.

"Get away from him! Didn't you hear me lad."

"I am away from him."

"Not far enough."

Tetra pushed past Calvin, so that the group were standing between him and the traveller. "Declare yourself," he said.

"He won't respond," said Calvin. "He's…"

"I can see what he is," Tetra responded. "By law, I'm giving him the chance to confirm it." He turned to face the traveller, who was facing the opposite direction. "I said, declare yourself."

As Calvin expected, there was no awareness from the traveller that Tetra or the others existed. Or even that Calvin existed.

Tetra extended the drainpipe horizontally towards the traveller and nudged him, hard, in the side.

The traveller turned with the motion of it, as though he had been literally stirred, like washing in a tub of water, rather than with any comprehension that he had been poked.

"Declare yourself," Tetra demanded again. Without a response, he then looked to the other elders. "That's the third time," he said. "We can do no more than that."

The group exchanged glances. Calvin had a feeling he wasn't going to like what was about to happen. The traveller shouldn't be expelled. He was in no condition to look after himself. Although that still begged the question of how he had arrived.

Tetra turned to look at him. "You better get back to the settlement," he said. "We can deal with *you* later."

Calvin stood firm. "What's going to happen?"

"Nothing you want to know about." Tetra clenched his teeth. "You're too young for this. Too young to understand."

Calvin shrugged. "What's to understand? I know what he is, and he's harmless. We need to do something to help him."

Tetra couldn't help but laugh: a short bark that echoed uneasily amongst the rest of the group. "We can't do anything to help him. He's beyond help. Always will be and always was."

"But someone's helped him up to now," Calvin persisted, "otherwise he wouldn't be here. Would he? He should have been killed at birth."

"Ay, he should have been. And as you can see," Tetra poked the traveller with the downpipe without any reaction, "he's next to useless. What kind of existence is that? We take him in, we feed him, we get nothing back. You know our policy on travellers. Even those who bring stories bring little else. This one: well, this one has no purpose. It's only fair to do what should have been done long ago. He'll know nothing of it."

Calvin opened his mouth again, but realised he didn't have the arguments that might change Tetra's mind. He glanced at the other elders in the group. Rain dripped from their hair onto their faces like crocodile tears. But their heads were down, their feet nudging the moss. He knew they couldn't look him in the eye, but equally knew there was no question over their task. It was the way of the settlement. Calvin had been led to believe it was the way of all settlements, although the traveller's very existence and the story that Book had told several moons ago seemed now to disprove this.

"Go on. Get away with you." Tetra reiterated. "We can't be standing around here in the rain all night."

Calvin turned his back: on Tetra, on the traveller, and on the other elders. Even as he faced the settlement, he realised he was also turning his back on the settlement. He began to run, his feet slipping on the wet moss, squelching in the mud. Behind him, he heard the soft silent thuds as the men used their weapons to beat the traveller to death. Calvin fought the urge to turn around, to witness the spectacle. But he didn't need to have the atrocity cemented in his mind for the effect of it to harden. For some reason it was easier to kill a baby than it was a fully-grown man: he would have memories, experiences, possibly even expectations. Surely? But maybe this was the point. There had been nothing other than the need to eat which indicated the traveller had any understanding of his own existence. And perhaps it was the understanding of one's own existence that separated such entities from men. Yet if he were no more than animal, didn't animals also have the right to live? Again, Calvin knew animals only held that right when they were useful to the settlement: unless they were wild, like the birds and the vermin. The traveller couldn't survive wild, so perhaps Tetra was correct and they were doing the best they could for him. It was true that unless he could work they couldn't keep him in the settlement. Food had to be earned, it wasn't a right. Even the oldest members of the settlement sewed clothing or helped prepare food, with only the sick excused their duties.

Conflicting, confusing arguments ran around his head just as he ran from the elders.

There were no cries from the traveller, no yells from the elders. Just the soft soft thump of wood and metal on flesh, like a half-hearted beat of a drum.

7

Levi looked up as Calvin entered the food shack. His lower jaw dripped with broth from bread dipped into a meaty stew. He widened his eyes, indicating it hadn't been him who had informed the elders; then continued eating. Calvin imagined the warm chunks of meat descending down into Levi's stomach and he realised how hungry he had become.

Yet he ignored that hunger. Rather than walk over to the place set by him at table, adjacent to Citroen, he stepped forwards towards the cooking area, where Sky had watched him since he entered the shack.

So much was inside him – so much rage and confusion – that by the time he reached Sky the cocktail of emotions fell out of him through tears. Regardless of the eyes upon him, he leant within the folds of Sky's apron and sobbed whilst he felt her fingers run through his hair and her soothing words caressed his ears.

"It'll be alright, Calvin. Everything will be ok."

"It doesn't make any sense."

"Not much does. You'll understand this as you get older. You may even grow to accept it." Sky stepped back, looked into his eyes. "This is how life is on Heart. We look after our own, we have to. We couldn't survive if we did any less. And however much we might consider life is better in another settlement we have to realise that this is all we have. We have to protect what is ours."

Calvin remained quiet, his body shuddering with after-sobs. He knew what Sky said was true. But truth didn't equate to fairness.

She kept him close until his emotions subsided and hunger began to invade once again.

"Here." She pressed a bowl into his hands, his fingers warmed as soon as he touched it, rain water still dripping from his hair and face into the broth. "Now, go and eat. You'll need to get your strength up for when the elders talk to you later."

Her smile was half-hearted. Calvin wondered whether she regretted giving him the bread for the traveller, wondered why she had.

He took the bowl over to the table, then saw the gleeful expression on Citroen's face, and instead went beyond the others and leant with his back against the wall, eating the broth in peace.

It was good. Chunks of beef that had cooked for hours fell apart in his mouth upon contact, the juices warming and soothing him, the familiar taste grounding him in a reality where he hadn't been usurped, as though he were travelling into the past through his taste buds and the horrors of the world were still before him rather than behind him.

Yet there was still a feeling that nagged at him like meat stuck between his teeth or finding a jagged piece of bone amongst the broth. Tetra had seemed to understand his position – even if he hadn't taken kindly to it – and Calvin knew he was a good enough worker that expulsion from the settlement wasn't a question; however he knew and had known that he shouldn't have approached the traveller regardless of who he turned out to be. He imagined some kind of limitation would be imposed on him, and not only that, but his private thoughts had now been unveiled for all the settlement to see. Just the look on Citroen's face told him that he didn't want to remain there. But there was really nowhere else that he could go.

His perpetual dilemma about remaining in the settlement and accepting his fate against leaving and throwing himself to the wind was never more present. Again, he remembered Book's assertion that he had the calling. He felt that, for sure. But who exactly was calling him.

By the time Calvin had finished the broth and wiped around the inside of the bowl with his last remnant of bread everyone else had long finished. Only a handful had left the shack, however, and a circle of whispers ran around the tables barely audible above a hum from where Calvin was standing. He knew what they were waiting for: Tetra's return. Some to see what had become of the traveller, others to see what would become of Calvin.

There wasn't long to wait. As Calvin placed his bowl on the floor the door opened and Tetra and the other elders entered. They had left their weapons outside, and had also washed and changed their clothes. Tetra's eyes were drawn to Calvin's seat, and when finding it empty were directed by a nod from Citroen to where he now sat on the floor. His gaze washed over Calvin – neither annoyed nor aggrieved – before the group sat down at an empty table and waited whilst Sky spooned out the remnants of the stew.

Patiently, all present waited whilst the elders ate. Calvin noticed his father, Royce, slip into the room from the rear and place a hand on Sky's shoulder. She nodded, and glanced over to Calvin. His father's smile was forced, yet somehow reassuring. It had often been commented as to how similar Calvin looked to his father, as though he resembled him in miniature. Calvin was more than aware, however, of their difference in temperament.

With all the glances coming his way Calvin realised he was more conspicuous on the floor than he would have been at the table. But something solidifying inside him determined he wouldn't rise. Call it stubbornness, but he realised his wilful refusal to be part of the settlement was likely to ostracise him even if only for a short while. Nevertheless, he found he couldn't help but undermine his position in the community; perhaps he wanted out even more than he realised.

Tetra wiped his mouth with a crust of bread, then turned to face the room. "You might as well all hear this," he began, his voice low yet authoritative. "It wasn't a traveller on the moor, it was a body without a soul. We've disposed of it."

A ripple of whispers rang around the room again; soft susurrations of acquiescence.

"And if it wasn't for Calvin," Tetra continued, "we might not have seen him until it was too late. We owe it to Calvin that nothing serious has happened, despite the fact that he really shouldn't have approached the creature himself."

Calvin raised his head in astonishment. The first expression he caught was Citroen's: downturned. Over the past few seasons they had drifted further and further apart, their ideologies shifting. He sensed that Citroen had been hoping for Tetra to speak differently; an expectation that would have been matched by his own. Yet, he knew there was more to come, and whilst Tetra skirted over the details of the 'disposal' and encouraged the evening to continue as normal, Calvin couldn't help but feel that he wouldn't be going to bed any time soon.

As with the others, he queued with his empty bowl and took turns washing by the large sink. Placing the wet bowl with the others, Sky then took his arm and led him back into the corner of the room.

"Tetra wants to speak with you later," she said. "After it's quietened down. He doesn't want to make an example of you in front of the others. There's nothing to worry about, I'm sure."

Calvin shrugged. "You knew I was going," he said. He couldn't finish the sentence: *why didn't you stop me*, or *why did you allow it*. Sky knew the intention, however.

"Sometimes we want to understand things. Sometimes we need direct experience. I'm your teacher as well as your mother, Calvin. Even if your father occasionally considers my judgements ill-advised, I only want the best for you."

"The best for me here, within the settlement?"

"It's your place to be."

"But you want more for me too. I can tell that."

Sky sighed. She wiped her wet hands on a cloth. "Many of us want more than is available," she said. "But we can't achieve the impossible. Maybe I was like you once, and wanted to leave the settlement and make new discoveries. Maybe I didn't have the courage – or wasn't foolhardy enough – to do so. Your father suggests by encouraging you to experience new things I'm also encouraging that part of my self who didn't make those decisions in my youth. I don't know what to think about that."

"What do you want me to do?"

"If you have to ask me the question, Calvin, then you're not old enough to make the decision."

Calvin sighed. Their space in the corner darkened as Royce joined them. He was a tall, thin man; a full head-height taller than Sky. Like all men in the settlement his days were spent cultivating crops, tending their animals, or doing odd-jobs which always needed to be done. Unlike many of the other men, Royce did no butchering tasks. In the back of his mind, Calvin wondered if this was why he hadn't joined the party that had killed the traveller. Perhaps it was an unfair assumption; he decided to dismiss it.

Within the settlement, most of the men did the hands-on work, whereas the women held the cleaning and cooking roles, as well as looking after the children. For that reason – and for most of the children in the settlement – the mother's role dominated their upbringing. Or if not the mother herself, another woman. Calvin always felt that Royce was more involving than some of the other fathers, yet in other respects more distant. Often it seemed that the distance was deliberate.

"Calvin." Royce's voice pitched low, wanting no one to overhear. "Why did you go out onto the moor? You know it's forbidden. And to meet with a traveller..."

Calvin shrugged. "Curiosity. No more. No less."

Royce sighed. Calvin knew it was the end of the matter. Royce would defer to the other elders; understanding was lost to him.

The food hall was almost clear. Tetra remained sitting, and once he was satisfied they were sufficiently alone he beckoned Calvin over to sit opposite him. Sky also took a seat, adjacent; whilst Royce lingered in the corner.

"You understand our rules are put in place for your protection," Tetra began. "These creatures: we know little about them. And our ban on travellers – whether you like it or not – was discussed by all the elders for a specific purpose, to ensure the integrity of our settlement. I appreciate you could not tell the nature of the creature from the boundary of our settlement, and I understand your confusion with regards to his status. Few of us have seen a fully-grown body without soul before, although we have all heard the stories. Fact is, he had no right to exist and could have been a threat. We have to protect the settlement."

Calvin cleared his throat. "Am I a threat?"

"What?" Tetra sat back, his brow furrowed.

"Am I a threat? I could have led this *creature* back to the settlement. If I had my way, he would have eaten with us this evening. So, I ask, am I a threat to the integrity of this settlement?"

"Calvin..." Royce cautioned from the corner.

"No, Royce, let him go on," said Sky, her chin resting on her hands.

Tetra cleared his throat. "I covered for you earlier. I see no reason to admonish you in front of the rest of the settlement, particularly the children. That's not how we work here. But I would advise that you keep your head down and get on with your work. This is your first – and hopefully your only – aberration. And, as I said, whatever outcome you were looking for, you did bring this creature to our attention."

"But," Calvin persisted, "aren't you just treating me as you do the travellers? Banning me from telling my story, not indicating to the others what you really think of me, that's a form of censorship, isn't it? I thought our settlement was more open than that."

"We have to protect our interests. The children don't need to hear stories from beyond the settlement. You are a case in point. You've heard the stories and you want more. You could have jeopardised your life, and possibly that of others in the settlement. It might have escaped your attention, but there aren't many of us here. We need you. We need all of you. And we need to focus on the settlement itself. This has been agreed by all of the elders, Sky and Royce included." Tetra had kept his voice low until now, but with each word the pitch increased, involuntarily, through emphasis and exertion of the point.

"But we can learn from the travellers," persisted Calvin.

Tetra shook his head. "All we can learn is that there is somewhere other than here. That doesn't help anyone." He paused for breath. "Look, it could have been dangerous earlier. That's the bottom line. What we have here could be overturned at any moment. We know of illnesses in the past that have wiped out settlements on Heart. We just have to be careful."

"But we know of those illnesses from the travellers!" Calvin couldn't help raising his voice. "That's where we get our knowledge from. And if you dismiss it as rumour, then you do the same for the concerns you have over the creatures. That they are malevolent, or flesh-eaters, or some such. Whereas when we first get the opportunity to study one, when we can see up close there is no danger, we become so afraid that we kill it. How is that progress?"

Tetra sighed. "Do we need progress? Do we really need progress? Those travellers you are so proud of have told us stories of how progress crippled Heart. Is that what you want for us?"

Calvin shook his head. "I don't know what I want."

"Exactly." Tetra stood. "Let's leave it at this: you know the settlement's policy towards travellers and that's no contact. Don't do this again. Meantime, I've covered your back." He stuck out his hand. "We need you, Calvin. Don't disappoint us."

Calvin looked at Tetra's hand. The last time he paid attention to it, it had been gripping the downpipe. He held out his own hand, shook it.

Tetra moved his chair back from the table. "Glad that's sorted." He turned and left the food hall.

Royce walked over and placed a hand on Calvin's shoulder. "You held your ground, but you can see what's right. I'm proud of you."

Then he, too, left the food hall.

Calvin looked at Sky. The corners of her eyes held tears at the point of departure. His face was reflected in them.

"I'm proud of you too," she said. "When are you going to leave?"

8

Calvin struck out when the moon was full and the sky was cloudless. Bushes stuck out like wild haircuts; some moved in the dim light, revealing themselves as rabbits. On his back, Calvin had several days' supplies of food; as much as Sky dared to provide. Also within the bag were a change of clothes and some bulbs, seeds, and roots for planting should he find himself in a situation to do so.

The ground underfoot was still wet from the rain. The night carried the memory of moisture, and the evening was cool, as though invisible ice particles permeated the air. Calvin's steps squelched as he walked, his feet slipping from side to side on the uneven surface. He walked in the opposite direction to that which the traveller had come – he had no desire to see the creature's remains; was unsure if he would have been buried. In any event, it was Book he was following – although that trail was many moons cold. However, in Calvin's mind, it was a progression forwards, not backwards that he wanted to achieve.

With each step he walked, the vastness of the land before him and the distance from what had gone became ever obvious. He wondered at what point he would no longer be able to return. At the edge of the settlement? Once he was simply a dot on the horizon? At sun up, when it was realised he was missing? How many steps would it take for him to become exiled? He moved each foot forwards as a countdown for destiny. One of those steps would be the one which sealed him permanently from his settlement. Was it this one, or the next one, or one of the next fifty?

Isolation, estrangement, the surety of becoming outcast: none of these were favourable. Yet Calvin countered these with freedom, excitement, and knowledge. Despite any forebodings, as the settlement dwindled in size behind him, the vastness of the future became immense. He understood more than ever how Book embraced this existence, even if he hadn't seemed to take great pleasure in it. Understanding that he was the first in his settlement to take this journey also inspired him. He wondered what stories he might tell to those communities his path would cross. He wondered what stories might be told about him, in the settlement he had left behind.

Sky understood his need. But as she held him for the last time tears streamed down her face and her warm body racked with sobs. Calvin had hesitated before deciding not to mention his departure to Royce; however he had popped his head into the workshop where his father was working, bent over a piece of metal that glowed bright in the fire of the kiln, and told him he *was off*. He knew Royce would understand that phrase as *off to bed*, and he was given a nod in acknowledgement; but in his heart he knew his goodbyes were done.

He also considered mentioning his departure to Levi, but decided he didn't want to make him complicit in the act. As for Citroen, he hoped his absence might make him realise how shallow his views were becoming in relation to the status of the settlement; something that Calvin had come to regard as sterile and backwards-thinking, rather than a strong bond of community.

Yet community ran within him just as did the desire to leave. The evidence of this came when he lifted his sister, Acorn, above his head and rubbed his face into her tummy. She smiled and giggled, spoke his name in the peculiar way that she had, her pronouncement of all the syllables not yet exact. Then threw her arms around him with the usual hug, made all the more poignant by Calvin knowing it was their last. Unless she should travel – and even if she did – in all likelihood he would never see her again. When it came to his mother and father their status, looks, and demeanour would forever be fixed in his mind as adults, but with Acorn he knew she would change beyond recognition. Not seeing that change brought a lump into his throat.

"Be well," Sky had said. He had never been hugged so hard in his life.

"Am I a fool?" The words stuck in Calvin's throat; knowing the answer as he did.

"Man has always been a fool," she answered. "It is why the past exists as it does but it is also why the future will exist as it will. I support you. Go out and find new things. Your memory will always be here with me."

If Calvin wondered again why his mother seemed to understand his needs and didn't try to suppress them, then he didn't think about it for long. Dwelling on the past would negate his future. Taking his leave from Sky, he had set out into the night.

With only the darkness for company, memories of his departure ran round and around his head as he walked; replayed in the back of his mind, their accuracy blurring through repetition and amendment. Already he found himself struggling to picture what Acorn was wearing as he lifted her aloft, how her giggle sounded, how exactly she vocalised his name. And memories of Royce in the workshop were patch-worked from previous encounters, the specifics streamlined in his memory as to how he imagined they had said goodbye. Even his memories of Sky were fading, just as the night sky itself segued into daytime and then the pattern repeated until distinctions between different days and nights could no longer be made.

Maybe this would be the focus of his first story, he mused, when he was invited into another settlement. How travelling unravelled you.

He walked for some time, until his settlement was lost in the past.

It became so quiet that he could only hear his own breathing.

Night coloured the sky. Shades of darkness fluctuated. Calvin found himself growing weary. Not only with the effort of walking in the dark over uneven ground, but with the mantle of emotion that he carried. When he felt that the moon was at its highest point in the sky, he headed towards the silhouette of some trees on the horizon and using his bag for a pillow lay down to sleep.

Dreams invaded his mind.

He was lying on his back, spread-eagled, pressed against the earth as the world spun ever faster; a force pinning him to the ground as the stars blurred and then dominated the sky in an ever-increasing whiteness.

The scene changed. He was looking through a piece of dirty glass towards some autumnal trees. The underbrush a pale green, the tops of the leaves golden yellow and in some instances pinky-red. Looking hard, Calvin could make out the shape of a face amongst the redder leaves – the brunt of forehead, a gap for an eye, the elongation of both a chin and a snout. The harder he gazed the more vivid the face became; then a breeze blew the shape sideways, distorted it, turned the face towards him. He shuddered, almost awoke from the dream.

Finally he was falling, the ground opened underneath like two halves of an egg: his body the white, the yolk his soul. As he poured into hollow earth, the white and the yolk pulled to separate, their varying viscosity at odds which each other, until, as it appeared he was descending into a point, into a cone, he reached an area of absolute blackness and could not tell whether he was whole or broken, intact or dissolute.

When morning came – pale white clouds against a pale white sky – Calvin awoke with cold inhabiting his bones; stiff, goose-bumped, and fearful.

Whereas the night had cocooned him against the expanse of the moor, daylight revealed its extent entirely. Gorse bushes and scrub decorated the landscape as far as the eye could see, their colours an amalgamation of his dream: green, golden, and red. White rocks peppered the surface, half-buried and speckled with moss. Stubby trees grasped skywards, all angles and points. Whilst it wasn't barren – signs of life simply subdued due to the season – it was hardly hospitable either.

Calvin dug into his bag and pulled out some bread, which he soaked into the oily residue of broth held in a plastic container. The taste seeped into his mouth, the cold broth heartening on an empty stomach. Corners of the bread were already hardening, however, and Calvin realised that as a traveller the continuous hunt for food would be one of his main daily tasks. How far was it between settlements? This was a question he had never raised with Book or any of the other travellers who had passed through their community. And whilst his own settlement had been comfortably self-sufficient, there had been occasions when food shortages occurred and he was well aware of the subsequent hunger and associated health problems. These could only be magnified out here on the moor.

He rose. Shook out the stiffness in his body. When he urinated the colour was as golden as the leaves and keen in odour. In the daylight, the direction he had come from looked as much as the direction he was going, but he wasn't lost. If there might be a sense to the word 'lost' when he had no place in particular to be.

Lost, the word played in his mind. Usually it was associated with objects rather than people: this was the most common phrasing in the settlement. Occasionally it related to their livestock. Only twice had Calvin heard it associated with people. Once when Citroen's sister had gone missing; through the natural wanderings of a three year old. And once when an elder named Bosch had left the settlement and had not returned. Bosch had been permanently lost; reason unknown.

Rumours ran rife: he had fallen and been incapacitated, he had been attacked by a body, he had left to become a traveller, he was ill and hadn't wanted to infect the settlement, he was collecting the loose livestock and wandered too far to return home. None of the rumours were satisfactory. No one left the settlement to search for him. His absence put down as *lost*.

Calvin wondered whether he was classed as lost from the point of view of the settlement, despite himself knowing where he was.

Another word: *settlement*. Or perhaps more precisely, two words:

the settlement. Calvin considered how long it might be before those words in relation to his home lost their meaning. And connected to the musings he had the previous evening, in addition to the way in which the faces of those familiar to him were gradually fading away, he wondered how soon his internalised map of the settlement would disappear. For now, the fixidity of the buildings, the narrow pathways, the vegetable patch, were more embedded in memory than the shifting expressions of the people. But surely, as he saw more and more places, the interstices between the old and the new would blur, until they all became disparate, or alternatively they all became one.

Packing everything in his bag and slinging it over his back he realised that he tended to think too much. Thinking, in fact, had brought him here this morning: in the middle of nowhere with only somewhere to go.

He began walking.

The day warmed as the sun rose. Wisps of mist steamed off the ground as the earth dried. The moor was familiar yet unfamiliar, different yet the same. Each step hardened Calvin's resolve to see new things. Not that there was any question of returning. The horizon curved ahead of him, as though he were walking on the treadmill that drew water from the ground back home and as if he were turning the distance towards him whilst remaining static underfoot. The vastness of his surroundings played tricks with perception. Objects that seemed close, turned out to be further away than he had thought. It was a full day before he stopped to rest, his feet and ankles aching with the constant pressure of his journey, his stomach aching in anticipation of the food that he had saved. In that time, whilst he had covered quite some distance, he had seen nothing spectacular or any signs of life. He wondered whether it might be possible to never see another person again; only birds and rabbits assuaged his increasing fear.

On the second sun-up the going was harder, the emptiness in his stomach more prolonged, the blisters on his feet more prominent, the excitement in his heart less sustained.

A pattern developed over succeeding days, a rotisserie reverie created upon waking: stand, stretch, eat, walk, sit, gaze, walk, eat, sleep. All interspersed with imaginings and musings that tended towards the unreal the further he was distanced from the settlement. It was as though reality had been tethered there, and was now unspooling like a dropped ball of wool. Calvin knew through the repetition of tasks he was anchoring himself as closely as possibly to reality, just as the lack of food and water threatened to pull him towards fantasy. Determination kept him forwards, through the cycle of day and night, sun and moon; until finally, at a distance and time imprecise to him, he came upon the cross.

He had seen it in the distance, on a ridge. Initially, through eyes so tired they were little more than slits, he believed it was a person, another traveller. If he had had the strength he would have waved his arms above his head, shouted. Yet his cracked lips dissuaded his voice, his dry throat suffocated the cry. Once nearer, the *body* resolved itself into the cross, the *head* transformed into a circle. Calvin had never seen anything like it before, yet he knew what it meant to him. Life. It meant there was a sign of life. Of habitation.

He removed his bag, which — whilst becoming lighter as his supplies dwindled — had recently seemed much heavier, and rested on the ground with his back against the structure. It was made of stone, situated on a hillock overlooking a dip in the landscape. Lichen decorated abstract patterns on the surface, weather had worn the angles smooth, pockmarked the façade. Calvin reached into his bag, pulled out the final piece of bread and attempted to soak it with the vestiges of broth juice to no avail. It was hard in his mouth, the sharp edges of the bread cutting his lips, causing them to bleed. Calvin grimaced, swallowed the bread with the blood, licked the residue from his fingers, then stood again to regard the cross.

The base was embedded in the earth. The tallest part of the cross was that which rose from the ground, whilst the sides and top were equal in length. Each side broadened towards its end, in the intimation of a fan. The four points of the cross met in a circle; a hub. Extended from the cross, a larger circle linked the middle of each of the arms. Calvin drew a comparison with a four-spoked wheel where the spokes extended beyond the wheel itself. In any event, it was clearly man-made. Symbols were etched onto the structure — not those which he had seen in books, but curlicues, patterns. He wondered if they held any importance.

Considering the object as an artefact made him remember the gift he had received from Book. He removed it from his pocket. The rougher outside, white and bright, contrasted with the smooth pale pink interior. As had become habit, he ran his finger over the sheen, wondered whether repeated movements by other fingers had erased something similar to the exterior roughness. The object comforted, had become a talisman to him during the colder nights and the hungry days. There was a patina to the sheen that recalled puddled rainwater. Calvin returned it to his pocket, paid his attention again to the cross.

It was then, through one of the loops of the circle, that he saw the wisp of smoke.

His heart thudded loudly. He could almost feel his blood coursing through his veins. The smoke didn't necessarily indicate a settlements or another traveller, yet the possibility of nature's own fire seemed unlikely considering the wet conditions. This wasn't the height of summer, after all: the moss and bracken weren't kindle dry.

He stood. The cross was the same height as himself. Using it as a shield he followed the line of smoke from sky to ground. There was a ridge obscuring the source. Hunger drove Calvin towards it. For good or ill he needed company; had to restock his supplies.

His strength wasn't sufficient to break into a run, but he did so in his mind; his imagination in overdrive. He pictured a small wooden settlement, tiny streets, the tantalising odour of freshly baked bread, children running aimlessly dragging kites in the mud. He imagined a traveller's welcome – hopefully more favourable than his own settlement had been giving. Hot food, maybe a warm bed. And as he imagined this, all he had lost impinged on his consciousness. All security was now denied. And it had only been a matter of days.

The blisters on his feet felt like broken glass. Calvin spurred himself on with such an intensity of spirit that he wondered if he truly believed in the smoke, or whether he felt it to be imaginary. Or worse, that the settlement was fixed on Heart for a limited period of time, and if he didn't make it soon enough it would disappear in a puff of the very same smoke and be replaced by the barren landscape.

Each of these cumulative reveries gained substance as he approached the ridge, vying for position in his mind. He knew they were born out of hunger, necessity, but it made them no less real all the same.

Finally the settlement was revealed. It was smaller than Calvin had imagined, possibly smaller than he had hoped. A clutch of buildings were held in the grasp of a small valley, like a toy town held in the palm of a hand. Flanking the settlement, two small fields held sheep and goats. Behind it, a vegetable garden sprawled backwards onto the heath. There couldn't be more than twenty or thirty inhabitants, Calvin thought, judging by the size of the buildings. Being the first settlement he would ever visit as a traveller he was unsure whether its size was for or against him: food would be limited, yet there was less chance of animosity. Whichever might be the case, there was no question of turning back.

Two figures emerged from one of the buildings as he approached. He raised an arm and it was immediately reciprocated. Friendly, then. The remainder of his steps were lighter, the pain in his feet less intense. The closer he came to the settlement, the greater the number of people to greet him. When he was within distance to determine their expressions, however, he noted they were tinged with disappointment. Brows furrowed, eyes hooded.

Calvin realised he was unsure of protocol. Having never been with the party of elders who had greeted a traveller he wasn't sure what he was supposed to say. In the event, someone spoke for him.

"He's just a boy. A lad."

The woman had large breasts, her arms folded across her chest accentuated them. An off-white apron indicated she had been cooking before he arrived. His stomach ached from hunger, and his heart ached from loss – there was something about the woman that reminded him of Sky.

"Speak, traveller." A man had stepped forwards; his beard appeared woven. Wisps of grey flourished at the ends, like curling smoke from the fire. He didn't look unfriendly, but Calvin froze. "Speak," he repeated, "if you are a traveller you must have a tale."

Words accumulated at the back of Calvin's throat. He imagined them as children, pushing and cajoling each other to the front. Eventually his head cleared, he ran his dry tongue over his cracked lips: "Of course, a story," he found himself saying. "But first of all, if you don't mind, a glass of water."

9

Calvin sat cross-legged in front of the fire. Five children semi-circled him; faces dirty, clothes torn. All were expectant. Behind them, adults formed a wider semi-circle; all standing. Their frowns were replaced by curiosity. Evidently none had seen a traveller so young, and now Calvin thought it through he realised he hadn't also. Yet the welcome had become warm, and in addition to the water which had soothed his cracked lips, he had also been fed a hearty slab of mutton and three slices of warm bread. The large breasted woman had also tended to his feet, tutting softly as she did so.

"My oh my. You're a poor thing, a poor looking thing."

Calvin had winced as she first wet then dried his soles, anointed them with the sap from a plant he didn't recognise, and then bound them with fabric before replacing his shoes.

"A poor looking thing, to be sure."

She looked up at him; concern etched her face. He wanted to look away, but knew it would seem rude given the hospitality. When he smiled, his lips hurt.

"Did you choose this, or were you cast out?" she whispered.

"Choice!" Calvin replied a little too forcibly. It closed the conversation down and she heaved herself to her feet and left him with the mutton, bread, and water to eat in peace.

Now, with the expectant faces turned towards him, Calvin knew he had to pay for the meal. And once it was over, a soft bed would beckon until night fell and he would find himself on his way again: in a pattern to be repeated for the remainder of his days.

He racked his brains. There was but one story he could tell. The only story that was beyond the realm of ordinary experience. The story of the soul-less traveller.

He spoke swiftly, ensuring brevity to the tale; giving only as much as he needed, leaving questions unanswered but not unsatisfied. He narrated third person, didn't make it Calvin-specific. There was no need for the assembled company to become aware of how he began travelling – that wasn't part of the deal. What was clear as he told his tale, however, was that he gained as much as he gave. It was evident that this settlement had not experienced something similar, and he realised this knowledge would become useful the next time he told the story.

One boy seemed more inquisitive than the rest – Calvin wondered if he would have the *calling* as he grew older. If it could be that noticeable.

"What happened to the body?" His hand had shot up as soon as Calvin finished the tale.

"I'm not sure," he answered truthfully. "I imagine they buried it on the moor."

"But how would they know it was dead? If it has no soul?"

"A body isn't just a body. It can move. It has life. It just seems to have no understanding of its surroundings, no sensation of self." Calvin paused. "It can be killed."

The boy nodded, thoughtfully. Calvin looked around for other raised hands, but there were none.

"My story is told," he concluded.

He stood. The semi-circle of adults dispersed with only the elder who had addressed him and the large breasted woman remaining. They shooed the children away from the fire. Darkness had crept up on them, the fire maintaining the semblance of day in its immediate vicinity. Perhaps because of his full belly, Calvin felt extraordinarily tired. The temptation to remain in the settlement was intense: there was a strong sensation of home. In the half-light, the elders who stood before him closely resembled those he had left. Calvin wondered how many pocket settlements on Heart were similar, how many were populated by familiar faces. Not for the first time he wondered why he had left simply to look for what he had lost.

"Interesting story," the bearded man said. "Is it true?"

"All traveller's stories are true," Calvin replied; simultaneously doubting the veracity of the statement.

The man nodded. "We had one here," he said. Calvin noticed the woman nudge him, a frown crossing her face like a cloud over the moon. "Not of that age, of course, but recently. We kept it for a while, a curiosity."

Calvin felt his mouth dry. "Aren't they supposed to be killed at birth?"

"Ay." The man shuffled his feet.

"Here," the woman held out her hand, "I'll show you where you're to sleep. There's a little bit of mutton left, but you'll have to be on your way before sun up."

The bearded man glanced at her, then nodded again. "Just trying to get information, Mercedes. Nothing wrong with that. We won't see this lad after tomorrow."

"We've filled his belly, we don't need to fill his head," she said. Her hand still extended, waited for Calvin to take it. "And he is just a lad, new to this life. He won't have many stories. We don't want to be giving him more."

Calvin took Mercedes' hand to end the approaching argument. Although his interest had been piqued, he was too tired for discussion. And if he had to leave during the night, then he wanted to make sure he had rested properly. Anomalies of nature could be considered another day.

The bearded man relented and stepped back, allowed Mercedes to lead Calvin away. The bed of straw he found was warm, if not soft. Smoke from the fire had stung his eyes and they felt gritty as he closed them. Nevertheless, within moments he was asleep.

Dreams ran songs through his head. Sky and Mercedes folded into each other, were overlaid, became one. Fecund earth mothers lying in the dirt: their breasts hillocks, their mons mounds. Babies levitated out of their insides, twisting like souls yet as tangible as bodies. They formed a circle in the air, hands holding hands holding hands. Their faces expressionless, their eyes blank.

Calvin woke shivering, realised a hand was on his shoulder. *Wake up*, he heard, repeated. He struggled his eyes against the dark, saw half a face and nearly yelled before the black of the beard separated in his vision from the black of the night and he realised he was being woken by the elder.

The elder raised a finger to his lips. He stood from his crouching position over the bed and waited for Calvin to join him. Then they made their way outside. The moon was obscured by cloud and the night air was warm. Visibility, however, was murderous.

"I want to show you something before you go," the elder said.

Calvin followed him between the buildings, his feet sliding on mud, his eyes adjusting to the delineations between objects and the spaces between them. Within moments the freshness of the air was replaced by animal smells: wet wool, faeces, musk. The elder stopped at a wooden building, pushed a sliding door to one side and immediately the smell intensified. He beckoned Calvin to enter.

Within the darkness of the barn it was almost impossible to see anything at all. The way was even slippier than outside, and Calvin found himself nudged by the sheep and goats as their scent invaded his nostrils. The elder had hold of his elbow, directed him to a corner of the barn.

"This is between us," he said. "Not all the inhabitants here are aware of this. But we decided to keep it. For curiosity, as I said."

Calvin swallowed. The smell within the barn was making him nauseous, the anticipation of what he might be about to see even more so.

"You've seen one, you see," the man continued. "Not many have."

"It was a story. A story I told."

"It was your story, as plain as the nose on your face."

Calvin wondered how plain his nose might appear in the half-light within the barn. They were approaching the corner of it now, darkness closing in further as the physical space lessened.

"Here," the elder said.

Calvin squinted. It was impossible to see anything. It was hot in the barn, the bleats of the animals accentuating the warmth – the homeliness – despite the stink. Gradually a shape formed within the bars of a metal pen. A baby; no, a child. Curled up. Possibly no more than fifty new moons old.

"Touch it," the elder said. "Touch it," he goaded; his voice urgent.

Mindful of the bag of food and water the elder was carrying on his behalf, Calvin leant over the pen and prodded the child. Its skin felt human, just as it should do, but there was no response. Nothing.

"It just lies there," the elder whispered. "If it gets hungry, it rolls onto its side, back and forth. But it doesn't speak. No sound."

Words were ragged in Calvin's throat. He had so many questions. It suddenly struck him that this was why he was travelling. To see such sights, however unpalatable. The elder obviously didn't care if the body were distressed, lying in the muck with the animals. But then why should he? Civilisation dictated that bodies without souls should be killed upon birth. With that as a starting point, without compassion, then any dealings with them if they survived could only be considered from that viewpoint. The more important question was what was it within Calvin's mind that found the situation disagreeable. For disagreeable he certainly found it.

"Is it like the one you saw?" The intensity in the elder's voice increased its pitch.

"Mine was older. Far older."

"So, they can survive. To what purpose, however."

"To no purpose," Calvin said, almost forcing the words out between his teeth. "They evidently have no purpose."

"Ay. You're right there. No purpose."

Calvin could feel the man's breath hot on the back of his neck. "Come on then, lad. Time for you to be going."

Calvin turned and left the body behind, the way clearer as the door was illuminated by moonlight now the cloud had passed. Yet, Calvin knew, it would always be dark in the barn for the body.

Even so, as his conscience weighed heavy, he knew there were no other options. The body couldn't function within the parameters of the settlement. It was humane to kill it at birth. Not to do so only prolonged a meaningless existence.

Yet – he couldn't help but continue musing – was the body even aware of its meaningless existence? Because if it wasn't, then alive or dead it made no difference. It was the soul that animated the body: a soul that would have dissipated once the connection hadn't been made. As for where the soul went, no one seemed to know. It was nebulous, insubstantial, ephemeral, intangible. The beauty of it was that it held the magic of life. Without it the body was no more than meat.

Once outside the barn the elder pressed the bag of food into Calvin's hands. "Go now," he said, suddenly eager to get rid of him. He pointed out into the darkness. "Follow the ridge of the sheep pen. You'll find the next settlement three days hence, assuming the travellers before you were telling the truth."

Calvin thanked him for the supplies, even as his feet began to ache. He turned back before he left, "Have you heard of a traveller named Book? I'm looking for him. He might have passed through here many moons ago."

The elder's shrug was barely perceptible in the dark. "We don't remember the names of the likes of you." His voice was harsh, disinterested. "Get going now, lad. There's nothing further for you here."

Calvin slung the bag over his shoulder and headed in the direction the elder had pointed. Welcomed, then outcast, welcomed then outcast: his future was mapped out as surely as the way ahead was undetermined.

10

And so it went. The settlements stacked up, one after the other, over ensuing moon/sun cycles. Moorland replaced moorland replaced moorland. The soles of Calvin's feet hardened as he adapted to his new life, providing an extra strip of leather besides his shoe. He became used to ensuring his resources lasted: eating slowly and spreading his meals throughout the entire day, harvesting rainwater and dew, utilising nature's crop whenever he was able.

It was not an easy life, but perhaps less hard than he had imagined. Life in the settlement had been a daily toil of tending the vegetables, cleaning, repairing, assisting. Whilst he missed aspects of that life, he knew in his heart how travelling excited him. Despite the repetition of the landscape – and in many ways, of the settlements – there was always something new to see, always another experience and another tale to be told.

Twice he had been refused entry to a settlement. On one occasion because he had been told they were diseased. They stressed it was for his own protection, and had thrown some bread and beets over a wooden fence before he then went on his way. The second time, his refusal had been gruff, then overturned when they saw his age. For the moment, his young years were on his side. He was sure the treatment he received inside the settlements was in excess of that afforded to the regular travellers. The women, in particular, were effusive over his needs.

During this time, however, he had yet to see any other travellers. Neither at a settlement itself, or even at a distance. It caused him to wonder whether they were necessarily separated by time and space – if there were some cosmic force which ensured they never met, causing their rations to be distributed fairly, for stories to always be distinct. He often mused thus when on his back on evenings spent alone, watching the night sky and the pinpricks of light, which were always there but never touched. And despite the temporary camaraderie within each settlement and his memories of home, it was at these moments – under the night sky – where he was at his happiest. Where, in fact, he felt more complete. Where he felt truly home.

This affinity to the sky didn't surprise him. Very occasionally there was movement above, a tiny light would slowly traverse the blackness before winking out. He saw himself as one of those lights, moving between the settlements, exploring the length and breadth of Heart.

Not that he knew the extent of Heart, of course. All he understood about the ground he walked on came from a handful of travellers. And not all they knew did they tell.

His experience of bodies within the settlements was sporadic. Only once since Mercedes' clutch of buildings had he witnessed a body kept alive. It had been a distressing experience. The body had been allowed to grow – almost to adulthood although much younger than the one he had first experienced on the moor. It had been chained in full view to the side of one of the buildings. Children took turns throwing stones at it, the adults barely paying any attention. It had become part of settlement life. The creature indicated no signs of distress at its predicament, nevertheless Calvin couldn't help but find his morality tugged towards it; as stones bounced off its skull and children ran screaming towards and then away from it.

Calvin also learnt during this period to ask no questions, to not challenge the different workings within the settlements. From the big questions – the handling of the body – to everyday tasks – such as discrepancies in the way he would have tended the beets if he had been part of a settlement: all these were taboo. He was best to sit and listen, to observe and await information or conversation to be volunteered to him. He was a guest, but one entertained grudgingly. He was only as good as his stories and his rewards reflected this, tempered with the good fortune of his years. It didn't serve to tamper with the fragility of his existence. To annoy one settlement might mean not being provided with any victuals or a soft bed – it could mean at least another three sun-ups without food.

Just like the stars, the settlements appeared spread equidistant from each other. None were within two day's walk, none were over four. If there was a pattern it seemed more luck than design: as if, again, there was some cosmic force which made the settlements perfect for a traveller's needs. But again, he dismissed this as nonsense. It was not up to him to understand Heart; it was his role to live in it.

Night's temperature decreased. When he woke he found the moors brittle, dew hardened by the cold. Days were warm despite the freshness of the air – the physical exertion of walking incubated him. But the nights increasingly chilled him – he woke often to eject a stream of urine, the sweet smell breaking the monotony of the dark, acquiring it a vision – before folding himself back into his clothes, trying to regain a little warmth before sleep.

It was on his mind that snow would come. It would bring with it an abundance of clean water, yet would take the harvest from the land. From his own experience he knew the settlements paid no attention to the weather when it came to the treatment of the travellers. Fair or foul, they were listened to, fed, and cast out all the same.

One afternoon, with heavy grey clouds hung low and threatening to bring the fabric of the sky down with them, the first flecks of snow descended to the surface of Heart like falling softened stars. Calvin welcomed the beauty, feared the danger.

The previous few days he had noticed a change in the landscape. The scrub and brush of the moorland changed with subtleties which weren't simply seasonal. Calvin saw plants that he didn't recognise, trees that were unknown to him. Stone peppered the ground, stretched to the horizon. He came across a few solitary abandoned dwellings, indicative of times past. He had been tempted to take shelter within them, but something about the buildings discouraged him in ways he couldn't quite understand. It was too far to suggest there was a presence there, but he couldn't overcome the sensation that these buildings were homes to souls who had never been united with their bodies.

As these first flakes melted on his clothing, wet his hair, dissolved on his skin, he wondered whether he would have to utilise those buildings in the months to come, despite his no doubt irrational fears. At least their actuality gave him the choice, rather than freezing into non-existence on the harshness of the moor.

The day of these first flakes, however, brought another surprise.

Cut across the moor, like a snake whose scales had been replaced with rocks, a black line meandered southwards. Overgrown, interspersed with belligerent vegetation, buckled and broken, the line was still clear despite its status. Once Calvin had approached it, he bent to his knees, touched the surface. The texture was odd. There was a non-natural feel to it. He was reminded of burnt cake, of one time when Sky had become distracted and left one in the oven too long. The top had blackened, broken off in dark chunks, wedges. This material resembled that cake. It also crumbled in his touch.

Calvin stood on the *snake*, looked one way then another. Whilst he perceived it headed southwards he realised that in fact it also stretched out to the north; although the way was more rugged and due to the undulation of the landscape the black line wasn't so distinct. Something about the Snake tugged inside him, as though the line were a rope which, once he had touched it, exerted a force.

He stopped and thought for a moment.

For some time now he had meandered from settlement to settlement, doing his best to ensure he was moving in one direction but unaware other than the position of the stars in the night sky and the movement of the sun as to if he were making anything that might be called progress. This randomness excited him, yet despite his enthusiasm for new sights he had begun to feel dislocated. What if he were moving in one big circle, what if the next settlement he came upon was that of his birth?

Whilst the possibility was unlikely, he realised that even whilst travelling he needed some kind of anchor, a purpose. The Snake seemed to give him that purpose.

He sat on its damaged surface. It was clear that the Snake had once been a solid object – the vegetation which pushed through tessellated the material but it was clear that the pieces which remained might be reassembled jigsaw fashion. Calvin recalled the puzzles he had played with in the settlement when he was younger, simple shapes cut from wood which interlocked in a particular order. He pulled out his plastic container that contained beet and leek broth from the previous settlement, and dunked chunks of dry bread into it. The broth was cold – too cold for comfort, in truth; but it was hearty and filled his stomach completely. Swigging from his water bottle he watched the sheep-white flakes melt on the surface of the black Snake as though it were warm.

Standing, he decided to follow the black line whilst it was still visible, before the snow fell heavier and obliterated the track.

11

After a few days, Calvin began to realise that following the Snake had been a bad idea.

With his food supplies running low, and the snow sporadic yet increasing in cover, it was becoming clear that no settlements were anywhere near the black line. Certainly none in habitation, in any event.

Dotted along the Snake, however, were further signs of earlier occupation. Larger structures than the abandoned buildings he had seen recently shouldered the line: buildings made of material which wasn't quite wood and wasn't quite plastic and which certainly wasn't stone. Broken glass lay strewn inside the properties, making them dangerous to enter, although the wind and snow blew through the rectangular openings which Calvin assumed had housed the glass and didn't make them hospitable regardless of the interior. Glass crunched under his feet in competition with compacted snow. Whoever had lived there had certainly done so some time ago. The vegetation subsumed most of the properties, many were flattened, shadows of their former selves. Markings similar to those Calvin had seen in books were etched on the sides of some of the buildings, their colour bleached white by the sun.

Occasionally, also by the side of the Snake, metal skeletons rusted. Calvin could understand no purpose with regards to these elongated box shapes. After examining one closely, he decided to leave the others alone.

One night, with the snow particularly heavy, Calvin forced himself to take shelter inside one of the abandoned buildings. He chose one smaller than the others, where the openings onto the Snake were narrower and so the wind only pushed the snow in as triangular drifts that formed in one corner of the room. The structure creaked with the wind, added a supernatural dimension that unnerved him even as he understood it. He wasn't alone. Mice ran back and forth along a back wall, and bats hung from the ceiling; immobile in hibernation, wavering only in the breeze.

Calvin tightly pulled his clothes around him, but still the cold bit hard; as though disembodied souls of the mice and the bats had penetrated his clothing and were fixing their claws and teeth through his skin, fastening on bone. He shook his head, almost to dispel the vision, but also to maintain movement. Dark had descended like a wet blanket, through the building's open spaces snow twisted in animal shapes against the blackness. Calvin buried his head, thought of home and warmth and friendship.

Morning returned a bleak whiteness. The snow had reached its apex during the night. Upon leaving the building Calvin's eyes narrowed as he squinted against the sun reflected on the white. Two primary colours – white and blue – were all that he could see. The delineation between the two blurred, like colours running in a paint box, frustrating the clean sweep of the horizon. The fresh snow was unbroken save for the tiny footsteps of birds, creating broken-twig shapes, or malformed arrows. As for the Snake, it was buried. If it weren't for a similar building up ahead Calvin would not have been able to determine in which direction it ran.

Walking out into nature's expanse his shoes became soggy, his feet colder. He picked up soft handfuls and threw them back at the building he had left, attempting to direct them through the narrow openings and into the interior. When this bored him he scooped more of the snow together and filled some of his containers. As it melted and he drank he felt the cold throughout his arteries. He imagined it freezing inside his body, stiffening him with ice.

There was no point in continuing his journey, yet hunger tore through him. He couldn't remember how many days it was since he had eaten. He rued the idea of following the Snake, but didn't know which direction to traverse in its stead. And with the whiteness disguising landmarks, rendering everything the same, Calvin almost resigned himself to curling in a corner, to die.

Time blurred like the landscape.

Wet snow kept him alive just as it detained him.

There was no question of finding help.

Lack of sustenance fed into dream.

He was back in his settlement. Sky and Book were copulating in one corner of the sleeping quarters as his father, Royce, looked on. His expression was blank – literally. He had no facial features but Calvin recognised him as his father just as he recognised the tall girl sitting on an upper bunk with her legs unnaturally elongated, her feet dangling to the ground, as Acorn – his sister all grown up.

The moans from Sky segued into his own as he shivered against the cold. He became aware of the transition briefly before falling back into slumber. A plethora of dreams followed, as chaotic as a box of memories falling from the sky, bouncing and scattering across the landscape. Attracted by a girl he had never met, Calvin found himself led through room after room lined with beds. The girl sat on one of them and pulled up her top, but before this fully registered an elderly male wandered into the room; disorientated and distressed. Calvin realised the man was no more than a body, and following him back through the rooms of beds became a parade as more and more relatives joined them; until finally the man was led out of the back of the hut into blinding white light. Calvin looked down and realised he was only wearing a short shirt.

Other dreams thwarted his sleep: misshapen rabbits, malformed humans, chases through muddy corridors, blankets of leaves. And food. Calvin woke one morning after a banquet of rich meats, cooked to melting point in delicious stews, populated with tender vegetables and coloured purple by beets; of bread warm in the roof of his mouth, its smell teasing and intriguing to his stomach; of fresh peas popping against his tongue – their clean green taste reminding him of childhood.

One morning his wakening was accompanied by the lack of breath clouding from his mouth. His limbs were stiff – but from positioning, not from cold. The frozen snap that had dug into the land for several days seemed to have lifted. Snow melt puddled and muddied the floor of the shack. Through an opening Calvin could see that the limbs of a nearby tree which had been iced with snow were now bare; drops of moisture hung from the underside of branches like miniature bells. He forced himself to a sitting position, then to his knees, and finally to his feet. Everything ached, from the soles of his feet through the emptiness in his stomach to the knotted hair on his scalp.

It was a brief respite, he knew this. The sun had hung low in the sky for some time, and the days were much shorter. If he were to survive on anything other than melted snow then he had to keep going. Pushing himself out of the shack the glare of sunlight on snow had been replaced by sparkling water on heather. The black line of the Snake had returned visible to the landscape, its darkness accentuated by the wetness, the glare somehow blackening the line, as though the Snake itself were absorbing the energy of the sun. When Calvin bent to his knees and touched it, he found it warm to the touch.

He gathered his bag and selected a fallen branch that was half his height from underneath one of the trees; one that didn't snap when he put his weight on it. His legs were weak, too long curled up underneath him in sleep, but with the stick he found himself able to forge forwards. All he might question now was direction.

It now seemed lunacy to follow the Snake. It had led him nowhere but into disused buildings, no settlements in sight. Yet there was a pull to the Snake that kept Calvin married to it. It held a purpose, that much was clear; and to deviate from it threw just as much wilderness to either side as there might be ahead of him. With his head down, following the blackened broken surface, he stumbled forwards, forcing the memories of the dream food out of his head and trying not to concentrate on the space in his stomach which sapped his strength equal to the lack of sustenance itself.

The wind had dropped as well as the inclement weather. Calvin steeled himself against traitorous thoughts, shut down his mind until it focussed on the Snake and nothing else, as though the landscape around him had closed in, enfolded him in a sack, carried him unbidden across the surface of Heart with no intention of letting go until he found another settlement.

This sensation lasted much of the day. Calvin turned his artefact repeatedly through his fingers: rough and smooth, rough and smooth. His journey to date had yielded nothing exciting to trade, his bag was next to empty save for some odd-shaped stones. In truth, artefacts had always been unimportant to his original settlement; travellers had been welcomed through hospitality and the exchange of a story, little else. Yet he hoped to one day amass a collection of interesting objects that he might carry around with him in the manner that Book and others had done. If nothing else, he figured they might amuse him on long evenings between settlements, as he puzzled out their former uses or attributed functions to them which they might not have had.

Currently, however, the lack of weight in his bag held the most appeal and he was thankful his searches had been fruitless.

The Snake widened near day's end, splitting into twos and threes. Calvin kept to the straight path. Derelict buildings piled up the further he journeyed. Some apparently on top of others. It was as though Heart had buckled from underneath, cracking the Snake and destroying the buildings; although in truth, Calvin had no understanding of how or why things were as they were. And from any of the buildings he entered, there were no indications of habitation, either current or historic.

In the back of his mind Calvin recalled Book talking about large settlements where crumbling shacks rose to the sky. If he remembered correctly this was where artefacts were to be found. He wondered if the Snake might be leading him to such a destination. He wondered if he might find anyone living there.

As darkness encroached he sought shelter in one of the shacks. Once movement stopped, all the hunger and tiredness flooded through him; a weight that couldn't be lifted. The walls of the shack were blackened, scorched by fires from long ago. Stumps of formed wood were scattered about the room, like half-remembered furniture. Ash remained inch-thick on the floor, but Calvin didn't mind. It insulated the cold ground, and – despite the wind that had picked up again as the sun fell – the room itself, whilst not snug, was relatively warm.

He pressed himself into a corner, willed sleep to come fast. The soles of his feet ached as if they had been planed flat, the muscles in his legs hardened, the weariness in his eyes heavy. And the interminable hunger in his stomach could not be satisfied. He had come far today – further than he had thought possible – but to what avail? He forced out of his head those memories of his former settlement: of warmth, food, and laughter. Instead he folded into his mind possibilities of what tomorrow might hold: finding a settlement, finding food, finding salvation. As sleep took hold those past memories and future thoughts blurred into one; until his brain regenerated repeated images of food. Food food food.

<h1 style="text-align:center">12</h1>

After a short exploration the following morning Calvin came across a vegetable garden at the rear of one of the shacks.

It had gone to pot; obviously hadn't been tended for some time. But winter vegetables were a hardy crop, and fuelled by expectation Calvin dug around the hard, compacted earth; his fingernails filling with dirt just as his heart filled with hope. Finally, wrenched from the ground like a baby from the womb, three parsnips – elongated and thin – lay on the ground beside him; whiskery roots at their pointed ends like the inquisitive snouts of mice.

He dug elsewhere, unearthed a couple of stunted turnips. Taking his knife from his bag he scraped the vestiges of dirt from their skins, then stood on shaky legs, looking around at the disused buildings that followed the Snake to the horizon.

It took time, but within one of the buildings he found a battered pot, its handle loose but serviceable. Starting a fire from some heather that had blown into one of the shacks and was therefore dry he filled the pot with the remainder of his water and set it to boil.

Dicing the parsnips and vegetables into small pieces, all the easier for them to cook, he added them to the pot and waited.

Without seasoning he knew the broth wouldn't be especially palatable, but even so his stomach ached with an almost tangible ferocity as he watched the vegetables cart-wheeling within the boiling water. Prodding them with the tip of the knife, willing them to soften, he couldn't help but think back to previous meals and the sustenance they contained. He was aware his body was deteriorating as it strengthened. His physicality had improved since he had left the settlement. Not that he had previously been frail: his upper body strength had always been sound. But when the furthest distance he needed to walk hadn't exceeded beyond the range of the settlement his lower body, whilst supple, had never gathered the strength of muscle that it contained now. Yet, conversely, without sufficient nutrients, without regular unbroken sleep, without a purpose of mind, and through his recent hardship he was also wasting away.

He mashed the vegetables with the side of the knife and ate them before they were ready. The mush slid slowly down his throat – hot and sticky. He could almost feel his internal organs processing the food, kickstarting themselves and sending the nutrients out to each part of his body. Despite the blandness, despite his haste, it felt good. Calvin repeated the procedure over the next two days, until the vegetable garden was spent and his energy was restored. It was only then that he leant against the side of the shack, looked up at a sky pregnant with snow, and realised he would have to do it all over again.

He pressed on. The further he followed the Snake, the closer the buildings came together, the more frequent the vegetable gardens, the more prevalent the cooking equipment. Despite the often hurried flurries of snow, none settled as they had that first time when he considered himself near death. But the memory of it kept him aware. Whenever possible he stockpiled water and food. Nothing was left to waste. He walked, ventured, gained: kept on the move. After several sun-ups he saw buildings on the horizon unlike any he had seen before. Despite their distance, they towered over the landscape.

And from that distance they appeared to be intact, but the closer he journeyed the more obvious it became that they were in the same state of disrepair. For the first time since he left his settlement, however, a flush of excitement coursed through his body. This was why he had ventured: to see such sights, to gain some understanding. He wondered if Book had seen this settlement, or whether he was the first traveller to come across it since it had fallen beyond its use.

The Snake fled in many directions simultaneously. Calvin kept to the main route that led into the apparent centre. Buildings were made of substances that were unknown to him. The network of paths were myriad. The expanse of civilisation colossal. On an almost clear blue day he sat and watched the clouds play against the background. The conical tip of one of the buildings appearing to pierce the cloud which nevertheless passed by unhindered.

Who had lived here? Numbers more numerous than all the settlements he had visited thus far. Hulking skeletal cages of metal rusted beside the buildings, smashed glass strewn underfoot glistened like manmade dew, gaping holes in the buildings resembled the maws of dead beasts, massive chunks of stone dented the Snake where they had fallen; all strangled by vegetation, virulent despite the season.

Calvin moved cautiously. The way was dangerous underfoot. He might easily slip and twist an ankle, break a leg. The Snake underlay every part of the settlement, was omnipresent. Here and there, long metal structures pointed skywards, bent at the end like insect feelers. Thin black lines were strung from rooftop to rooftop, in a disjointed spider's web. Whilst most of the buildings were of the same colour, others bore traces of previous garishness now subdued over time. Ochre, pale pink, green. Some of the Snake-facing buildings were littered with what Calvin realised were metal chairs. Seeing something familiar yet different attuned his mind to possible artefacts, and he darted here and there inside the buildings, looking for items to place in his bag, to trade, should he get the chance.

Within a short while he had a cup with a faded green and white design of a face with wavy hair and a star over her head, a replica in metal of the cross he had seen prior to finding the first settlement, a tiny glass bottle miraculously intact with symbols *l*, *v*, *k* and *n* visible on the side, another piece of twisted metal for which Calvin couldn't discern a use, and a book.

Calvin handled the book carefully. A strip of paper that was wrapped around it almost fell apart at his touch. A faded image was almost discernible – two rising silver figures set against what once might have been a blue background. He carefully peeled the paper away from the harder plain black cover. Gold-coloured symbols ran down the side of the book, and inside the pages turned stiffly and were rife with other symbols. Disappointingly there were no pictures. Calvin wondered what the symbols were for. They obviously had a use, but no one – villagers or travellers alike – had the knowledge to understand them. Some of the pages were wet, some stuck together, a couple fell from the book as he handled it, disintegrating and spinning like sycamore leaves.

If the book had contained pictures then it might have told a story. Travellers had told stories from books when visiting Calvin's settlement, but it was a rare occurrence. Most, like Book himself, simply told stories from experience.

There was little food to be found within the expanse of the large settlement. Calvin decided to remain there whilst winter took hold. There was shelter aplenty, and much to explore; but forays into the surrounding countryside were necessary for sustenance. Due to the decreasing number of sunlit hours, these trips often took the best part of the day. He found a barrow, rusted and wobbly, in one of the buildings and used it to transport the vegetables from the fields into an area suitable for a storeroom. Pickings were scarce and stunted with no one to tend to them; but with only one mouth to feed Calvin's future seemed assured.

Those days where he wasn't foraging were spent exploring the settlement.

The nature of the Snake constantly made the going difficult. Rarely was it smooth. Mostly it was buckled – chunks of stone were tripping hazards hidden by vegetation. The buildings themselves were dangerous, prone to collapse. One morning – a brisk wind affecting debris, Calvin's eyes collecting rubble – an entire two-storey block came crashing down. He had passed it on previous days, noted the way that it leant to one side, like a child with a leg kicked out from underneath it. A ball of dust rose from the ruin, was collected by the wind and bore upon him, almost personified. Once it passed, his clothes retained a whitened tint; a brick memory.

Throughout his exploration, however, there was no sign of recent occupation. No stores of food like those he had amassed, no campfire traces, no noise other than that provided by nature. This corner of Heart was desolated and forgotten. Calvin couldn't help but speculate on the reason for the settlement's demise or on the fate of those who had occupied it. How long ago had it been populated? Where had the people gone? His knowledge of Heart had been entirely limited to his previous surroundings. It had only been through traveller's tales that he was aware such places existed.

Winter embedded. Snow flocked in doorways and through windows. As it had on the moor, the snow removed all traces of the Snake and the dangers underneath. If it were not for the close-coupled buildings, potential pathways would be obliterated. As it was, Calvin found a spade in one of the buildings and cleared those routes necessary for his daily routine. And he kept to that routine. It was important to keep busy, to keep fit, to keep sane. Repetition reminded him of his settlement, away in the past. And by creating a semblance of home he created home. Not that he had any intention of staying once the season had changed.

Book – or the other travellers – had failed to mention their isolation when travelling: the sense of loneliness, futility, desperation. Their tales were of new sights, unexplained places, found objects. They didn't detail the creeping dread which traversed their bodies, their longing for a human voice, for a touch. From a communal environment to being a sole player in the game of life, Calvin now understood that being a traveller was more than a calling, it was a cage. A cage from which there was no escape.

In essence, despite his soul, he had become just a body to those settlements he visited. A body to feed, a body to entertain, to stare at. The nature of his soul – what made him individual – was rarely of interest. Of course, story was paramount and story *was* individual, but beyond the story itself their interest in him and his way of life was negligible. Leaving his settlement had caused him to leave his soul, his anchor to self. Yet also, it had strengthened his soul, had caused him to focus on the nature of his own reality and his perception of self. Without others' trappings, he could be himself in peace. Unfortunately, that peace had side-effects.

He began talking to himself. Briefly to begin with, some cuss words when the spade slipped or the barrow tilted and spilled beets onto the Snake. Then a sentence, then a few strung together. In the darkest days of winter, when the sun curved over Heart for but a few hours a day and when daylight was shrouded in cloud in mimicry of night, Calvin practised his stories with himself as audience. Paring here, adding description there; he pretended to hone his craft but in reality served to keep himself company. And when this failed, he became adept at masturbation.

White snow became grey became black. Compacted ice became sludge became water. As the weather cleared so did the settlement. Calvin decided to remain just a short while longer, and forged himself into exploring once again.

Hitherto he had restricted himself to those buildings that were of one level. His safety was paramount – any injuries sustained should a building collapse might lead to death even if he wasn't killed outright. But familiarity with the settlement had brought him some confidence. Assurances had been created within his mind as to which areas were safe and which were dangerous. And boredom had set in. Becoming a traveller had pushed himself to the limits of existence; he should also push himself within those limits to encompass his role effectively.

One morning – with blue sky stretched pale and thin overhead like a cloth pulled tight over a saucepan – Calvin woke determined to scale one of the tallest buildings in the settlement.

He chose his target carefully. Those buildings that covered the greater ground space appeared more liable to collapse. Whilst their weight spread over a wider surface area Calvin felt less safe with them for reasons he couldn't quite identify. However, some buildings were intact that soared upwards from a single point on the ground. For him, there was a sense that their centre of gravity was focussed to such an extent that they were forced to remain standing. He drew an analogy with sticks he'd pushed into the ground when growing peas. The sticks might bend with the wind, but they rarely broke. Other complex systems necessitating several sticks and string used to tie rows of tomato plants together often collapsed and had to be reset. His logic might be flawed – Calvin had no real precedent for any of it – but it was all that he had.

The subject he chose appeared to be made of more ancient brick than the surrounding buildings. From a flat base, part of the building extended backwards from the Snake, whilst the other half rose skywards culminating in a point. Having re-examined his found artefacts the previous evening he realised it resembled the symbol *l* from the small glass bottle lying on its side. The building hadn't been immune to disturbance, he had to pick his way over stone shapes worn with age but apparently sculpted with faces. Looking upwards, he could see breaches in the stonework which indicated they had fallen from a great height.

There was a circular opening halfway up the main façade of the structure. As Calvin entered through large wooden doors glass crunched underfoot. This wasn't unusual, glass littered the settlement, but he was puzzled to see that these fragments held colour. Unlike many of the other buildings he had examined the interior of the building wasn't subdivided. He had expected to find steps leading upwards – the height of the building had led him to anticipate several floors – but here the ceiling stretched high above his head and only came to a halt at the roof which was damaged with holes.

Disappointed, he was about to turn back when a door alongside one wall caught his eye. Half-opened, he glimpsed some steps in shadow.

He walked towards the door. The floor was covered in ash. He imagined much wood had once been burnt within the interior. Windows on both sides were oddly shaped, their glass long gone but again underneath each one coloured fragments glittered ineffectually in the half-light. At the far end of the building vertical metal pipes, rusted and tarnished, were set into the structure of something he couldn't determine. Off to one side, a large stone bowl, presumably used for cooking, contained rainwater, ash, and leaves. Calvin felt uncomfortable within the vastness of the structure. The building had a history that seemed to transcend the others he had previously visited. He felt uneasy as he looked around, and once he reached the stairway focussed his thoughts on the ascent and nothing else.

The steps curved around a central stone column, and were worn smooth. As Calvin journeyed upwards – for the first time in his life – he was reminded of his artefact that Book had given him. If he stood it on one end it might resemble the structure. It crossed his mind there might be a connection.

Openings were set at intervals within the outside wall. Calvin resisted the urge to peek, instead focussing on the slippery steps, fighting claustrophobia and fear the higher he went. Above him, the roof seemed to narrow as though he were within a cone, whilst each turn of the steps removed him further from reality. Without sight of the ground below or the sky above it felt he were in an ever-perpetuating circle. This thought alone was almost enough to make him backtrack his steps, as his fingers sought handholds in the stone and he fought his legs from shaking.

About half way up a room led off the stairway. Here the floor was wooden and most of it was gone. Calvin didn't dare to try his weight against it. Massive beams formed part of the ceiling, and rope descended towards an area beneath that he had yet to view. From this distance up, he could see the shining hulks of large metal shells far below, and decided to take a more detailed look once he was back on the ground.

Again, he ascended. After the same distance had passed the steps stopped and a circle ran around the central column with four openings until he returned to the steps once more. The space was tiny, just enough for one person – but of course, it was all the space he needed. Moving to a position opposite where the gaping stairwell descended, he leant his back against the stone column and then gradually slid to a sitting position, resting his legs. It would have been simple to look out at the view, but after the strangeness of the climb he needed a few moments to compose himself. No one he ever knew had ever looked out at this height: it was a moment to be savoured as well as feared.

It was in such moments, however, that he found himself. Where Book's calling came to fruition.

He heaved himself to his feet. It was colder up here than on the ground, the wind whipped through the opening and threw sunlight into his eyes.

It was a clear day. Calvin looked out upon the expanse of the settlement, his mouth hung open catching the breeze.

His fingers gripped the stone.

Below him the buildings were tiny, their mostly roofless structures lined up like teeth on sheep skulls. From here, there seemed a pattern to the layout; a grid which hadn't been obvious from the ground. The settlement itself, whilst reaching towards the horizon, suddenly stopped short just as he expected it would. Yet to see it from this height, to view it as simply a mass of buildings forced onto the landscape, pinpricked just how finite civilisation once must have been on Heart. And as the vegetation encroached, it was clear just how quickly that civilisation might be subsumed.

If this was a shock, so was the height in itself. Calvin's stomach cart-wheeled as he looked out through the stone opening; as though his soul were falling, pulled towards the ground. He breathed faster than necessary, once again his legs began to shake. He was level with the birds.

He worked each window in turn, views overlapping, until he was once more by the stairwell. He had detected the passage of the Snake through the settlement in its myriad forms, eyed each line as far as he could; its substance all the clearer given the height, as though the overview made the vegetation invisible. He followed the Snake back in the direction he had come, but it disappeared with Heart's curvature before he could trace the source.

There were no other settlements within view. Buildings flanked each branch of the Snake, as they had done on his journey into the settlement, but none appeared populated. There were no wisps of smoke on the horizon, nor ant-like figures on the ground. It confirmed his suspicion he was alone in this large settlement.

He descended cautiously, the way feeling far more dangerous downwards than it did up; the fear of slipping quite tangible as his eyes followed the darkness under his feet.

At the bottom he discovered another side door and found the chunks of metal he had viewed from above. The structures were the height of a man, but much wider and hollow. The stone underneath them had broken into myriad pieces, the metal punched through from the height of the fall. Calvin ran his fingers over their smooth coolness, wondered at their purpose. But it was unfathomable. He considered that the lives of those of previous generations must have been frivolous. From his experience, the only objects that needed to exist were those that were fit for the immediate purpose of living, growing food, eating and sleeping. There wasn't any need for anything else, as the almost never-sale of artefacts proved. Calvin left the building shaking his head. He had enjoyed the experience at the top of the building, although it was a retrospect pleasure, but even the purpose of the building itself remained a puzzle.

Night time warmth came from the crackle of his fire. He poked at the wood that split and spat, watched brilliantly lit embers dance and fall; the white yellow flame seeming to dissipate into smoke that rose and became one in the darkness above him. After his climb, he had spent the remainder of the day exploring some of the other taller buildings, emboldened by his action. But none had the height or the mystery of the first. Whilst he collected a handful of other artefacts, it was impossible to imagine that he was the first to have visited there; the absence of anything of much use made that clear.

What was also clear was that a decision needed to be made. It was tempting to remain in a place that had kept him safe, that had become home; but also it went against his very nature to stay somewhere devoid of people, to be static rather than to travel. There was comfort to be had, but unless he made plans for a permanent camp – including a structured growing of vegetables – his life there would be pointless. In some respects, he imagined the massive settlement would be a beacon for other travellers – and remaining here he would be more likely to find others. But then what would be the purpose of it? He just had to keep moving.

He wondered how the light from the fire illuminated his face. Wondered how Sky, Royce and Acorn were coping without him. Wondered what Levi, Citroen, and the others would say if they could see him now. Wondered in what direction he might head.

From the top of the pointed building it had been evident that the Snake stretched out in multiple directions, all leading to the horizon without an obvious settlement in sight. So which route should he take? Which would be safe, which would be dangerous? As the flames fled the fire Calvin saw each as a Snake, all emerging from the same source and disappearing Heart knows where.

For a few desultory days he returned to the pointed building, climbed the steps, attempted to plan a route, and searched for other travellers. The view from the top remained unchanged.

13

Time passed.

Calvin travelled.

With the large settlement behind him he had struck out at random, determined to follow the Snake despite the paucity of settlements in its wake. Occasionally he found those who had chosen to live in abandoned buildings rather than making shacks of their own. These people tended to be few: groups of no more than twenty at most. In many instances they had facial or bodily disfigurements, although with these groups he saw no evidence of any bodies without souls. The stories he told there were grudgingly received – they did not favour travellers, yet they were not unkind. It was rare that he was turned away from a settlement, and again he thanked his age as the probable cause.

Sometimes, when given directions, he ventured away from the Snake, and found much larger occupations. These were always constructed afresh, without any ties or acknowledgement of the past. Here the food was better prepared, the people friendlier although remaining at a distance, the children always eager to hear his stories. After three cycles of the seasons Calvin found his tales became more complex and detailed; yet sometimes there was an urge to elaborate and every so often he simply made things up. This blurring of fantasy and reality appealed to him, created a version of him in his mind as a storyteller rather than a conduit for history. He saw no moral argument against this service: who knew how much the other traveller's stories he had heard were fact or fiction? His travels had corroborated some of their tales, confounded others.

The landscape changed during his journey. Heath and moor gave way to rolling fields of green, pockets of dense woodland, flattened former settlements. In some instances, the material which formed the Snake covered great swathes of land, Calvin could no more determine its purpose than any of the artefacts from the former settlements. He wondered how many years had to be thrown into the past until his own life would no longer be understood. For as sure as surety could be, once the people who lived in the abandoned places had lives that were as vibrant and as *now* as his own. Yet, those civilisations had crumbled to dust without any indication of how they once ran.

During this travelling time, at each and every settlement, he asked after Book and news of other travellers. Little was forthcoming, and Book's name was unheard of. Calvin wondered if he had chosen a different direction, or simply gave different names at every settlement. He wondered how vast the expanse of Heart must be. How long he would need to travel before he saw everything.

And in the winter months he made it habit to seek out the larger settlements. As the days cooled he made efforts to re-track the Snake, should he have spent time drifting from its black line. Invariably following the wider widths led him to greater buildings. And within several of those that he visited, pointed buildings still stood standing, affording views of the surrounding countryside, with only subtle differences between them which made him realise the previous occupants of Heart must have had a way of sharing their resources, that in the past the methods of communication had to have been more frequent and succinct. He developed a fascination with piecing together fragments of his discoveries; yet knew he could not resolve all the discrepancies in his mind, that the answer would never be found.

The pack he wore now was larger, its material unknown. Straps fitted over both shoulders and under his arms, with a supporting strap that could be tied around his waist. He needed the space. The artefacts he had collected filled two thirds of the bag, the remaining space available for spare clothes, food, and water. He had become adept at living from the land, his abilities with beet, parsnip, and turnip unsurpassed. Occasionally he traded artefacts for extra food, although realised now that it was often unnecessary. The trade itself was immaterial to the amount of food and duration of shelter that he had been likely to receive. Sometimes he didn't offer the artefacts at all, mostly he disliked parting with them. He had come to consider these belongings to be part of who he was.

Another season, another winter. Calvin woke one morning huddled within a shack on the outskirts of another large settlement. Fresh snow had lain overnight, traitorous white falling through a clean black sky. He had woken and stretched; put on a pan to boil some water. For five sun-ups he had been alone. The settlement he had left had provided much food and directions. Whilst none of them had been outside of their own enclave, they had been told of the existence of the settlement from travellers before him.

It crossed Calvin's mind how people might know of wonders without wishing to experience them.

The shack he had chosen, one of a series that lined the Snake as was familiar en route to a large settlement, had retained its door, which had provided a welcome deterrent for the wind. Calvin opened it now, braced himself against the day. The sky was clear blue, the whiteness hurt his eyes which took some time to focus. Once they had, however, a hammering started in his chest and he sucked in deep breaths. Clear in the fresh snow were footprints.

He looked from left to right. From right to left. Then again. Other than the sunken tracks there was no indication of another presence. The single line indicated a solo traveller. It couldn't help but cross his mind it might be Book.

Yet, like a shadow, he also recalled the shambling body he had first encountered outside his home settlement. Although the straightness of the footprints dispelled that notion, as they seemed not without purpose.

He re-entered the shack, stuffed his belongings into his bag, and headed out into the snow.

The tracks were easy to follow. Snow had fallen the previous evening, then hardened overnight. His feet made crisp crunchy noises as he walked beside the prints, not daring to actually walk *in* them. They seemed a little smaller than his feet, the stride shorter too. They were definitely human. Unless they belonged to an animal of a kind he had never seen.

But there was a purpose to them that would be afforded to an animal. They were heading in the direction he had intended, following the line of the Snake under the snow.

Calvin walked for some time. The early blue sky was replaced by low-slung clouds. He was fearful of further snowfall that might obliterate the tracks, so kept up his pace. His calf muscles began to ache, his breathing more ragged. As buildings accumulated so the depth of the snow increased, funnelled into the paths between the ruins. Calvin barely looked up to register the massive settlement that was forming around him – probably the largest he had ever seen. Despite the size, however, few of the taller buildings remained standing. Rubble under the snow made the going tough, the footprints harder to follow. They were persistent, though; yet Calvin knew they would stop soon. No one would pass through the entire settlement without stopping. His heart began to beat faster in anticipation, in expectation.

Just as the first few flakes began to litter the sky, the footprints turned off the Snake and headed towards one of the buildings. Calvin stopped and followed the line with his eyes. The building looked sturdier than some of the others. It had a wide frontage, open to the elements. Above the façade strips of paper, that appeared to have been stuck to the brickwork, were peeled and torn. Symbols v and e were writ large over the entrance in pale pink. Calvin sucked in a breath, scanned the dark interior although it was impossible to know if he were being watched. Yet there was nothing for it but to venture inside.

He removed his backpack, leant it against the wall just inside the doorway, saw no reason for encumbrance.

The interior appeared wider than the exterior. Like several of the buildings he had previously visited the floor space was covered in material which squelched under his feet. Alongside one wall ran a curved section of wood with a space on the other side. Four slopes led up to a series of galleries with large intact double doors leading off them. As with most of his travels, Calvin wondered what the building's purpose had been. He suspected, again as usual, that it was alien to anything he would have experienced, and also superfluous to the daily necessity of living.

Snow had not been driven into the interior, due to the direction that the building faced outside. There were no telltale prints to indicate which door the person might have chosen. Inside, despite the open frontage, quiet reigned. Calvin walked up the nearest slope and rested his hand then his ear against the door. Swallowing something which felt like his heart, he pushed against the wood. The door was heavy, but with force it swung open, and he moved inside.

Once his eyes adjusted to the dark, he never expected what he saw.

Rows of seats in a semi-circle faced an open space.

Distracted for a moment from looking for the owner of the footprints, Calvin walked between the seats, running his fingers over the fabric which caressed and momentarily held his skin as he passed. The interior of this part of the building was black, the space deceptively smaller at first glance than was apparent. The open space filled one side of the room. Fabric lay bunched on the floor at both ends. A white expanse was strung from the ceiling, torn in several places. It appeared to be the focal point for all the seats.

Calvin walked to the end and looked back to where he had come. Despite the emptiness, a shiver ran up his spine, as if he were being watched. He returned the way he came and checked the next double-doorway, which revealed an exactly similar space. There was no one there. Continuing to the next in line, he entered the blackness, let the door shush closed behind him. He could hear breathing before he spotted the traveller — or perhaps he could simply sense it, was attuned to it. He looked across the rows of seats and saw a figure three rows from the front. He had no idea as to whether they knew he was there, wasn't sure whether to call out or to walk towards them. He didn't want to scare anyone, yet didn't want to be scared either.

For a moment he stood in silence. Then a voice said: "I know you're there."

He let out a breath, realised he had been holding it in. The voice was unmistakably female.

Calvin had never known of a female traveller. All those he had previous contact with at his settlement had been male. He had never questioned this before; had taken it as fact. These thoughts ran through his mind as he began to walk towards her, the knowledge that this would be the first time he had met anyone outside of a settlement crowding his head.

He sat down in the first row, turned to look at her.

She seemed to be of a comparable age to himself. In the darkness, illuminated solely by a few holes in the roof, her long hair was knotted and braided with objects tied into it – ribbons and plant life. Her skin was as white as his, her eyes too dark to see. She appeared to be smiling.

"Hello," Calvin said.

The word almost had to be pushed out of his mouth. His heart wouldn't stop hammering.

"Hello." The girl held out her hand. "My name's Moss."

Calvin looked at her hand. The fingers were long and slender, the nails bitten to the quick. It was as engrained with dirt as his own.

"In some settlements," Moss said, her voice soft, pitched low, "the taking of a hand is seen as an indication of friendship, not of hostility. Would you take my hand?"

Calvin reached across the seats and held her hand in his. It was cool to the touch. Now that he had established contact, he was loath to let go, but the gentle pressure of her fingertips against his palm suggested he had held on long enough.

"Have you got anything to eat?"

He nodded. "Vegetables, no meat. There's not been any meat for some time."

"Would you mind sharing it with me?"

Calvin looked back to the doors. "It's near the entrance," he said. "Shall we set up camp?"

Moss nodded. She stood. Calvin could barely detect the shape of her body within the multi-layered rags that she wore. She picked up a small sack and flung it over her back. "Lead on."

Calvin returned to the building's entrance with Moss in tow. His bag was still by the doorway, and when he turned after picking it up he saw Moss in greater definition via the sunlight that now flooded the scene.

Her eyes were a light brown, like deer fur, although they weren't doe-eyed. Her nose an upturned knuckle. Her lips were red and cracked. She looked vulnerable yet strong simultaneously. He wondered what had caused her to travel, knew he would ask her later. For the moment, food was on his mind. He wondered if she had any supplies of her own.

He made her a meal whilst she looked through his collection of artefacts. She was dismissive of the book – "they're so revered yet so pointless" – but she adored the replica of the cross: "so pretty".

He watched her turn the object in her hands. Suddenly he wanted to give it to her. Between them he felt a connection that ran deep but which he couldn't quite trust. Being alone for so long, even within a settlement, made him wary of establishing a sudden relationship. But when he looked at Moss he knew that if she had lived in his original settlement then maybe he wouldn't have left.

Although, was it his mind playing tricks? Looking for connections which weren't there. Which might not be connecting the same way in Moss's mind. Something pitched over in his stomach: the possibility of loss. Now he had found Moss he couldn't imagine leaving her, going their separate ways.

He shook his head. It was ridiculous. They had only just met. He snuck a glance over at her again, watched her delve into her own bag where she pulled out a thin metal chain. She threaded it through a loop at the top of the cross.

She caught his gaze. "May I have this?" She pulled the two ends of the chain around her neck and fastened something at the back. The cross hung against her chest as an ornament.

Calvin felt his mouth dry. He nodded.

"I'll exchange, of course." She rooted around again in her bag; pulled out another metal object that fitted in her palm and handed it to Calvin.

It resembled the cages of metal that he had frequently seen lined up against the Snake and in various parts of the large settlements. Yet if those were broken, this one was intact. It was longer than its width. Two tiny doors opened out on each side. Wheels, such as those on a barrow, were fixed in each corner. Clear plastic fronted the gaps that would otherwise be apparent between the metal frame. Looking inside, he saw a tiny plastic figure resembling a person moulded in white sitting behind another wheel.

"What is it?" he asked.

"I don't know," Moss said. "But look." She took it from his hand and ran it along the floor of the building. The wheels turned ineffectually, its progress slowed by the wet material on the ground. But the purpose was evident. And not only was it evident, but it paved the way for thought about those metal cages.

Calvin picked it up again. "This is a clue to the past," he said, his eyes examining it more closely. "All those hunks of metal I've seen. They moved people."

Moss's eyes sparkled.

They returned to the main seating area to consume the parsnip broth. It was a thick concoction that slowly made its way down their throats, but it was ok. Calvin had a small amount of bread left from a previous settlement which he broke in half and shared with Moss. He did this unthinkingly, in the expectation that they might at least spend the winter together and would pool their resources. Moss had contributed some dried rosemary, which added a little flavour to the broth but was really too old to have much effect.

Questions formed in Calvin's brain as they ate. There was so much he wanted to know: why she was travelling, where she had been, what she had seen. But by the time the soup was finished they were both ready for sleep. Moss curled up across three seats and Calvin followed likewise.

Just as he was drifting off her heard her say goodnight.

14

It was so dark inside the building that when Calvin woke he couldn't remember where he was nor guess at the time of day.

He sat bolt upright. Listening. For a moment he couldn't hear Moss, couldn't see her. Then he realised she had slumped off her seats and was on the floor between them. It was easy to remain quiet, and shortly afterwards he became attuned to her breathing, thankful she was still there.

He stood and stretched. Hunger flicked at the peripheries of his stomach. Exploring some of the other doors leading off the main building was a small room where he toileted. He had seen similar rooms in other buildings and it appeared that they once might have had a mechanism dispersing waste into the ground. If so, this no longer worked and usually he toileted outside. But the day was so cold, so bitingly fresh, and the ground so hard he decided against it. Not only that, but he didn't want Moss to see him. It was an odd notion, but he trusted his instinct and stuck to it.

Whilst waiting for her to wake he peeled and sliced two potatoes. He had enough vegetables for another couple of days at most, and expected they would need to forage before he could hear her stories. He realised his expectation was that she would want to remain with him, but he could make no assurances that she would be better with him than without. Taking the food back into the seating area he could only hope she would want to stay.

The smell of the cooked potatoes returned her to consciousness.

"Hey."

Her voice was soft and light.

"Sleep well?"

"Not bad. How did I get down here?"

"You must have rolled off. I never heard you."

She smiled. "Breakfast, too."

They shared the fried potato. It tasted of nothing much at all. It tasted good.

Calvin still felt hungry after he had eaten, but he said nothing. Moss had had the greater share.

She sat back and stretched. A smell rolled off her that he hadn't previously detected. He no doubt smelt much the same himself. It had been several settlements back since he had had a warm wash. This never bothered him before, but it did now.

"I've got so many questions," he said. "I don't know where to start."

She looked at him curiously. "Do we travel for questions or do we travel for answers?"

He shrugged. "Sometimes I'm not sure why I travel."

"Because you have the calling," she said. "As I do."

Calvin started at the words. He thought for a moment, then said: "Have you met a traveller named Book?"

Moss shook her head. "No. Should I have had?"

"It's just that he spoke those words to me. *The calling*. I understood the meaning, of course, but I didn't know if it was his description or something from a wider source."

"I don't know either."

They sat in silence awhile, the limitations of their knowledge greater than the sum of their experience.

"Have you met anyone else, travelling solo?" Calvin couldn't quite keep an unexplained edge out of his voice. He wanted to be the first.

She didn't answer straightaway, but he noticed her fingering the cross that she still wore around her neck.

"I saw someone once," she said. "From a distance. But I decided to hide. Is that silly?"

He shrugged. "I don't know." Then he thought. "Was that me?"

She laughed. "No, I don't think it was you. It was some time ago. How did you find me?"

"I followed your footprints in the snow. You must have walked by me during the night. I was sleeping in a shack just outside of this settlement."

"Settlement?" She thought it over. "This is a little large for a settlement, isn't it? Surely this is a city?"

"A city?" Calvin had never heard the word.

Moss seemed amused. "Have you never seen anywhere this big before?"

Calvin felt his cheeks flush, as if his manhood had been called into question. "Yes, I have. I always spend the winter in a city. But I've never met anyone who called it that before."

Moss's amusement broke into laughter. "I've never met anyone who called it anything different."

Calvin leant back. He was enjoying the conversation, but he couldn't lose sight of necessity. He stood. "We need to forage."

"Supplies running low?"

"Enough for a few days; but I don't want to wait 'til they run out."

Moss nodded, thoughtfully. "I understand. I'm with you."

"With me?"

"'Til winter's end. Right?" Her eyes caught the outside light and sparkled; or maybe it was Calvin's imagination.

"Right," he said. "'Til winter's end."

They made a sweep of the city. It was vast, sprawling. Many of the buildings had been reduced to rubble. There were entire areas blocked through brick fall and a violent buckling of the Snake. Calvin held back on descriptions. It seemed Moss had knowledge that had eluded him and he didn't want to appear foolish or naïve. As they traversed the *city*, he repeated the word inside his mind. It was meaningless, of course; but through repetition it would become apt, and once that happened there would be no other word for the over-sized settlements that he would see in the future.

Occasionally, they saw rats scuttling through the debris. Moss picked up a couple of bricks and slung them half-heartedly, but Calvin had never known anyone who had caught a rat, much less eaten one. Meat was a farmed substance, animal husbandry carefully maintained. Over the time that he had travelled he had rarely seen wild animals, outside of rabbits. A handful of deer, a couple of horses; little he could capture or kill. And birds, often there were birds, but mostly he paid no attention to them.

Despite the size of the city it didn't take long for confirmation that there was no food to be found. Calvin began to worry. Whilst it hadn't snowed again, they could see the surrounding countryside was whitened with it. Crops would be deep underground, if they existed at all, and not readily harvested. The nearest settlement – the one he had previously left – was several sun-ups away; and there was no question of returning. No traveller retraced their tracks – at least, none that he knew. Of course, he might direct Moss there but that could mean losing her. It was selfish, but if he had to starve he wanted her by his side.

They ventured out of the city boundary, armed with spades they had found. Cloud cover anticipated the darkness to come. They were silent. Shifting snow, forcing the blades into the hard earth, leaning back to wrench the soil free from Heart's embrace. Nothing was discovered. They tried in several places, but the city's size meant that so many Snakes ran towards it that it was impossible to determine where gardens might exist. As clouds became subsumed by the night they returned empty-handed. Moss a few steps behind Calvin. In a sudden unexplained frisson of fear, Calvin imagined Moss swinging her spade...

He turned and waited for her to catch up. "We have enough for this evening, at least."

"I'm hungry."

"I know."

He looked at her hands, raw from the cold, clinging to the handle of the spade. He remembered touching them. Wanted to do so again. Wondered what it might accomplish.

Later, nestled again in their temporary home, they cradled containers of parsnip broth, warmed their hands. Their portions were greatly reduced from the previous evening. Calvin realised he had been rash with supplies. Even so, Moss seemed upbeat. She questioned him over his origins, what he had seen, where he had been; and he answered her as best he was able. Whilst he explained that Book had been his spur, and the body the final straw, he held back on his personal artefact, even as he turned it in his fingers within his pocket as he spoke.

"Bodies," Moss mused. "I've seen a few in my time. Totally, utterly, useless."

"But nevertheless, people," insisted Calvin.

"Oh, I'm not sure. Without soul they are nothing. I saw one trained to work. Nothing difficult. Picking up potatoes and placing them in a pot. It took forever. Was comical, really."

"I'm not sure we should laugh at them. If the soul had been present at the birth they would be just like you and me."

"But they're not, are they? And that's the difference." Moss folded her arms. Calvin wondered whether that was to keep warm or confirm subject closed. He pushed it.

"We see the body, but we don't see the person. We don't know where the soul goes. Maybe it could be reunited. There's so much that we don't understand."

Moss sighed. "Resources are limited. Even bodies have to be fed. And for what? It makes sense to exterminate them. Believe me Calvin, they are worthless."

There was more Calvin wanted to say. He couldn't explain why he wanted to defend the bodies: Moss was right, without question. But morally he couldn't stomach the idea of already-grown bodies being despatched. At birth, he could understand it. A body without a soul was like a still-birth and could be discarded. But once grown: he couldn't conceive that over time it would have developed no consciousness, despite common opinion that this wasn't the case.

And where did the souls go? No one had an opinion on that.

He held back, however. Arguing on the second day with someone he really liked, who he wanted to spend the winter with, made no sense. Moss had become disinterested anyway. Bodies held no attraction for her. Instead, she was examining the cross she now wore.

"Where did you get this?"

He related the story: *somewhere*, a long while ago.

"I've seen this symbol before. Carved on stone. Maybe I was there too."

"How long have you been travelling?"

Moss sighed. "It's difficult to determine time, isn't it?" She reached within her bag, pulled out a small circular item and handed it to him. "Do you know what this is?"

He took it from her. Shiny metal ran in a circumference around the object, polished to a sheen. A convex piece of glass was held within the metal, and underneath it he could discern a white background with symbols evenly spaced around it. Some of the symbols seemed repeated. One was similar to another, but upside down. The interior of the object was so dirty, however, that discerning much more than this was difficult. When he turned it in his hands, two black lines moved from side to side, until they aligned themselves downwards.

"I haven't seen this artefact before," he said.

Moss took it from him and replaced it in her bag. "This was given to me by a traveller," she began. "When I was in my home settlement. He told me people used to measure time with it. That it was called a watch."

"But it doesn't work now?"

"No, it doesn't work now. And he didn't know how it worked either. I've been trying to puzzle it out but it makes no sense to me. Time is measured by days, by sun-up and sky-fall. I don't see that we need more than that, other than our own growth, from birth to death, which signifies the timeline of our lives."

"A watch." Calvin turned the word over in his mind. He wondered if the object had to be watched in order to work. Meanwhile he filed away the word *sky-fall* as another – like *city* – which he hadn't heard before, not wanting to embarrass himself by revealing his lack of knowledge. At least it was a word he could understand.

"But, to answer your question, I've been travelling for two winters. I mean, this is my second. The first I almost starved."

"We won't starve this one," Calvin said, emboldened. But he knew, in truth, that they might.

They headed out again the following day. There was no further snowfall, but a cold snap had frozen everything: from the droplets on the underside of trees to large expanses of water that filled indentations in the ground like circles of glass. The top layer of snow was frosted, stepping on it cracked the surface, led to discoveries of surprising depth. Bright sunlight reflected from every surface, so that emerging from their home temporarily blinded them each and every way they looked.

In a different direction to where they had previously journeyed they found a small orchard with the shrivelled remains of apples and pears. They bagged them, continued their search. Moss persuaded Calvin that nuts contained in tiny prickly cases that were growing from several trees were also edible, and again they massed a collection of them. As the buildings became smaller the further they journeyed, they realised the large spaces at the rear were gardens, and underneath the snow in one of them were found large next-to-rotten potatoes and a healthy supply of beets and parsnips. Suddenly, what had seemed would be unproductive turned on a chance, and they returned home with bags full which, if carefully prepared, would last them for some time to come.

It didn't escape the back of Calvin's mind, however, that if he had been alone then this haul would last longer – despite not knowing about the edibility of the nuts. He wondered if Moss entertained the same thoughts.

Later, the nuts roasted in a dry pan and mashed into a sweet delicious paste, they lay back in the seats where they had set up their home and looked up at the painted blackness above them, punctuated by occasional stars that could be seen through the holes in the roof.

"I wonder what's up there," Moss said.

Calvin looked across to her, at the way a moonbeam caressed her face and gave her skin a milky sheen. "It doesn't matter," he said. "What matters is what's down here." He paused, drinking in the moment. "How big do you think Heart is?" he asked. I've travelled for three winters and it's all been the same: settlement, landscape, city, settlement. How long do you think that goes on?"

Moss shifted in her seat, leant towards him. He wanted to feel her heat but it was impossible through their joint layers of clothing. Nevertheless, there was a frisson from the briefest of contacts. "I don't know," she said. "I've seen a lot. I've seen where the ground pushes up towards the sky, where deep valleys seem to go on forever, and where water has flooded the world as far as the eye can see. But I haven't seen the end of things. I haven't seen where Heart stops and something else begins."

"Maybe it doesn't," Calvin answered. "Maybe Heart doesn't stop."

Moss shrugged. "We will never know."

Calvin thought over what Moss had said, realised she must have come from an entirely different direction to get where she was today. It crossed his mind that she would want to leave in another direction, and conversely, he wanted to see the places she had seen which seemed vastly more interesting than his journey had taken him to date.

"What are you looking for?"

Moss smiled. "I don't know. Do you know? No, of course you don't. What we both wanted was to be somewhere other than where we were. And now we are. Now we are here."

She slouched a little further in her seat, shifted towards him. Her head rested on his shoulder, just under his chin. He could smell a wiry must to her hair, see the dirt ingrained within tiny lines on her forehead. Desire, of a kind which he had never experienced before, ran through his chest to his loins. He realised with a start that he wanted her to conceive.

Sky had spoken to him about the impulse to breed, only one season prior to his leaving the settlement. She had explained how it was the pull of human nature to procreate, to continue the species. Calvin had barely wanted to understand at the time, he found the entire subject embarrassing even though he had watched the animals rut and seen newborn creatures and people alike. Yet now he had travelled, now he had seen how populated Heart must once have been, he realised that without new life there could only be further deterioration. *What was he looking for?* He was looking for a reason for being. It might be hasty, but with Moss he wondered if he'd found it.

His heart beat faster and he realised despite the cold that he was perspiring. "These nuts are good," he said.

Moss smiled. "They're chestnuts. There were always a lot of them around in my original settlement, although I haven't seen any for a while."

"Our staples were root vegetables. Potato, beets, parsnips, swede, turnips. I was assigned to duties as a gardener. I also took care of tomatoes, peas, cucumbers. I enjoyed it. I like tending the garden, seeing things grow."

"And what did you do with the vegetables that didn't develop as they should?"

Moss's voice was so soft that Calvin could barely hear her.

"We never threw them away," he said. "They were used for soup, or at the worse, compost."

"Soup or compost," Moss repeated.

Calvin sat a little straighter. He could detect a subtext and guessed where it was heading. "Everything has a use," he said. He paused. He didn't want the conversation, yet he wanted the conversation. "The body you saw picking up potatoes, why did they have it doing that if it was so slow?"

"The settlement was tiny," Moss said. "Only two families lived there. I guess they needed as much help as they could get. He wasn't the only one, either. They had two or three of them lying around."

"Really? For what purpose?"

"For none, as far as I could see. Soup or compost. Compost is all they're really good for."

Calvin could feel the hairs in his arms bristling; confusion reigned over the sudden shift in feelings that he had towards Moss. He chose his next words carefully, not wanting the surge of anger that he felt to be reflected between them. Meantime, their position on the seats looking at the stars remained, was contained. "What if you were pregnant," he said, "and the father wasn't there for the birth?"

She snorted. "He *would* be there. I'd be sure of it."

"What if something happened and he couldn't be. What would you do to the child?"

She turned her head to look at him, her nose crooked from that angle. "We both know what we would both do," she said. "We would know what we had to do."

Calvin's mind reeled as he wondered about his own response, if it came to the quick. But also as they fell quiet his mind lingered on the word *both*. Their fate had been sealed, he was sure of it. They were going to have a baby.

15

By the time the snow had melted Moss was pregnant.

They had spent winter in the city, managing to find food just as it seemed their supplies would run out, and generally having the luck of it. In one quarter, where the buildings were all composed of a pale yellowish brick, they had found a structure with a pointed top still intact not dissimilar to the one Calvin had first climbed. Up they went, giggling and holding onto each other through the spiral, until they reached the top and gained the familiar nauseous feeling coupled with the incredible breadth, scope, and beauty of the view. Moss indicated the direction in which she had come, Calvin likewise. From this vantage point they chose the direction they would head once spring arrived. They had already decided they would journey together. Calvin realised in retrospect there had never been any question of it.

They made plans for the future. They agreed whenever they came near a settlement that only one of them would approach it, taking this in turns. They agreed that when the time was ready they would create their own settlement and raise their child there. These agreements were made playfully, in the depth of the winter when the snow piled so high against their home that they didn't venture out; but they were serious too. Because now they were on a path of no return. Their lives had been sealed within a moment.

Their coupling had been awkward, yet natural. Making a fire in a part of the building they rarely used, as the heat of the flames increased so they divested themselves of their clothing. Calvin's fingertips ran traces over Moss's skin – over scars, dirt, and blemishes – exhibiting a tenderness that came from inside him, which surprised him. Moss's mouth engaged with his, her tongue darting in and out in the manner he had seen the occasional lizard do as it basked on a stone in the hot summer sun; yet he enjoyed it, tongued her tongue back, mashed his face against hers as their passion rose and they created the universal shape of two animals in rut, silhouetted by the flames against the white-screened expanse that flanked the wall opposite the seats. A shadowplay of sensuality.

Afterwards they knew they had created a baby. They had interwoven in much the same way that tapestries were formed – their initially separate threads combined to make a bigger picture. As Moss's periods ceased and her stomach started to swell they developed a closer relationship; Calvin insisted on performing most of the manual work, but Moss was not about to be defined by her pregnancy, and after a few gentle arguments she held onto their shared roles as she had before the conception.

Spring revealed all that had hitherto been buried under the snow. They saw the gardens they had milked were close to exhaustion. Whilst Calvin had been toying with the idea of remaining in the city for the duration of the pregnancy, Moss wanted to strike forth. They were travellers, she reminded him; and he wondered if she would continue to travel after the birth, despite their talk over creating a settlement. Whilst he wanted to see Heart's expanse, his role as father made him more protective. It made sense to find somewhere, cultivate a garden during the spring and summer months, and to have established themselves by autumn when they expected the baby was due. Moss could be hot headed, determined; sometimes Calvin wondered what she was running away from, for it seemed the concept of a settlement and domesticity was abhorrent to her.

The night before they left the city he decided to raise the question of her travelling. Of what had started her on that path. She had always been evasive, putting it down to *the calling*. But Calvin knew that as with himself and his experience with the body that had been battered on the outside of his birth settlement, that there would have been some impetus to kickstart her journey. Now she was pregnant, however, she had become less secretive. So she told him, over tea they had made from plant leaf and cinnamon sticks; the latter Moss had along with the rosemary in her backpack. Spices had turned out to be her forte.

"My settlement contained a structure of glass," she began, nestled against Calvin in their usual spot across the front row seats in their temporary home. "Until I began travelling, I assumed every settlement had one of these, but I've seen so much broken glass since that I consider it a miracle. Within this glass structure we could grow as many vegetables, spices, and plants as we desired. The glass magnifies the heat of the sun and the enclosed building contains it. I've never seen anything like it since. Maybe we were blessed, but generations had farmed in our settlement in this way. Much of what we grew there I haven't even seen since. The cinnamon, for example, that flavours this drink, is of a completely unknown bark to the trees I have seen elsewhere. In hindsight, it was a magical place, but also because of this I had to get away.

"Travellers came to our settlement and were wowed by us. They told such tales of ravagement elsewhere, of survival against the odds, of places where vegetables had to be farmed out of hard ground, where meat was the mainstay and when it failed people starved. They told these stories so vividly that I felt compelled to see these places; even knowing that I was leaving my charmed life behind.

"And it's been hard. Harder than you can imagine."

Calvin wrapped his arm around her, noticed tears on his sleeve from where he had brushed against her face. "Could you find it again? Maybe we could go back."

Moss jutted out her chin. "Travellers never go back," she said. "We know this."

"You'd have a baby, you'd have me; maybe it would be different."

"It couldn't be different. I didn't leave under the best of circumstances. I did more than run away." She paused. "I escaped."

Calvin gave her a squeeze. "Escaped?"

"They saw me talking with the Traveller. Esquire, his name was. In our settlement it was only the men who were allowed to speak to Travellers, unless we were children asking questions during story time. One of the elders overheard part of the conversation. I think they guessed my intent. That night they were waiting for me. They hustled me into the glass house. It was the height of summer and stifling in there. It was so hot the air was full of water." Moss saw Calvin's puzzled expression. "I can't explain it if you haven't experienced it. Anyway, I paced up and down whilst I saw them talking about me. Eventually, I went to the back of the glass house and charged against it, smashed right through the glass and kept running and didn't stop."

"Heart. You were that desperate to get away?"

She sighed. "Maybe I wasn't. But in that moment I was. Do you understand? They actually forced me into doing something I had only been toying with. I changed from a child to an adult as I breached the glass."

Calvin kissed the top of her forehead, noted her subconsciously touch her belly with her right hand. Moss tasted like moss: there was a fresh green sensation that came with kissing her. They had been foraging that morning for supplies to take away with them, and the outdoor spring weather seemed to have affixed itself to her skin. He continued kissing, down the length of her nose, around her neck, brushing his lips against her mouth which retained a touch of cinnamon from her tea.

Those cinnamon kisses continued as their love enwrapped and enveloped them; they became pockets of each other's coats, memories of each other's flesh, designs within each other's fingerprints, growths within each other's bodies. The spring weather had dissolved within them nodules of the rut, and despite Moss's already convex condition they cemented the love for each other repeatedly, a love which would be endorsed through their baby's birth, through the conjoining of body and soul, through the expectation of the future as seen through the past telescoped through the present.

Calvin had never been happier.

AUTUMNAL BURIAL

1

Spring brought an early unexpected warmth. Calvin and Moss set out, away from the city, in a direction neither of them had headed before. Moss insisted on carrying her own pack and Calvin fought the urge to be overprotective. He slid easily into that role, however, as though it were made for him. He realised that fatherhood brought responsibility with it, and that this was natural and not something that needed thinking about.

Flowers that had lain dormant during the winter months began to push their way out of the soil. The heath land was now long behind them, the landscape that Calvin was familiar with had been hidden under snow and when it was revealed he saw that it had changed. Pockets of woodland flanked large expanses of grass. Broken wooden fences half-heartedly enclosed these areas. As they journeyed, fields of brilliant yellow stunned their eyes; emanating a rich odour that caught in their back of their nostrils and throats. Calvin didn't like it, but Moss did.

"This crop was close to our settlement," she said. "It's rape. You can make a viscous liquid out of it which enhances cooking."

Calvin nodded. Looked out at the fields of yellow and didn't understand.

Then it struck him how good the surface of Heart was to them. It provided food, sustenance, water. Some places provided natural warmth and shelter. Whereas the vestiges of a previous civilisation had assisted him during his travelling, those settlements he had encountered had all been self-sufficient. He mumbled a *thank you* to Heart under his breath. He wondered if this serendipity of cohabitation between people and the natural world was coincidental or by design. It seemed almost impossible for it to exist without intervention.

Occasionally he had overheard conversations between the elders about the nature of existence and whether there was more to life than the cycles of birth and death. As a child he had paid little attention. In any event, nothing had been said which was anything more than a nebulous discussion of being. Some had pointed to the existence of a soul as proof that there was more to a being than simply a body. For it was true that without a soul at birth the body was no more than a useless object; but when a body died what therefore happened to the soul?

Calvin had not witnessed death first hand. Within the settlement, some had stated that the soul left through the mouth of a body during death, others that it wept through the pores of the skin, still others that the soul simply was no longer apparent and therefore died at the same moment as the body ceased functioning. For those who believed the soul left the body, opinion was divided as to whether it then still existed as an entity with consciousness or whether it simply dissipated. And this, of course, led to arguments as to whether a soul that left a body after death had the same properties as a soul that couldn't connect to a body at birth. If they were one and the same, in essence, then did the soul body-hop from death to birth? It had made Calvin's head spin to think of such concepts, yet now he was due to father a child himself, such things were promoted to the forefront of his mind.

As Moss grew the body of their child, so he was aware of changes inside himself to develop the soul.

Moss had asked him how it felt, after a morning of such sickness that they had to rest before continuing their journey.

"Do you feel the sickness, in the same way that I do?"

Calvin thought. "I feel a queasiness, not a sickness. I don't want to be sick, but I have an awareness of sickness as a concept."

"As a concept." Moss spat contemptuously onto the grass. Calvin didn't mind her mood, he knew it came with the territory. "I wish I knew it as a concept."

"It's an imagining," he continued. "There's a sensation, like nervousness, that hovers in the pit of my stomach. Maybe it's anticipation. It's the kind of feeling I used to get when I was aware there was a traveller on the edge of the settlement: a feeling of trepid excitement. It's almost like movement inside me, but not quite."

Moss nodded. "I have none of that yet," she said. "Only the absence of blood and the sickness." She tried to stand, but Calvin watched as her legs visibly shook and she returned to the ground. "Not yet," she smiled.

Calvin placed a hand on her arm. "We're in no rush," he said.

Moss smiled again. They sat and watched a few white clouds scud across the sky. "I wonder what it will feel like, for both of us, when the baby is due. I can't imagine it being pulled from my body, to hear its first cries, to hold it for the first time. And for you, too, how will it feel as the soul leaves your body and joins that of our child. Will you feel a wrench – a physical detachment, or will there just be an absence: a hole where something was?"

Calvin shook his head. "We won't know these answers until it happens."

But Moss needed more. She found it impossible not to constantly question the changes within their bodies, or what might happen once the baby was born.

"We will need a settlement, of some kind," Calvin had said. "A midwife should be there."

Moss shook her head. "We can do it alone."

"Seriously?"

"Seriously. I'm sure that we can."

Calvin shrugged. "Have you ever seen a birth?"

Moss shook her head.

"Me neither," he said.

It was during these moments that the enormity of their choice of life as travellers overwhelmed them.

If they could view themselves on Heart, maybe from the vantage point of one of the stars in the night sky, Calvin imagined that they were no more than blades of grass. Yet if they were utterly part of things, they were also completely *apart* from things. In all their travels, other than each other, they had neither met nor conversed with any other travellers – and whilst it might have been that his age improved the hospitality he had received at various settlements, and no doubt Moss's gender and latterly the fact that she was pregnant would also enhance her reception, he had never been in a situation where it appeared even remotely likely that a settlement would adopt him permanently. And not only this, he had yet to see another settlement – other than that of his home, from which he had left – where he would want to live.

These concerns played on his mind. Would they continue to travel after the baby was born? And if they settled, could he support them? He determined they would have to find a base where they could bed in some crops, possibly barter some artefacts for a couple of animals; because whilst spring would segue into summer and would in turn segue into autumn and the birth of their child, it wouldn't be long before winter came around again and harsh realities would need to be faced.

Moss, however, was more concerned with keeping moving.

"I love this life," she said, one evening when it was warm enough for them to lie on their backs looking skywards at the stars. "I know it's difficult, but there's so much to see. And now we have each other it's not a lonely experience – there's so much to share. There's places I've been that I'd now like to return to, with you, to show you. There are new places out there that I want to discover with you. I want it all."

Calvin nodded, unsure if she could see that movement in the dark. "I love travelling too. I wouldn't be here if I didn't. We both gave up so much, took such a risk, to get to where we are." He thought: without the travelling, they would never have met. It seemed an impossibility. "But I'm fearful for the child."

"We can create our problems or we can create solutions," Moss said, quietly.

Calvin wondered if other travellers met, paired up, continued travelling together. He wondered if there were any other female travellers. He wondered if Book ever wanted to settle down. Whilst their meeting had been so transitory and such a long time ago, he couldn't help but consider Book as the catalyst for his travelling. He would always be a reference point for the basis of speculation. Surely like himself and Moss, Book must have met other travellers during his journeys. Calvin considered this even as he knew it had taken him three solitary winters to see *one* other traveller. Couldn't a scenario be envisaged whereby whole communities might move from place to place, in transitory encampments, so that they got the best out of settlement life and travelling life? He wondered if there was ever a precedent for this. But even as he considered it, he also realised the impracticalities of farming and feeding a settlement on the move. And whilst settlements might happily feed solitary travellers, they would not consider doing the same for large groups of people. The idea was as unfeasible as it was desirable.

He concentrated on the sky above and the pinpricks of light. They co-existed but never touched. He reached out and held Moss's hand.

"Do you see that," she said.

"Hmmm?"

"Up there." She let his hand go and pointed. "Do you see *that*?"

Calvin followed the line of her finger. The stars looked no different to him; their places fixed in his mind as well as in the firmament. She knocked his elbow: *there*.

"I can't see it. What am I supposed to be looking for?"

"There!" Moss's insistence forced him to look harder. He strained his eyes until it seemed they might see through the black expanse and journey beyond. At the point where he didn't believe he would see anything at all, he realised what she was indicating. Up there were two lights on the move: one white, one red. They were tiny, smaller than those surrounding, crossing from right to left across the sky. Both lights remained equidistant from one another.

Calvin sat up. Then lay back again, for the best vantage point.

"What is that?"

"I don't know," whispered Moss, all the excitement drained from her. "I've never seen anything like it before."

They remained silent as the lights traversed against the black backdrop. Eventually, they faded.

It was only when they had disappeared that they realised a low level hum had accompanied its progress.

"Maybe it's a sign," Calvin said. He reached into his pocket and rubbed his fingertips over his artefact, finding the alternation between the rough and the smooth reassuring.

"Maybe it is," Moss agreed. "But a sign of what?"

Calvin had no answer.

They remained watching the skies in silence, but by the time their eyelids drooped heavy and Moss had drifted off to sleep in Calvin's arms the anomaly hadn't returned.

2

Their experiences at settlements were fraught and anxious.

Whenever it was Moss's turn to play the role of storyteller Calvin found his insides twisted until such time as she safely left the settlement. He had to stay out of sight. They couldn't risk being seen together in case it compromised the traditional understanding of the role of traveller. Two together would be an unknown concept, and whilst they might equally be welcomed it wasn't a risk they were prepared to take. Nevertheless, Calvin spent those solo nights skirting the rim of the settlement – for Moss couldn't return the same way she had come – muttering under his breath and wishing they had decided only he should play that role.

Conversely, on those nights when Calvin became storyteller, his mind was elsewhere, worrying about Moss and her condition and how she was spending the night alone – particularly when the weather was against them. It was as though their status as travellers, which they had both embraced as ways to free themselves from society's constraints, had now defined them to the extent that they were more restricted than they had ever been.

At each place they visited they made enquiries as to other travellers, but never heard of anyone within twenty sun-ups. None of the settlements had heard of a traveller called Book, and from the reaction to his question Calvin often thought that no other travellers ever asked. At a couple of settlements he once again saw maltreatment of bodies, which seemed to have been kept alive for nothing more than amusement. Moss also reported that she had seen one being ridden like a pig. She had laughed when she told him, and Calvin buried his distaste. She was – after all – the carrier of his child.

Calvin found he dwelt on these anomalies frequently during periods of separation from Moss. He wondered what her reaction might be if he wasn't present at the birth. Not that the circumstance was likely to arrive, but nevertheless he hoped that her acerbic consideration of bodies would change as the pregnancy progressed.

One late afternoon, with the sun streaming low through the trees striping Calvin's vision, he stood at the edge of a wooded area and watched Moss – obviously pregnant, her hands resting on her belly – walk towards a settlement of around twenty shacks that sat on a small hill in the distance.

As usual, he felt tremors of anxiety. Her increasingly diminished

90

form seemed to vanish from his memory at the same time as she slipped out of view. He remembered his feelings of disassociation when he had first left his settlement. Nowadays it was hard to envisage his family and friends – their mannerisms, looks, tone of voice. He didn't want the same to happen with Moss; ever.

They had arrived in the wood the previous evening, too late for Moss to venture out and storytell. Building a fire was too dangerous – they didn't want to attract attention – but the evening was warm and eating some broth and bread they had left over from a previous settlement was fulfilling despite not having it warmed through.

Calvin had rested his hand on Moss's stomach. It was still too early to feel anything, but he found it reassuring.

"What shall we call it?" he asked.

"I don't know. Of course, it'll depend whether it's a boy or a girl."

"Don't you want to think of some names beforehand?"

Moss shook her head. "I haven't given it any thought. Is that wrong?"

Calvin didn't know. In his settlement, names were assigned well before the birth – although of course they were discarded in those few instances where the soul didn't join with the body. No one named a body.

"Where I lived," Moss said, "the mother and father had no input in naming the child. It was something the elders decided. In fact, after the birth, the father didn't have much of a role in the upbringing at all. The mothers nursed the baby in turn."

Calvin ran his fingertips along the length of Moss's arm; she shivered.

"It was similar in my settlement, although the parents named the baby. My father, Royce, kept to himself much of the time. Although my mother, Sky, was my main carer. Certainly the other women dipped in now and again, but I always knew I was her baby; it was evident."

Even as he spoke the words Calvin felt a deepening sorrow for all he had left behind. He tried to bury it under the knowledge that for their child he would have to be a far more hands-on father than Royce had been.

"My mother's name was Tomy and my father's name was Amstrad. Have you been thinking of names?"

Calvin shook his head. "It just occurred to me. I think about the baby a lot."

Moss smiled. "I know you do."

Calvin remembered the conversation as Moss winked out of view. A small crowd had gathered at the edge of the settlement as she approached, and her form became amassed with theirs. Calvin often wondered about her reception, how it would differ from his, considering she was female.

They were taking a risk, despite her insistence, in allowing her to journey into the settlements alone. If Calvin could see she was pregnant, then it wouldn't be long before that became evident to outsiders who weren't expecting it. A female traveller was unusual in itself. A pregnant female traveller indicated that she might have run away from her settlement under difficult circumstances – that was open to all sorts of speculation. And a female without a male in tow who was pregnant could only expect to deliver a body – all sorts of dangers and moral complexities were tied up with *that*.

So as night descended and turned Heart black Calvin couldn't help but fret and bite his nails and not eat whilst Moss told her stories and fed heartily and hopefully would return with foodstuffs for the next stage of their journey.

To busy himself he watched the skies. His eyelids were heavy – he was fighting sleep. He made patterns out of the light but as his vision blurred and he shifted in and out of consciousness it appeared that the lights were dancing. Then he saw it again. He blinked twice, wiped his fingers across his eyes: there they were, clear against the blackness, one white light and one red light arcing across the sky.

He listened carefully, and once more heard the hum. For the duration of the visibility and for a little while afterwards the hum was steady and strong. Calvin couldn't begin to imagine what it was. He wondered if anyone had noticed in the settlement, but then it was rare for people to spend time outdoors at night. The days were harsh: hard work, early mornings, and the repetition of familiar tasks all tended to make for sleepy evenings. And within the settlement the hum would be no more than a whisper amid the noises of cooking, eating, and sleeping.

He scratched his head, now wide awake. Moss had suggested he get some sleep, then move around to the other side of the settlement to meet her at another outcrop of trees that mirrored their location. But this wasn't going to happen. They had dozed during the day, but his brain was buzzing with disturbed sleep, skylights, the worry over Moss and the settlement, and all their future selves. He decided to skirt the settlement early, stood, and made his way slowly in a semi-circle, keeping the trees behind him so they might shield him from prying eyes.

Before him, the settlement was dark, there wasn't even any light from fires, or visible smoke emerging through the roof. Calvin wondered what story Moss had told. He had a favourite of hers that went something like this:

"I had been travelling for one full swing of the seasons. Winter had set in and the ground crunched with each step underfoot, ice making puddles that broke like glass when I stepped on them, water droplets frozen on trees refracting light in weird patterns.

"I was drawn to a sound like the wind rushing through trees. It was an alien noise – repetitive, melodic, almost by design. When I crested a hill I saw before me the largest expanse of water you could imagine. It stretched as far as the eye could see, both to the horizon and to either side. It was like the surface of Heart ended with the water, was submerged into it. At the water's edge the land changed from green to dull yellow. The wind was harder and faster, bringing a chill off the water that whipped around my face.

"And the water itself seemed alive. On my travels I have seen smaller areas – some settlements are built around them – but none were of this scale. Imagine a river stretched wide: the water moves in one direction, over rocks, stones, around corners and through banks. We understand the movement of rivers. If we drop something it rolls – so it does with water. Imagine this stretched river – I can't even call it a *river* because the only connection is water – that does not conform to these properties. If it flows to the land then it pauses and returns – repeatedly; it curls and twists, froths on the yellow surface, drains back leaving bubbles which stretch and burst. If you watch it long enough it recedes, baring the land that exists beneath it, but like a temptress should you accept its allure and follow it then it undoes you, flows back inland, rushes forwards with that noise which is not air yet sounds like it, then repeats the entire cycle once more.

"And should you follow the edge of the water, along the yellow surface leaving footprints later to be reclaimed, you might find crumbling walls that appear manmade – maybe the detritus of old cities – battered by the water that smashes into it and then rises vertical, sweeping upwards as though in a dance, flinging droplets sky high before they fall and re-amass with the water again. I tell you now: this is mesmeric. I remained for several sun-ups, watching the rise and swell, the return, the recede; until the noise that repeated itself in my ears became song, became soothing, became inconsequential.

"I dared myself to touch the water. Each time I reached for it I found it ran away. When I waited longer it rushed over my shoes, wetting them, filling them with yellow grains. The water itself was salty on my tongue, like the residue of sweat on my forehead. The white froth seemed to taste of nothing different. The water seemed to pull at my feet as it moved away."

Moss told Calvin she always sat forward at this point, looking each of her listeners in the eye, before concluding: "You will never see such a terrible, awful, subsuming beauty."

Calvin related the story in his head as he skirted the settlement. He wanted to see the things Moss had seen, to experience her experiences. He wanted to show their child those things too. He realised then that however practical it might be to settle down, he didn't want to deny their baby the right to be on the move. Subliminally, through repeating her story, he realised Moss was slowly convincing him to follow her demands.

He smiled to himself. A smile that was broken by a sudden shout that rose almost visibly from the settlement and chilled him to the bone.

He paused in his tracks, his right hand automatically reaching to lean against a tree trunk to steady himself. *Was the voice female?* He couldn't be sure. He waited again, strained his ears against the dark, but could only imagine he heard the blood pumping round his brain and the hammering of his heart within his chest. Following the noise the air itself was deathly silent, as though even the wind had paused all the better to hear a sound.

Calvin wondered if it had been Moss. Once the idea was in his head he couldn't shake it. And as it couldn't be shaken then there was only one thing to do: investigate.

He turned to establish his position on Heart and dropped his pack by a tree with a distorted stump that he might easily find again. The skies were clear, moonlight lit the direction. He walked steadily towards the settlement, knowing that no travellers ever did this at night, knowing he might be open to attack if he were perceived to be a threat, knowing that if Moss were safe he might have to pretend he didn't know her, wondered if she would do the same.

The settlement was encircled by a fence. Its only use was to restrain livestock and therefore presented no barrier as Calvin climbed over it. Goats bleated softly as he moved between them, their animal scent warm and fresh against the smell of the cool night air. Calvin pressed himself against the wall of the nearest shack and listened again. He could hear a low murmur: conversation. Then a dull thud and a muffled cry.

Again, it was impossible to determine the sex of the cry; but Calvin was taking no chances. He edged around the building until he found the door and then peeked inside.

The interior was darkened, but not unlit. Fires on sticks lined the walls, and shadows created more people than Calvin eventually realised were there. Caught in the light of the fires, a body was crouched down on the floor, hands over its head in a pose that tore at Calvin's insides. It was a pose that *understood* threat. It wasn't Moss – she was sitting amongst a group of elders in a semi-circle around the body. The body itself was naked and obviously female. It faced away from Calvin, long hair draped on either side of its head, knees on the floor. It emitted a noise that Calvin could only describe as a whimper: a soulful sound derived from pain.

He caught his breath, was determined to remain quiet. Around the body lay a variety of objects: small sticks, stones, rounded wooden shapes he recognised from his own settlement childhood games. A circle around the figure had been drawn in the dirt. As he watched, Moss was handed one of the wooden balls and she threw it – hard, not half-heartedly – at the body's back. It bounced off with that dull thud he had heard outside the shack, and was followed by a low moan from the body. Bile rose to the back of Calvin's throat. He glanced back to Moss's face: she was smiling.

Calvin closed the crack of door he had spied through, leant back against the side of the shack. This wasn't his business. If he interrupted what was happening then the settlement would turn against him; possibly against Moss too. He had no right to interfere in how they treated the body. Yet, simultaneously, he felt a surge of moral duty. The body could *feel*. It was aware of its treatment. It wasn't simply an inanimate object, which might be used as a target. It was precisely because it *was* a body that it was being abused. It sickened him. He tried to push Moss's role in the game to the back of his mind, hoped she had been coerced; but knew from her expression that she saw no wrong in what she was doing any more than the regulars did.

And if he did make a stand? He ran the risks already considered, plus the possibility of losing Moss, and even if he were successful on all counts and got the body out of there what would he do with it? He rested his head in his hands. The truth was, the body was in a better place crouched on the floor and being beaten than it would be anywhere else. It was totally bounded by circumstance.

Yet he continued to think through the possibilities as he walked back through the goats to the fence, made his way over it, and returned to the treeline where his backpack awaited. What would it take for him to go, now, and leave Moss alone?

He slumped against the foot of the tree, resting against it. What if he were to scare Moss. To make her think he had deserted her and their baby, to cast her out alone upon the landscape knowing that without him she would birth a body without a soul. Would that make her understand how awful it must be to be a body? Not that he could go through with it, of course, but maybe for a few days, to trail her at a distance, just to hammer home what he considered to be her cruelty.

But then he looked inside himself. No one would choose to have a body over a baby. However much he might profess to care about their circumstances he naturally wanted his and Moss's baby to be the perfect union of body and soul. Was it hypocritical, therefore, for him to criticise her attitude? But then he remembered the smile on her face as she lobbed the stone and knew it went beyond simple ethics. Moss's attitude, like most of the people he had ever encountered, was ingrained. They viewed them as mostly useless – which, indeed, they were. Of course, in his settlement a body without a soul was killed at birth. This could be the only fair option. But if that didn't happen, what would be fairer? Should he go back into the settlement and kill the fully formed body which was being tormented? Whilst it might put an end to its suffering, would that really be the right thing to do?

He could feel the dampness of the soil seeping into his clothing. He knew he would do nothing.

He sat awhile, then sighed, rose, and continued the semi-circle trek around the edge of the settlement. No further noises were set against the night, but they repeated inside his head: a dull thunk and a low moan of pain.

3

They continued from settlement to settlement, taking turns; Calvin never mentioning what he had seen.

Some days they couldn't stop talking, other days they said nothing at all. Buds pushed up green from the ground, trees blossomed in a frenzy of soft colour, wildlife became more obvious. They pushed on: destination unknown. Some days they rested, when Moss's sickness became too great and she speckled the ground with the previous evening's broth. Other days they went faster than Calvin thought possible: running up hill and down dale. Those days were when laughter was paramount and all his fears were forgotten. Those were the days when he felt blessed to be travelling.

The strange lights in the sky didn't reappear, not as spring segued into summer and Moss's belly extended and undulations ran across it whilst Calvin watched and Moss encouraged him to press his ear to her skin.

As the pregnancy became more evident, so Calvin took over the role of traveller. Moss acquiesced that her presence at a settlement might lead to disturbing consequences, but she did so grudgingly; Calvin realised how attached she was to the concept of being a *traveller*. If he had felt a calling, she had felt a summoning. As the time he had known her pregnant extended beyond the time he had known her not, so he understood her more. If he had to describe her, it would be something like this:

"Moss is a unique being. The only female traveller I have ever heard of, let alone met. She is capricious and inquisitive, she is open-minded yet fixed in her ideals. She needs me and yet she could exist without me. Sometimes it seems she wants to exist without me. Sometimes I know she never wants to be anywhere but at my side.

"She views her pregnancy as both a blessing and a disturbance. She both wants and doesn't want the child. She has a fear of needing to settle in one place, and fights against it at every cost. Yet she knows that she is the instigator of her own destiny, she knows the baby was created out of love rather than necessity, and she revels in it just as she finds it an encumbrance."

Sometimes they walked hand in hand.

One afternoon they lay on their backs in a meadow speckled with white petal flowers that held yellow circles in an embrace.

"These are daisies," Moss said. "We had lots and lots of these back at my home settlement. Look." She plucked one from the earth and with a damaged fingernail slit the green stem. Then she plucked another and threaded its stem through the hole in the first. Calvin watched her as she repeated the motion, until such time as she had a loop and she had attached the final stem back to the first to create a circle. She placed it over Calvin's head.

"These were worn when couples procreated," she said. "They're supposed to be lucky."

"It's a little late for that now," smiled Calvin. He reached up to pull it off his head.

"Keep it," Moss insisted. Calvin was sure he saw something flash behind her eyes. "It's lucky, remember."

The tone of her voice told him not to argue. They lay back on the grass, shielding their faces against the burn of the sky. Calvin rarely looked up during the day, it was the night that enamoured him with all its intricacies. The day sky, whether bright blue or cloudy, simply obscured the stars.

"Close your eyes," Moss said.

Calvin did so. He focussed on the heat on his face, tiny red lines striated the inside of his eyelids set against a glowing yellow background. The warmth of the sun was comforting, a reminder that they could tarry by the side of the Snake and relax without worrying about the cold or where the next meal might come from. These seasons were abundant with produce they could harvest; although he remained aware that they would have to bed in for autumn and find somewhere semi-permanent for a while, at least.

Moss touched his left earlobe. He gave a start, then settled as his body relaxed and gave in to her tenderness. Her fingertips were replaced by her lips were replaced by her tongue. The left-hand side of him goosebumped: arms through to legs. He shivered, despite the heat. Pressing herself against him he could feel the curve of her stomach. Her hand slipped inside his shirt, one of her legs entwined with his. Her fingertips pressed against his chest, she bit his earlobe. He became enveloped in the moment, open to sensation, to sensuality. Under the wide sky he became aware of her fingers around his penis. He hardened. Moss moved her mouth to kiss his, repeatedly, until he had speckled the daisies with his ejaculation and the centre of some of their tiny yellow suns were dotted white.

Moss laughed. "We haven't done that for some time."

Calvin slipped into sleep, warmth spreading throughout each pore of his body, breathing her in, breathing in the smells of their sexual activity.

And as he slept, he dreamt.

The scene was crystal clear, but the more Calvin looked the more he saw that each object in his vision was outlined in bright light. The trees on the horizon had silver edges, each blade of grass was backlit as if by frost, a scabby shack in the foreground seemed to glow. As Calvin watched, mesmerised by the panoply of light, the door to the shack opened and Book stepped out.

He, too, was hyper-real; the edges of his clothing etched in brilliant white. His expression was calm, inquisitive; as though he were seeing Calvin for the first time and was unafraid of him. *Should he be afraid*, queried Calvin, in his dream mind. Something nagged that maybe he was dangerous. He extended his arms, hands down at his sides, palms outwards. Book took a stride or two towards him, then stopped.

"How are you?"

Book's voice echoed. It seemed to be inside Calvin's head. Calvin suddenly realised Book's mouth hadn't moved. He was communicating in another way.

"I'm fine," spoke Calvin. His own lips moved. He hadn't even thought about his answer, it was automatic.

"Do you have the artefact?"

Calvin reached into his pocket, felt the familiar rough and smooth sides. He pulled it out. "Here it is."

Book frowned.

Calvin looked down at his hand. The object shivered and then collapsed into dust.

"It's been corrupted," Book echoed.

Calvin watched as the dust fell through his fingers onto the floor; each individual particle silhouetted in the same silver light.

"I don't understand."

"There is nothing to understand," said Book. "This is a dream. It doesn't adhere to the properties of reality. In the dream your artefact is meaningless."

"And outside of the dream?"

"It has as much meaning as you impart to it. But I repeat, this a dream. Why are you attaching any importance to my answers?"

Behind Book the shack suddenly imploded, collapsing in on itself, folding up, until it was no more than the size of a tiny box. Book turned and picked up the box, held it in his palm, and then offered it to Calvin.

Calvin saw himself reach out and take it. He opened the box. Inside sat his artefact. He took it out and replaced it in his pocket.

"Listen to this," said Book. His voice that had run around the inside of Calvin's head was replaced by humming. Calvin realised Book was singing to him. He strained to understand the refrain. Singing was familiar to his home settlement but he had rarely heard song since he had begun travelling. Yet this didn't sound like a song: it was a continuous noise, getting louder and louder and...

"Wake up!"

He opened his eyes. Beside him on the grass Moss was asleep. He looked around for who had called to him, but there was no one; it had to have been within the dream. He shook his head, rubbed his eyes. Then realised the noise remained. He looked up at the pale blue sky.

A silver object traversed his view.

He jolted; stood. Raised a hand to his eyes and shielded his gaze from the sun which backlit the object, gave its edges the glare from the dream. It was tubular in design, longer than it was wide or tall. On two sides, arms extended. Much as he had extended his, palms outwards, to Book. Instinctively Calvin felt in his pocket for his artefact and pulled it out. It was intact. He returned it to his pocket and rubbed it with his fingers for security as the object moved slowly through the air.

The distinctive hum faded as the object moved out of sight. Calvin looked down at Moss, still asleep on the ground, her body surrounded by grass and daisies as she made an impression in the vegetation.

He decided not to tell her what he had seen.

There had been a white light and a red light on the object. There was no question that this was what they had previously viewed in the night sky, its substance now revealed by the sun. Calvin looked back to the Snake, its cracked undulations followed the direction the object had taken. They had mused whether to continue following it. It was true that more settlements lay beyond the Snake. But they had sufficient food supplies for some time and Calvin was increasingly unhappy about leaving Moss alone overnight whilst he spent time in the settlements. He decided to persuade Moss they should continue to follow the black line, in a secret hope that it might also somehow lead them to the object.

Book was right: the dream might have no significance. But it could also be a portent, and Calvin thought it unwise to disregard it.

He bent and shook Moss awake. "Hey, it's getting late. We should be on the move."

She stirred. "Hmmm?"

It wasn't quite the hum of Book's singing nor that of the object in the sky, but it resonated within Calvin and the tiny soul that was growing inside him seemed to seize on it and recognise. There was a flutter, as though his heart were shot through with adrenaline, which gradually subsided.

"We have to keep moving," Calvin repeated. They had to get somewhere, had to make a home for themselves, because the birth wouldn't slow down, wouldn't stop. He shook Moss further and shortly afterwards she awoke proper. He pulled her to her feet and they continued their journey, the soles of their feet within their worn shoes almost burning on the sections of the Snake that were exposed through the grass.

4

They continued for several sun-ups, but there was no further sign of the object. Calvin spent one night in a settlement where he wondered if he should ask about the noise in the sky – it seemed inevitable the object would have passed overhead – but he had long since realised it was himself who should be the storyteller and that information was rarely obtained through direct questioning. He considered telling it as a story, but it seemed so far-fetched as to be unbelievable, and all successful stories required a modicum of belief. So instead he listened for scraps of conversation – amongst both the children and the elders – though nothing was forthcoming and his time spent there was fruitless.

Moss complained when he returned. She had moved herself to the opposite side of the settlement but was breathing with difficulty. They waited for her distress to subside before talking. Calvin placed his palms either side of her stomach. Moss had felt tiny kicks inside her, but these were yet not strong enough for Calvin to detect them. Some nights they just lay holding each other, waiting for the miraculous to happen.

"I think we should start entering settlements together," Moss said, once she had fully recovered. "It makes sense. I don't want to be left out here alone whilst you make merry and feed."

"I'm hardly enjoying myself," Calvin couldn't help retort; although sometimes he had found he needed the break from being constantly by her side, despite the worry it also contained.

"I know what you've said about it being odd there are two travellers together, but that doesn't mean it can't happen. We *are* together, it's a fact. And any female elders would be understanding when they see that I am pregnant."

Calvin nodded. It was something they had both fought against, but he could no longer risk being absent from Moss's side. Her minor ailment this evening had made that clear.

"Ok," he said. "We'll make enquiries at the next settlement. If they see two of us approach then I'm sure we'll be met before we enter. The elders will advise us what to do."

Daylight cracked the edge of Heart as they stood and resumed walking. Calvin noticed Moss often placed a hand at the base of her spine as she moved. There were practicalities to the pregnancy which they couldn't ignore. They would have to make a decision soon about settling down, for the long run of summer's end through to autumn and then winter. Time wasn't on their side.

The sun rose hot, then cooled towards the end of the day. They stopped and watched two squirrels cavort on the grass at the base of a tree. Both of them had eaten squirrel, although never together. Calvin couldn't tell what was going on in Moss's mind, but he had no intention of capturing these creatures. They reminded him of the two of them, building their lives together, moments captivated by play. The squirrels represented a certain freedom to be had whilst travelling – there were no set tasks to be performed, none of the restrictions of settlement life. Constantly foraging, the squirrels also bedded down for the winter. The similarities between them were obvious.

Calvin was pleased Moss didn't suggest capturing the squirrels or start throwing stones at them or in any way denigrate their existence. Yet it troubled him that this even came to mind.

They journeyed on. Day segued into night segued into day. They made a decision to divert from the Snake. All they had come across were old buildings, long fallen into disuse. Calvin wondered why more of these weren't inhabited, why settlements had begun afresh rather than reusing what had gone before. Whatever had happened in the past seemed to have impacted psychologically rather than just socially. Yet he knew that himself and Moss wouldn't be able to start from scratch, and when they did finally make a home – however temporary it would be – they would need to salvage what they could. They didn't have the tools or the manpower to do anything differently.

After another sun-up a mid-sized settlement came into view. It seemed perfect for their needs: not too large to contain a threat, and not too small for the residents to consider two travellers a burden. It nestled within woodland, flanked on either side with paddocks for sheep and cows, with a vegetable garden that stretched out from the rear and seemed well-tended. Calvin felt comforted by the clutch of trees that surrounded it. Depending on the people he considered whether it might even be suitable as a home. And in the distance, the familiar scrub of moorland with its summer purples and yellows provided memories of his starting point. In many respects, it was perfect. Glancing at Moss's face Calvin realised that she thought so too.

"Not bad, is it," he said.

Moss shrugged, her usual non-committal self. "It'll do."

They sat and watched the settlement for a while, unseen from the other direction. Children attended to their duties, sweeping the paths, working in the garden, bringing water back and forth from a small river which edged one side of the settlement. Elders worked the harder manual tasks: repairing one of the shacks, wheeling a barrow of vegetables from the garden through to what Calvin assumed to be a kitchen, and generally overseeing the settlement.

They sorted through their bags, placing the choicest artefacts on top, and digging a hole beside one of the trees where they hid the food they had hoarded. It didn't pay to arrive fully laden, their needs would not be seen to be great. They had already worked through their story: both that of their reason for travelling together and the one they would tell as payment for the hospitality. Finally, when they could be sure they had done all they needed and before the sun had reached a quarter point in the sky, they held hands and walked out of the wood, towards the settlement where they had been observers and would now be participants.

"I hope this goes well," Moss muttered, as they stumbled over the uneven ground.

"Trust me," Calvin answered; less sure of himself than he sounded. "There's no reason why it shouldn't."

At half-distance they were seen. Some of the children stopped playing and pointed. They waited, sure that a group of elders would advance; not wanting to appear a threat. And this indeed happened. After a short while and some discussion a party of six exited the settlement gate and walked towards them.

Calvin's heart beat fast. He couldn't help but be reminded of the group who had approached him whilst he had been in the presence of the body near his home. A couple of the elders carried sticks; but he reasoned this as a precaution rather than a warning. His reasoning was proven correct.

One of the elders raised a hand in greeting. "Hello."

"Hello," said Moss, before Calvin had a chance to speak. If this puzzled the elder it wasn't apparent.

"We're travelling together," Moss continued, resting her hands on her belly. "I know it's unusual, but can we both rest overnight?"

The elder shrugged, glanced around at those with him, and then opened his arms in welcome. "Please. Join us. We will expect two stories rather than one, however." He laughed.

Moss slid her hand into Calvin's as they walked into the settlement proper. He could feel her smiling.

The settlement was similar to the majority he had seen: wooden shacks separated by grassy footways divided into quarters for eating, sleeping, food preparation and storage. The elder who had welcomed them, Universal, gave them a quick tour; pointing out the vegetable patch he was particularly proud of and their cooking facilities which made Calvin's mouth water. Reassuringly, there appeared to be no obvious places where a body might have resided or have been hidden. Calvin did not want to be forced into a situation where conflict might arise between himself and Moss regarding a body's treatment.

Whilst they were being shown around, a large fire was built in the centre of the settlement, and the children and elders alike formed a semi-circle around the flames. Calvin approached them first. He had already decided the tale he would tell. He wanted to mention the lights in the sky.

"Sometimes," he began, "when Heart is still and night has fallen, a traveller finds the greatest solace in being under the sky watching the stars. These seem fixed in their positioning, unassailable; but there have been instances where changes have occurred. Maybe these pinpricks of light are not as static as we think. I have seen lights move across the sky, more so than the erratic twinkling which is sometimes suggestive of movement. I have discerned absolute physical alterations: lights of red and white.

"I have no explanation for these lights: whether they are portents or natural phenomena. Maybe I have been gifted with the right to see them, as I have met no one who has seen the same as I. Other than Moss, who stands beside me, who wonders at their progress across the sky."

Calvin fell back. He knew the story was weak, yet he hoped to gain some feedback from others who must have seen the lights. He had held back on the silver object he had seen during the daytime, and also on the humming noise. He had yet to tell Moss about the object, and he wanted others to mention the humming should they be able to validate his tale, without him imprinting it on their minds so it was reflected by repetition.

Moss stepped forward. Calvin wondered whether she would tell her favourite story, of the great expanse of water, or whether he would hear something he hadn't heard before. They had occasionally told each other tales, but of course he had never seen her perform. He put himself in the role of viewer, watched as she asserted herself within the group. All eyes were on her.

"I want to tell a story of necessity. When I first began travelling I did so under duress. I wasn't unhappy, yet I wasn't happy. I wanted to explore the surface of Heart, to see things I had only heard about from other travellers. As it happens, the settlement I left behind was more miraculous than any I have encountered since. Should I have been travelling and came across that settlement I would have wished to remain there. But fortune plays its own game and instead I have run from perfection and found only dissatisfaction.

"Some of you sitting here might also express a desire to leave your settlement, and have been glamoured by travellers who have told stories that you wish to experience rather than hear. Let me tell you now that indeed there is great excitement in living a hand to mouth existence, but there is also great hardship. I was fortunate enough to meet Calvin at a moment where my life was at its lowest ebb. And if necessity had thrown us together, so necessity has kept us together." She touched her hands on her belly. "And now we have created a new life: maybe a first for the travelling community. Perhaps this child will long to leave the life of moving from settlement to settlement and will wish to live as you do. This is the conundrum of life on Heart: should you stick with what you have or try something new."

She stepped back. The audience seemed even less enamoured by her story than they did Calvin's. He wished she had expressed some affection beyond *necessity* when describing their relationship; but maybe he would have found that embarrassing. Either way, their stories were told and Universal came to collect them and lead them into the kitchens where hot meat, potatoes, and broccoli were waiting.

They ate hungrily, although their supplies had been sufficient that they hadn't been starving they didn't want to give the impression that their going had been good. It was important to take away with them as much foodstuff as possible. Universal leant with his elbows on the table, watching them eat. About halfway through the meal, he spoke.

"So. This baby. When do you think it will be due?"

"Another season," Calvin answered. "In the autumn."

"And you intend to remain travelling at that time."

"Yes," said Moss. "We wouldn't have it any other way."

"And how do you expect it to survive?"

The breath caught in Calvin's throat at his bluntness.

"I mean," Universal continued, "winter will be upon us sooner than you think. A baby traveller: I've never heard of such a thing. It will need food, shelter, parents who aren't exhausted and scavenging for themselves. I can't see that the travelling life affords the security that the child needs."

"We'll manage," Calvin said, more to appease Moss; even though Universal was only raising thoughts he had already had and they had already discussed.

"And the birth itself. How will you manage without a midwife. How is this one," he gesticulated at Calvin whilst speaking to Moss, "supposed to deliver a child? You'll lose it. You know you will."

Moss stood. "We won't lose anything. This baby is ours and we'll take care of it."

Universal reached out for her wrist, pulled her gently back to a sitting position. "I don't mean to question your lifestyle. We've had enough travellers through here to know how entrenched they are in their life, just as we are in ours. But your pregnancy, well, you can see how that might alter things. Whilst your food was being prepared I had a chat with some of the elders. We have a suggestion you might be willing to hear."

"What is it?" Calvin asked.

"Well, you can't stay here, of course. Out of the question. But we have a midwife in the settlement. Dell, her name is. She would be prepared to oversee the birth if you remained close to us. There are some abandoned buildings nearby, should you need to use them. Just temporary, of course; until the baby is born and the winter has passed and you'll want to be on your way again."

"We don't need any help," Moss said, moving her wrist away, politely but firmly. "We're fine as we are."

"But we would like to talk about it between ourselves," Calvin said. He stared hard at Moss. "And we greatly appreciate your offer."

Universal nodded from one to the other, then stood and let them finish their meal.

Moss hissed: "What are you doing? We can't stay here!"

"I'm being polite. But we *do* need to think about it. It's not just you and me anymore."

"It's hardly ever been just you and me."

"That's not really the point. Moss, we can't keep going as we are. This settlement has welcomed us as a couple, but we can't rely on that. Both of us have been turned away individually before, and maybe it's because of the season and the plentiful crops, but when it comes to winter it's going to get a lot harder. We can remain here for two seasons, and then be on our way; but until then it would be foolish to continue. Let us at least check out this shack and speak to Dell and see if it's worth our while staying."

Moss picked at some meat that had stuck between her teeth. She was determined to travel, Calvin knew this, but surely reality had to kick in with regards to the child.

"Ok. Let's talk with this Dell woman. But if I don't like her then we're going."

Calvin released the breath he was holding. "Good. I think it's for the best."

"We'll see, shall we?"

They ate the remainder of their meal in silence.

5

Dell was matter-of-fact: "You need me." She tucked her top into her skirt where it had ridden up as she walked; her overly large shape accentuating the matronly nature of her work. "You can't do this yourselves. Not without there being some risk."

Moss pouted. "We're not stupid."

Dell softened her voice. "I didn't call you stupid. Tell me, between the two of you, how many births have you witnessed."

Moss fell silent. Calvin mumbled: "I have seen animal births: sheep, goats..."

"Those won't prepare you," Dell said. "A human birth is an entirely different experience. Unlike an animal, it's not just the mother giving birth. You know this. The father does too. It's not just a case of being there and hoping it'll all work out naturally. If Calvin is focussing on you, Moss, then he won't be able to properly identify the changes in his own body. I'm sure it's been done before, but the risk is too great. You need a third person, and that third person will be me."

Calvin glanced across to Moss. He could see that she was already warming to this forthright woman, not that she would admit it. Not yet, anyway.

"For you Moss, the physical birth can be traumatic and painful. You need someone with you who has gone through it before. Not only have I had three children of my own, but I have been midwife to twelve other children in this settlement. I haven't lost any of them. And for you, Calvin, the wrench that can be felt through the departure of the child's soul can be harrowing, alien, and unexpected. You will need reassurance that everything is natural. A moment of lost focus and the body and soul won't join. And we all know the consequences of such a missed union."

They did. Of course they did. It was one of the fundamental tragedies on Heart.

"So, we won't be having any disagreements will we? Of course, if you want to travel elsewhere, see if you can find a settlement as open as ours, or a midwife as caring as myself, then so be it. I can't stop you. But if I were a mother again I know what I would choose. Not what is simply best for myself, but for my baby."

Calvin looked at Moss again. "You know she's right."

Moss sighed. "Let's see this shack."

The following morning, just after sun-up, they set out towards the edge of the moorland that almost encroached on the settlement.

Dell journeyed with them, as did Universal. Calvin decided not to question how they knew an abandoned shack was beyond the visible distance that could be seen from the boundary of the settlement. They might have had information from another traveller, or maybe one of their own had journeyed out there looking for escaped animals or land fit for farming. For the meantime, they left the supplies they had stored at the edge of the wood before they had entered the settlement where they were. They didn't want Universal or Dell to know they had more than they had come with.

When they had journeyed sometime, until the settlement was no longer in sight, Calvin detected Universal's discomfiture as though he could taste it on his tongue.

Dell and Moss were walking ahead. Calvin spoke in a whisper. "Are you alright?"

Universal looked down as he walked, grounding his feet to the floor. "Yes. I'm doing fine. As you have guessed, I have never been this far from my settlement. It feels like I am unravelling. How do you do this all the time?"

Calvin thought. "I think the sensation you feel as unpleasant is the same I get as excitement. The unspooling of identity as you leave the settlement is akin to a dropped ball of wool. What I feel however is a sense of freedom, and once you arrive at a new destination you rewind the wool, make yourself whole again."

"It seems you are wise beyond your years. But for me, this sensation is deeply unpleasant. Without sight of the settlement, how would I find it again?"

"When you start travelling, unravelling, you don't expect to find your settlement again. But *you* will do so: you've noted the direction we have come, the landmarks such as the change in landscape, the hillocks, the trees. And you have Dell. She is walking as though she knows where she is going."

"Dell was a traveller once," Universal said; taking Calvin by surprise. "But then she found her vocation in midwifery and knew she had to regain somewhere permanent. She was lucky: we have a very open settlement. Of course, this was many seasons ago. I don't suppose we would be so willing to absorb travellers into our settlement now, but we are willing to help; as you can see."

Calvin thought over what Universal said. They had been very fortuitous to locate the settlement. They had the best of both worlds – independence and security. It really couldn't have worked out better. He decided to find out more about Dell.

"Dell says she has three children. Did any of them inherit the desire to travel?"

Universal shrugged. "It's impossible to know. She had two of the children in her previous settlement, before she came here. As for the other, he is but a few seasons old."

"So she left her children in her old settlement?"

"It would appear to be the case. I've decided not to discuss it with her. It's not in my inclination to pry."

"It makes me wonder if they would travel in order to find her," Calvin said. "Although no doubt they might be full-grown now, even with children of their own."

"Possibly."

"And the young boy, here. Maybe he will travel."

"I hope not," Universal said. "The boy is mine."

Calvin was about to acknowledge this when Moss called out. "Is that it? Over there?"

Dell nodded.

Calvin realised why Dell had been there before. It all made sense. Dell the traveller had probably stayed in the shack before finding the settlement where she now lived. This was how they knew there was something out here. From a distance the state of the building was difficult to discern, but it resembled a shack – no more, no less. They would have time to make it their home.

And the moorland on which it stood reminded him of his home settlement. For the first time in a long while he wondered how Sky and Royce and little Acorn were doing. He imagined it would be much the same as they ever did. He hoped Sky and Royce thought of him often; although it was now unlikely that Acorn would ever remember him. He hoped Sky told her stories about him.

They still had some way to go before they reached the shack. The sun beat hot on their backs. Calvin could smell his body odour rise out of his clothes. They had bathed the previous night in the settlement: a rare occurrence. But there had been no opportunity to wash and dry their clothes. He hoped the shack would have a nearby water supply, for it seemed to be a full day's journey to and from the settlement. This ran another thought across his mind.

"How will Dell know when Moss's time has come?"

Universal was about to answer, but Dell had overheard: "There are signs," she said. "I will visit you on occasion, and when the birth is near I will come to live with you for the final days. Don't worry. It will be fine."

Calvin nodded; completely unsure of the truth in it. Yet it was better than them being alone.

By the time they reached the shack they had already seen it was in a poor state of repair. It was not made of brick, but wood. Two side panels had fallen and no doubt rotted into the earth. The roof had partially collapsed. Rather than being divided into individual rooms it was one open interior space. Because of the season there remained a sensation of homeliness, with the sun giving the shack more warmth than it might otherwise maintain. But Calvin could see much work needed to be done to improve it, particularly before the cold weather set in. Fortunately they had plenty of time now that their travelling days were paused.

Moss ran her fingers over the walls. Calvin could see that despite her reluctance to settle, she was already forming an idea in her mind of the place where she would give birth to their child. He saw her casually rest a hand on her stomach. The reality of her condition was finally sinking home.

"This will do," she said, quietly.

The building had been the focus of their attention as they approached it, but now Calvin turned so it was behind him and took a good look at the view. Moorland stretched to the horizon on all sides. The ground was hard, but he knew there would be areas where simple crops might be farmed. Universal had already assured him that they could be supplied with sufficient foodstuffs, seeds, and roots to get started; on the basis that when they eventually travelled again they would leave behind what they couldn't reasonably carry for the benefit of the settlement that had sheltered them.

Calvin also had it in his mind to negotiate over a few sheep and goats.

He looked at Moss who was talking quietly to Dell, then he entered the shack.

It seemed so open due to the absence of wall panels and part of the ceiling, yet he could imagine it split into three sections: one for eating and cooking, one for sleeping, and one for toileting. He looked at the panels that had fallen into the ground. The wood was dry, split; the damp earth over the winter months had caused a lot of damage. But there was enough to patch, and he was sure they could obtain supplies either from the settlement or through some trees that could be seen from the rear of the shack. The roof was another matter, but it would happen. For the moment, in the hot weather, it wouldn't be a problem. They could lie in the shack looking at the stars.

The thought suddenly coursed excitement through Calvin's body; dissimilar to the excitement of travelling or finding Moss or discovering her pregnancy, but excitement of the future rather than the present. They were going to build something here: in wood, in flesh and in soul. They were going to build something permanent, something to last.

Moss was standing beside him. He put an arm around her shoulders; pulled her in for a kiss. She tasted raw. He kissed her again.

"Hey." She made the pretence at wriggling from his grasp. "Dell and Universal are just outside."

"So? You're pregnant. They know what we've been up to."

Moss giggled. "Sssh. Just keep it quiet."

They returned outside. Universal and Dell were sitting on the ground side by side, their lunch spread between them.

"We'll have to go back soon," Universal said. "But Dell has something to tell you."

Calvin held Moss's hand as she manoeuvred herself to the ground – it was already becoming difficult for her. They would eat later.

"Your story yesterday," Dell said, nodding at Calvin. "Those lights. I've also seen them."

Calvin let out a breath in an O. "Recently?"

"Not many sun-ups ago. I had delivered a child. It was late, dark. I went outside, leaving the parents with the baby to give them some space. In the sky above me I saw two lights – white at the front, red at the back. They moved across the darkness accompanied by a humming noise. I wondered whether it signified the birth of a child."

Calvin knew she was telling the truth, because he had left out the noise when he told his tale.

"Did you tell anyone?"

"Only Universal." She laughed. "He thought I was going mad!"

Calvin smiled. "What do you think, now?"

Dell's face became solemn. "I think there are things happening that we know nothing about." She bit into her bread, chewed for a moment, then swallowed. "I heard Universal tell you that I used to be a traveller. So, you and I and Moss, we all know that things exist which those who remain in the settlement are unaware of. Things that they never need to be aware of, in fact. But I have never seen movement in the skies, other than that generated by the wind: debris, leaves, those momentary flutterings. And birds, of course. But the lights and their movement seemed neither wind nor nature made. So I don't know what to think."

Calvin hung back, once again, from describing the silver shape.

"Another thing," Dell said, "a story is a story is a story. We all know travellers embellish the truth, sometimes make things up; but we have a responsibility to those we leave behind. Strange lights in the sky might panic some of the more single-minded people. When you do travel again, I suggest that's a story you stop telling."

Calvin started, surprised at Dell's reaction. But then he remembered Book's story of the settlement where all the inhabitants were indifferent to the wonder of human life, where bodies were created indiscriminately, minds left to rot. It was a story that had affected him. If he hadn't travelled, would all such tales sit inside the pit of his stomach and gnaw away; would they frustrate and terrify him; would they undermine the safety of his existence?

He nodded. "I wanted to know if anyone had seen what we had seen."

Dell smiled. "I understand. We tell a story in order to gain information, not simply to provide it. Even so, we must have an understanding of how our words can affect others. Particularly others who have had no direct experience."

Moss leant forwards. "Did something happen?"

Universal coughed, spat some hard bread onto the ground.

All of them were aware that Dell had been silenced.

Calvin sought to change the subject. He wanted to know if she had met Book, but didn't wish to ask her directly. "When you were travelling, Dell, did you meet any others? Did you have any strange encounters because you were a woman?"

Dell hefted herself to her feet. Calvin wasn't sure if this was because she had simply finished eating and needed to stretch or whether she was positioning herself in the traditional storyteller stance. No travellers he ever knew told their stories sitting down.

She looked to the horizon, seeming wistful. "Until Moss, I had never known of female travellers other than myself," she said. "Woman are the child bearers. True, men are an absolute necessity to carry the soul, but for a settlement to survive they need their women amongst them. I imagine few women travel because of this – because of their moral commitment to the continuation of the human race. As soon as a woman leaves her settlement she abandons her right to have a baby. This is true for men, of course, but there will always be a man to carry a soul for a woman."

Calvin was confused. He understood what Dell was saying, but it was equally important for a man to carry a soul as it was for a woman to carry a body.

Dell continued: "Maybe I'm not expressing it well, judging by the expression on Calvin's face. From experience, the reaction to a woman traveller has seemed much harsher than the reaction to a male. A woman travelling has consigned herself to a life alone, without the accompaniment of man or child. Men can live without children, men can live without women; women can live without men, but women find it hard to live without children."

Calvin saw Moss nod. He knew she had been forced by circumstance out of her settlement, and wondered what would have happened should she have remained.

A wind picked up over the surface of Heart, tugged at the heather, their fronds pointing in the direction that the wind was headed.

"It's a lonely life travelling," Dell said. "I was lucky to find this settlement – just as you are lucky. Maybe it is the location, but they seem to understand the needs of travellers greater than elsewhere I have been."

"The location?" queried Moss. She looked around as though Heart might reveal the answer.

"We are apparently at a crossway," Universal said, his low voice reminding the others that he was listening. "Travellers have told us such, and according to what they have said we seem to have been visited more frequently than other settlements. Some have said we are in the middle of Heart, at the crux of North and South and East and West. We have travellers visit at least once every fourteen sun-ups. Those travellers tell us that most settlements have far less visitations."

Dell nodded. "I have seen more come and go here than my experience of other places suggests."

Calvin also nodded, but he was thinking how limited their knowledge was. No one really knew anything, other than what they were told or experienced. All truths had to be relative to other truths and were only true whilst the other truth remained so and was not disproven. Should one truth be shown as false, so the others would tumble.

Settlements gained their knowledge from travellers, travellers gained their knowledge from settlements. Neither of them spent enough time with the other to pass on more than cursory information. For all he, Dell, Moss or Universal knew, there might be thousands of settlements compacted together, still populated cities, or even places where estranged bodies and souls lived independently of each other. Anything was possible. It simply hadn't yet passed into the sum of their consciousnesses.

"So what was your experience as a female traveller?" Moss asked.

Dell sighed. "It wasn't easy. The first three settlements I came upon wanted nothing to do with me. They believed I was bad luck, that the reason for me travelling was that I had become estranged from my settlement because I must be barren."

"Isn't that a little harsh?"

She shrugged. "In some ways. Yet in a tiny settlement where babies are the key to survival a woman who cannot bear children is more of a burden than a use. Even though, other than you, who is obviously not barren, I never met other female travellers nor indeed ever heard of any, for those settlements the reason for my travelling appeared as obvious to them as though they had encountered it before. If you give someone a seemingly irrational situation you can guarantee within moments they will find and firmly believe a rational argument. Particularly if these are the closed minds often found in settlements: those people who do not want to believe anything other than the certainties of their existence.

"So, in those settlements where I was seen as a bad omen, I found neither food nor shelter. I would have starved if it wasn't for the fourth settlement who – despite their own insecurities over my role – took me in because it was clear I would be dead without their help. Even so, the following day after rest, shelter and food I was cast out again – no favours were to be found until I came here."

"We can expect no such favours," Calvin mused. "We have chosen our life and we know the rules attached."

"Agreed," said Dell. "I'm not making excuses for my decisions. I am simply telling you my story."

"I know what she means," Moss said. "Imagine how you felt when you first became a traveller – how alone, how scared. But imagine if you had also always known the hospitality afforded travellers and knew you would find solace once you found a settlement. Now, keep it in your head that every traveller you had ever known or heard about was male. Imagine now being a female traveller and throw all the initial uncertainty together with your gender into the mix. Embracing freedom is as terrifying as it is liberating."

"I understand," Calvin said. "I mean, in some ways I can see that being a woman traveller might be in your favour, but in other ways it throws up other barriers. A traveller's life in general is a difficult one."

Moss slid her hand into his. "But even so, it's a life that we chose and care about."

Universal stood. The wind continued to weave its way through the heather. It was a hot wind, warmed by the summer sun, and it carried with it the promise of rain. "We need to be going," he said to Dell. "It's a long way back."

Calvin could detect his anxiety as clearly as the coming storm. It fair crackled off him.

Dell nodded. "You've got all you need for now," she said. "I'll be back in a few sun-ups just to check how you're doing, and then after that you'll be on your own for a while. If you need anything, you know where to find me."

Moss hugged Dell before they left; then she and Calvin watched as the two figures walked until they were no more than bobbing heads on the horizon which finally popped out of sight.

"Well," Calvin said, turning back to the shack. "There we have it. There's the place our baby will be born."

Moss leant into him. "It hardly seems real, does it?"

Fat raindrops stained the side of the shack a darker hue.

Calvin pulled Moss's arm. "C'mon. Let's get inside."

They ran between the drops as best they could. It wasn't until later that Calvin realised he hadn't asked Dell specifically about Book.

6

Calvin spent the remainder of the summer working on the shack. Within a few sun-ups he had repaired the sides, hammering the wood he had managed to salvage from that rotted into the earth against the existing panels. It soon dried out in the sun, and whilst it had shrunk, blistered, and twisted, it proved a sufficient repair. Come winter he would cover the sides with branches, stacking them high to add warmth and additional shelter. Whilst travelling in a circumference around the shack he had found the remains of an old vegetable garden. Peas withered on an arrangement of vines, a few root vegetables were embedded in the soil, half-crops of potatoes on their way to harvest. Calvin dug around, and despite the inappropriateness of the season planted what he could. Some of it would take, some wouldn't; but they would need as much as they were able.

It was near the vegetable garden, which was some way from the shack, that he found an area that appeared to have been used for items no longer required. Residual unpleasant odours clung to the air. The ground was littered in broken glass, foul plastic containers, twisted pieces of rusted metal, heavy wheels, and an assortment of items which Calvin couldn't identify – whether through age or defunct use. Within this melange, however, he found some clear plastic which he hauled back to the shack, pushing or pulling depending on the ground, and eventually was able to install as a roof. Whilst it made a hellish noise when it rained, on clear nights they could lie on the ground looking up through the plastic at the stars.

The plastic was tarnished, white streaks smudged the surface, but at night time these became invisible. Darkness somehow accentuating its properties of clarity.

Moss loved the plastic: both the texture and its use. She hugged Calvin fiercely. "It's like we're outside even when we're inside. We have the best of both worlds."

Calvin smiled. He placed his hand on her extended belly and felt the baby kick into his palm. "I know. I knew you would like it."

When they looked up at the sky Moss kept one hand on her belly and held Calvin with the other.

Neither of them said anything, but each knew the other was looking for white and red lights.

Calvin ploughed himself into the fields. Sunlit hours were at their maximum, the days longer and more useful for work. Whilst Moss busied herself in the shack, making minor improvements to the structure that they had separated into different areas, preparing the vegetables for their meals, Calvin worked hard tending the crops. Dell had returned as promised, a few sun-ups after leaving them, with four sheep and a goat in tow. Calvin had tethered them to a tree and then begun the task of making a fence. He had learnt much of this work from Royce, and whilst it was rudimentary due to his lack of tools, he had managed to dig holes into the ground of sufficient depth to hold branches that were then woven together with vines. He continued to tether the animals, just in case, but at least they were contained should they work themselves free.

The work was hard, but satisfying. They obtained milk from both the goat and sheep and Calvin knew that come winter they would kill the animals and have meat for the cold season. Moss's belly swelled further, her breasts became larger, they copulated occasionally but it wasn't essential for their well-being. They were satisfied with the lives they had created, with the life they were creating. Dell visited occasionally, but otherwise they were self-sufficient and glad to be left alone.

One night they ate berries after the evening meal, the sweetness popping into Calvin's mouth, juicy and refreshing. They sat outside under the stars, a cool breeze taking the heat off the day. Calvin was ingrained with dirt, his fingerprints holding black marks like rivulets in mud. Moss leant into him, her legs extended, pointing in the direction of the settlement. Occasionally he leant forwards and kissed her cheek, ruffled her hair.

"I wonder what Heart will be like when our baby grows up," Moss said. "I wonder if it will be like this."

Calvin shrugged. "I imagine it will be much the same."

"I could never imagine it being different," Moss said, "until I began travelling. And then I realised that the past held lifestyles vastly different from ours. You've seen the cities. Can you envisage what they must have been like, populated. Probably larger than all the settlements you and I have ever seen put together. What happened? Where did all the people go?"

"I'm guessing it was a very long time ago," Calvin said. "Things change. But if you're thinking if those days will return, then I would assume it's going to be far ahead in the future. It'll be nothing for us to worry about."

"Who's worrying? I'm just speculating. What will the future hold for the child of our child of our child of our child? I imagine those people who lived in the cities in the past would never have believed

Heart could have abandoned those places. It would have been unthinkable to them; just as a reversion to those times would be unthinkable to us. It's a shame they no longer exist. I would have liked to have seen them. I would have liked to have known what use some of those buildings were put to: the place where we met, for example. And other things, like how they managed to feed everyone."

"Life was different," Calvin mused. "And that's all we need to know. Of course, as travellers our thirst for knowledge is insatiable, but also we can't torment ourselves thinking about things for which the answers can't be found."

Moss heaved herself off Calvin's lap, leant on one elbow. "You're changing," she said. "You sound so boring sometimes. Where's the Calvin who left his settlement pushing for new experiences?"

"He's inside you. Inside your body. Inside our baby. My priorities have changed now you're pregnant: it's all about the baby."

"I wish I hadn't fallen so quickly," Moss said. "Maybe we should have had more time travelling together before you made me pregnant."

There was little Calvin thought he could say to that. She was right and wrong, simultaneously. Just as Heart had a past filled with bustling cities and a present which contained small self-sufficient settlements, so he had a past full of wonder which had condensed into focussing on one single happening. Within a settlement, life was linear, and followed a defined path. When travelling, there were no paths. The two things could not be combined. Just as Moss was either not pregnant or pregnant: she couldn't be both. Their futures had changed irrevocably once they had copulated successfully. Whether they should or could have waited was irrelevant. The deed was done and they had to respect it.

"No regrets though," he asked Moss, wary of her answer.

She patted her belly in response. "No regrets," she said.

Calvin sighed, allowing happiness to course through him. He could detect the light fluttering of the baby's soul growing inside his body, a surging and ebbing of energy. It was a totally new experience, one that amazed, excited, and sometimes scared him. There was no precedent for this feeling, either from direct experience or through discussion. Few people in his settlement talked about pregnancy and birth: it was a sacred thing, only to be revealed when the time came. He had overheard some discussions between Sky and Royce when they were pregnant with Acorn, but had paid little attention. It struck him that Royce would have felt what he was feeling now, when Calvin's soul was inside him waiting for Sky to birth his body. Suddenly he felt an incredibly powerful connection to his father that he hadn't previously accepted. Then sadness pulled over him in the knowledge that he would never see his parents again.

He couldn't imagine their baby not being by their side. Moss was right, they had to keep travelling, they had to instil in their child a way of life that would mean it wouldn't want to leave. Even if, simultaneously, he couldn't quite imagine them being three.

7

The days began to get shorter, cooler. Mornings were crisp, cloudless. The blue of the sky enlivened the ground. The dead heat of summer was tempered. Calvin harvested the softer fruits: he had managed to grow cucumbers, tomatoes, and had salvaged the pea plants. They ate these fresh, without cooking, retaining their goodness. Near the field he used as the vegetable garden a small brook played noises over the stones. The drinking water was brackish and they preferred the goat's milk which had a pleasanter flavour, but having the brook also meant they could wash regularly and the grime which had been a daily part of their lives revealed broken, worn, hardened skin underneath. Skin that enjoyed being caressed by the breeze, the water, and each other.

Calvin had rarely seen Moss naked. In the winter months it was too cold to shed clothes, at other times she preferred some decorum. But when they washed in the brook they always did so together. Calvin enjoyed the sight of the water running through her hair, between her breasts, and over her stomach. Her pubis glistening with water droplets like frozen berries. Under the dirt her skin was pale white, almost translucent. In some respects he preferred the cover, found it slightly disturbing to see the blue tracks of her veins. He had assisted in the slaughtering and gutting of many an animal to have some understanding of the workings of the body, but always pushed these thoughts out of his mind when it came to people. It didn't seem appropriate, somehow.

When he wasn't in the vegetable garden Calvin was patching up the shack with found items from the rubbish pit. They needed to ensure there were no spaces that the wind might enter during the winter season. He had already begun to cut down some of the branches and smaller trees within their immediate vicinity, and stack them against the sides of the shack. They maintained a supply of firewood in the area he had partitioned off for their toilet, and food which wouldn't readily spoil he kept in a dark container he had found in the pit, a rectangular wooden box with a hinged lid that had remained intact. They were doing all they could to ensure their baby would be protected, although in the back of his mind Calvin wondered whether Dell might suggest they return to the settlement once it was born so that the care might be extended. In some respects, this seemed unlikely, but he couldn't shake the thought from his head.

Because, although he knew they were doing their best, he also felt hopelessly unprepared. The encroaching burden of fatherhood weighed heavy. Around this time, just as Moss became settled at their location, he felt an almost insatiable desire to travel and to shake off the incoming responsibility.

These thoughts he kept to himself.

Dell began to make more frequent visits, attending to them every seven sun-ups. She would kneel beside Moss on the ground, placing her hands either side of her belly, and push harder than Calvin thought necessary. She would place an ear to Moss's flesh, always smile when she felt movement. The baby's kicks were ever stronger, Calvin could clearly see distorted shapes under the skin. Dell would also check and sniff Moss's urine, squeeze her upper forearm and place her fingertips at the pulse in her wrist. It was only when she was satisfied that she then turned her attention to Calvin.

He found his examination to be unnerving. Lying on his back he would bare his stomach. Dell would place her rough hands against his skin as he fought embarrassment. Only Moss and Sky had ever touched him so delicately, and Dell fell somehow between his partner and his mother in ways that confused him. Her fingertips lightly ran across his stomach, tempting reciprocation from his insides. At this point, the fluttering within him always became more intense, as though his stomach were a mirror and Dell's finger movements were being copied by their reflection. When she was satisfied she would lay a palm against his skin to calm the movement, then she would check his own urine, sniff it, and allow him to rise.

"You're both doing fine," she would say. Then she would unload a few provisions that they would have been unable to harvest. Bread and meaty broth were luxuries.

They would sit and eat, feeling the day warm as the sun reached its highest point, silently speculating how long it might be before Dell's services were needed to their fullest extent.

After one such examination, Calvin remembered that Dell had never answered his question about other travellers. He also remembered how Universal had seemed to close down her replies about the lights in the sky, but these had not been seen in such a very long while that he had discounted them. Other travellers, however, were another matter entirely.

"There's been something I've been meaning to ask," he said, dipping his bread into the oily lamb broth and waiting whilst the drips fell back into the pot before pushing it into his mouth.

Dell looked up, wary. "Go ahead."

"When you were travelling," Calvin said, "did you see others like ourselves? Other travellers I mean. We seem to be few and far between. Even though Universal said that the settlement was at a crossway, we haven't seen anyone pass by us since we've been here, neither near to nor in the distance."

Dell snorted dismissively. "There are many routes into and out of the settlement. Just because you haven't seen any travellers doesn't mean there haven't been any. Since you were there, I believe we've entertained at least five."

"Five?" Calvin was surprised. "In such a short space of time?"

"It's not predictable," said Dell. "They come and go."

"Were there any interesting stories?" asked Moss.

Calvin knew what she was thinking. Once you became a traveller you stopped hearing stories. You missed them, despite living them.

Dell paused. "A couple mentioned lights in the sky," she said. "But they had no more information than you or I. They could have been recounting those tales, rather than having direct experience. As a previous traveller myself you tend to work out which tales are truth and which are embellished or retold."

"Anything else?" pushed Calvin.

Dell shrugged. "Someone told of a settlement where order is disarrayed. Bodies are born without souls and nothing is done with them. The population appear to be in a state of unconcern. We get these tales from time to time. I wonder whether they're told to remind us to maintain the equilibrium. I never saw such places myself when I was travelling."

"The traveller who told that tale," asked Calvin, "what was his name?"

"Name? I don't remember names," laughed Dell, showing her misshapen teeth in a brown grin.

"Have you ever met a traveller called Book?"

Dell's laugh stopped abruptly. "What do you know of Book," she said.

Calvin popped another piece of moistened bread into his mouth, chewed slowly. "Book was the traveller who set me journeying," he said, once he had swallowed.

Dell nodded. "I know of Book. He passed by here many seasons ago. I also knew him from before, when I was travelling. For a short while we journeyed together."

Calvin couldn't quite believe his ears. But then he didn't know what to do with the information. For such a long while finding Book had been important to him. He hadn't really considered the reason why, although he knew he wanted to show him that he had followed the calling, perhaps expected some validation because of it; but now he had met someone who had also known Book the point of his minor quest had evaporated. Dell would no more know his current whereabouts than he. And without himself meeting Book once again, Book would remain unaware he had travelled.

Calvin saw Moss looking at him. Her expression seemed to be urging him on. But he couldn't think what to say.

Moss spoke for him. "You and Book," she said to Dell, "were you travelling like us? As a couple?"

Dell tucked a stray piece of hair behind her ear, years fell off her. "For a while, perhaps, I suppose that was the case. This was a very long time ago."

"What happened?" Moss had put down her bread, she was no longer hungry.

"I left my settlement with Book," Dell said, quietly. She looked at Calvin. "Book was also my reason for travelling. I went foolishly and willingly but the life wasn't for me. In fact, it was a horrible mistake."

"You left two children behind," whispered Calvin, remembering what Universal had told him.

Dell nodded. "I can't explain the complexities of emotion. What seemed compulsive at the time now is just regrettable. Even though I've since had a child with Universal, those first two pull me back to a settlement I could never find again, regardless return to."

"Did Book treat you well?" asked Moss.

Dell smiled. "Yes, I had no complaints. He knows the land and how to use it. He had much more experience than you two. But he couldn't unravel the knot that tightened inside me every time I thought of Pringle and Sure. And when the string between us pulled taut, that's when I left Book and stopped travelling. Or rather, started travelling in reverse, trying to retrace my steps."

"But you never found your original settlement," said Moss. "You came here, instead."

"Yes, I did. There was no way to find where I had gone. And Book, well, he wasn't interested. I wouldn't say he abandoned me, but he allowed me to go. Maybe he shouldn't have. But I couldn't continue as I had been. With each day my two children moved further and further away from me. There's only so much distance from your loved ones you can take."

Calvin nodded. "And then, you saw him again."

Dell smiled, wanly. "Yes. I attempted to return home over several seasons, but only *once* did I find a settlement I recognised. You would think it easy, but you know the distance between places, and we had passed through several cities and not followed a straight route through them. It's easy to get lost on the surface of Heart. So, I came here. They were kind. They understood I needed stability. They realised the initial reason for travelling had gone, and that to continue would only lead to madness. Universal was very good to me, and so eventually we had our child together. As dear as he is to me he can't replace what I had. But then he's not intended to be a replacement. My grieving is over."

"And your experience at midwifery..." began Calvin.

"...was invented when I came here," Dell admitted. "I laid it on thick, I needed another reason to stay. But since then I've found the role is natural for me. Each child I deliver safely is a gift to Heart to subsume the guilt I feel at leaving mine behind."

They fell silent, each within their own thoughts; the broth growing cold between them. Thinking of what they had once had.

Calvin realised she hadn't answered his second prompt about Book returning. Although she now seemed lost in thought, he needed to know. He had to know which direction he had travelled.

"You say Book came here, several seasons ago?"

Dell flicked a glance at him. "Yes. He wasn't looking for me, of course. In fact, he didn't see me."

"He didn't see you?" Calvin couldn't keep the surprise out of his voice.

"I saw him first," explained Dell. "I couldn't bring myself to speak to him. I told Universal – we have no secrets from each other – and he ensured that our paths didn't cross whilst he stayed."

"Do you know in what direction he left?"

Dell shook her head. "I know nothing more than what I told you. But listen, Calvin, there is no use in chasing the past. For whatever reason you want to speak to Book his answers will only disappoint. No one can give you the answers you're searching for, because they cannot be given; they can only be found, within yourself."

Calvin stood. "I'm not even sure why I want to see him again, but I've always asked after him."

"Well then. There you go. You've partially answered your own question."

Calvin fingered his artefact in his pocket: the rough against the smooth. He decided to show it to Dell.

"Book gave me this," he said.

He pulled the artefact out of his pocket. The coned shape caught the sunlight, blinked it back brilliant white. The spiral interior threaded the rays through it. In this light, the interior shone a pale pink.

Dell reached into her own pocket. "I have something similar," she said. "He must have found a few of these on his travels."

She pulled out an object greyer than that Calvin held, but its shape was similar although squatter, its surface more rough than smooth. There was no disputing it though, each were of the same ilk.

"If you're asking for meaning," Dell said, "I'm no wiser than you."

Calvin was about to speak when Moss stood and took his artefact from his hand. "You've never shown me this before." But her reproachful tone was tinged with amusement. "Keeping secrets from me, were you?"

"No, I..." but he didn't have the words to finish the sentence.

"It's ok," she smiled. "And *I've* seen these before. Lots of them. Remember the vast expanse of water I told you about, Calvin, and the yellow ground? The land was speckled with these. Sometimes I saw small animals living inside them: soft bodied and sharp clawed. They're natural, whatever they are. And they've come some distance. I imagine for Book they were an indication of how far he had been, of what places he had seen. They were meant as a spur to keep you moving."

Calvin and Dell exchanged their artefacts, examined each others, and then returned them to their pockets.

"Well," Calvin said. "Now we know."

He wasn't sure whether he was happy Moss had revealed the secret. As Dell had said, some answers were best found out yourself. Yet, together with Moss's revelation and Dell's understanding of his need to encounter Book and then dismissal of it, maybe it was what he needed to forget his fruitless search and to concentrate on his own life without the encumbrance of the past.

Dell looked up at the position of the sun in the sky. "I best be getting back," she said.

Calvin helped Moss up from the floor, her bloated stomach often made simple tasks difficult.

"It won't be long now," Dell said. "I will be back when the first leaf of autumn falls. Thereafter it should only be a matter of a few sun-ups before the baby is born, so my intention is to remain here until that happens. I imagine this sits right with you both."

Moss nodded. Calvin could detect a shiver of excitement laced with fear run through her body as he held her. Or maybe it was his own emotion, transmuted through the growing soul inside him. Either way, it wouldn't be long before their child arrived. A new life for Heart. A new life for them both.

8

The intervening weeks passed inexorably. Calvin continued to busy himself in the vegetable garden, Moss tried to do as much as she could but other than continuing to exercise and cook she was too heavy and stiff to carry much or help with the other chores. In fact, there was little for her to do. Calvin now had all the sides of the shack protected against the incoming weather, and whilst on some sunny days the interior was stifling, Moss knew that they had needed to prepare and couldn't have waited for the conditions to change before they got on with things.

She appreciated Calvin. He was the right father for her child. She wasn't quite sure what would happen once the baby was born, how travelling together would work, or to what extent they might have to settle down; but for the time being she was happy with their situation, and had come to appreciate the stability he had fostered on her. Some nights, when they were curled up together, even though they could no longer comfortably entwine their bodies, the warmth that they shared filled her soul as well as her heart, and she – quite fiercely – desired him with a passion that her body with the body inside it couldn't fulfil. Not that Calvin appeared to be concerned. She knew he felt the closeness as strongly as she did, and whilst the fluttering of the soul inside him couldn't be felt externally, the simple knowledge that it was there, that the breath of life which would give their child a personality was being carried by Calvin, was enough to keep her happy.

The season began to turn. The days didn't start quite so brightly and they finished dull, as though twilight were colouring the sky before night fell. Mornings were crisp: frost clung hard to grass blades giving it the superficial sheen of snow. When Calvin set out in the morning he was accompanied by a crunching noise underfoot as though he were walking over glass, his breath emanating from his mouth like tiny ghosts. Even as the day warmed the hint of cold didn't completely escape the air; and the evenings benefited from the trapped warmth within their shack, confirmation his preparations had been both necessary and essential.

The days were shorter and he spent more and more of his time in the vegetable garden. Often it was dark before he returned to the shack, a hessian sack of root vegetables over his shoulder, dumping them into the wooden container he had created which served as their larder. He would be greeted by cooking smells, his stomach surging with the hunger that he had managed to hold at bay for much of the day. Moss would fall asleep soon after his return – a sleep punctuated by the repeated need to toilet, inevitably disturbing Calvin's own sleep so that when he resumed his daily tasks it was always with a headache and a yawn and an increasing weariness in his bones.

It wasn't quite before the first leaf fall that Dell returned. Calvin caught sight of her mid-morning: a tiny dot on the horizon, moving staccato-like due to his perspective and the angle of the earth. He had gathered together a box of leaves that he planned to turn to mulch, to conserve the moisture and improve the fertility and health of the soil. They were slick and oily to the touch, like organs carved fresh from a newly-dead animal. It reminded him that he had planned to kill one of the sheep later that day. He wanted to make sure Moss fed well in the lead up to the birth, and it was important to ensure Dell also didn't go hungry, given the hospitality the settlement had already shown them without expecting anything in return.

He continued working: heaving beets from the ground, purple-white orbs dragging free from the earth in a manner not dissimilar from a baby leaving the womb, the soil stretching around them at their widest point and then falling back and partially filling the hole. Once the work was done, he sharpened his knife on a piece of flint he had taken to carry around with himself for that purpose, and then walked back to the shack where the animals were tethered nearby.

He knew which one needed to die. Not the eldest, because the meat would be too tough; but not the youngest either, for reasons he couldn't quite determine but thought might be linked to his impending fatherhood. It made no sense: slaughtering animals was part and parcel of everyday life, it was how he had been brought up. Yet, that tug which he had felt when he had seen bodies being mistreated also flared from time to time when he thought of his animals. Shrugging it off was only a temporary solution, he couldn't get rid of a moral perplexity altogether.

Nevertheless, he entered the enclosure and picked up a large rock he had put aside for the purpose before cracking it down on the animal's skull. In some settlements he had seen sheep killed by having their throats cut without preamble, but he found it a cleaner and less distressful kill for the animal to knock it out first. Satisfied that the sheep was unconscious he took his knife and slit its throat through to the spinal cord. Blood poured from the animal which involuntarily kicked in panic, but the head blow had determined the reaction to be short and of little effect.

Calvin waited for the struggling to subside, then he pulled the sheep out of the enclosure leaving the remaining animals inside. Holding the back leg between his knees he pulled the wool up and cut the skin away down towards the rump. Then repeated the action with the second hind leg. Cutting around the leg joint, he then broke it and sliced through the remaining tendons. Turning the sheep around he performed a similar function with both of the front legs, pulling the wool up and cutting the skin away down to the throat. Then he broke the front leg joints, pulled the skin off the belly region and cut his way through the brisket.

He hauled the sheep towards a tree he had prepared with a hook and rope attached, then fixed it to the rope and pulled so it was raised in the air and hung head downwards. He cut the skin up the middle of the stomach, then punched the skin away from the flesh, forcing his fist repeatedly into the join between the two until he could pull away the entire fleece in a quick jerking motion. He left the sheep hanging with the skin attached to the head and the head attached to the carcass, sweat pouring down his back, his hands bloody and warm with the effort.

Washing his hands clean in a trough of water, he wiped them on his clothing and entered the shack where Dell was examining Moss.

"How is she?"

Dell rose from her kneeling position besides Moss. "She's good. It will only be a matter of a few days. Can you strip to your waist please?"

Calvin did as he was told, then lay on the floor beside Moss, instinctively reaching for her hand. Dell's fingers were warm on his skin. She ran them in a circular fashion, each hand moving opposite to the other. Calvin could feel the soul inside him reciprocate, as it was stimulated by her touch. Both himself and Moss had tried to do this themselves, with only partial success. Whatever Dell did she was obviously a natural. The movements were stronger than Calvin had ever felt before.

After what seemed like quite a while, Dell straightened and returned to her feet. Calvin replaced his undershirt and woollen shift, both of which were speckled with the sheep's blood. For some reason, this brought in a little embarrassment. As though killing something so close to the birth of their baby was a line that shouldn't be crossed. Dell, however, didn't even appear to notice it.

Later, after they had eaten and Calvin had cleared space in the shack for Dell to make her bed, they sat cross-legged on the floor and Dell gave them instructions to prepare for the birth.

"I have to stress this even though I know you are both aware of the consequences, but it is essential – Calvin – for you to be here, with Moss, at the moment of the birth. Late is late is late, do you understand? If the soul is not birthed at the same time as the body then I will have to destroy the child. We understand this, don't we?"

Moss nodded vigorously, clutched Calvin's hand tight. "We understand," he answered for them both.

"Because of this," Dell stressed, "you must be within shouting distance at all times. Giving birth is a strange beast – it can happen quickly, or it can happen slowly. A first birth is often slow, but there's no telling really, until such time that the baby seeks to make an appearance. I'll need your help too, Calvin, during the early stages. As for the birth of the soul, that's a much easier procedure. In fact, you will find that it will happen completely without intervention from me. In the heat of the moment, you might not even realise it has happened at all. But the result will be evident in the baby's eyes."

Calvin nodded slowly. Suddenly the enormity of their undertaking began to overwhelm him. It started as a tickling at the base of his neck that ran down to his spine and back again. Then his heart seemed to miss a couple of beats and he forcibly exhaled. Moss's grip on his hand intensified.

"Are you ok?"

Calvin paused, allowed his body to settle. "I think so. It's just that suddenly everything seems so real."

Dell smiled, a laugh withheld. "It is a big undertaking to bring a child onto Heart. Particularly if you two continue to go it alone. You won't have any of the community assistance that living in a settlement would afford you."

"We're fine with that," Moss said. "We know what we're doing."

"I know you do," said Dell. "But I wouldn't be a good midwife if I didn't mention it."

They fell silent for a while as darkness descended around their shack, like dropping a stone into a river's depths. Calvin poked at the small fire in the corner, the red embers burning fiercely despite the flame having gone out. The fire was surrounded by a metal container he had found, ensuring the shack wouldn't burn to the ground. Even so, one wall of the shack had scorched black. At night, it appeared darker than the dark itself.

The approaching birth dominated their conversations and, in the silence in between, each of them struggled to think of something to add to what had already been said, or to broach another subject which might be worthy of their time. If Dell had not been there, Calvin and Moss would have snuggled together, spent some quiet time touching Moss's belly, and reiterating their commitment to each other with soft, soothing words. But in Dell's presence, they felt awkward doing such things, so aside from asking about the settlement to which they had no particular affiliation their conversation was limited.

As usual, Calvin found himself wanting to ask questions to which he wasn't sure the answers would be forthcoming.

"Have you seen any more lights in the sky?"

It was getting too dark in the shack to accurately determine Dell's expression, but Calvin had a feeling that she grimaced.

Calvin persisted: "I had a feeling you had more to tell us, before. But Universal didn't seem as though he wanted you to continue."

"Universal doesn't like to hear things that can't be substantiated," Dell said, her voice low. "When you've lived in a settlement all your life you crave order – that sort of routine is your security. Damage that security and you damage everything you know."

"So there is more?" said Moss, her voice even quieter than Dell's.

Calvin heard Dell sigh. She could almost feel her urge to talk burst out of her body. Some stories demanded to be told.

"Book had a story," she said, carefully. "As far as I know, I was the only one he ever told it to. Although, who knows. Maybe he spoke of it before and maybe he's spoke of it since."

Calvin leant forwards, his tone confidential. "Will you tell us?"

Dell paused. "I don't know."

"We *are* fellow travellers," said Moss. "We understand how stories work."

Calvin knew Moss was referring to the nature of how a story is told, how it can become embellished and distorted, how you couldn't really take anything for granted. What she wanted was for Dell to tell the story as she recalled it from Book, and that we would understand that details wouldn't necessarily be accurate or true; yet we wanted to be the conduit for the story to remain alive.

"Ah well," Dell said, "so long as none of the details escape from this room..."

Calvin and Moss both assured her that this would be the case.

Dell made herself more comfortable. She lay on her back on the bedding they had provided and looked skywards at the stars through the plastic sheeting. For a while there was silence. Calvin even wondered if she might have fallen asleep, but then it became apparent she was simply gathering her thoughts, for a moment later she began.

9

"When Book told me this tale it was obvious how much it had affected him. I could tell how true it was from his turn of phrase, his tone of voice. I have never heard such a story before or since, and I'm hoping I never have to hear it again.

"Before I ever saw any lights in the sky I knew to expect them. Why? Because Book had told me about them. But Book had seen more than a white and red light pulsing across the night's expanse. He had also seen them in the day, seen what object they were attached to. And he had seen the object on the ground, also; seen what came from inside it. What's more, he told me he had spoken to the person who had been inside the object, that he had spoken to him on the ground."

Dell could tell that the atmosphere inside the shack was charged with emotion. For the moment, all thoughts of the soon-to-be-born baby had been forgotten.

"Book tells it this way: He had seen the lights in the distance one sun-up, just as the sky was shedding night and daylight was on the horizon. He says the object between the two lights was revealed through the process of sunrise, as if night had deliberately cloaked it. Even so, it was a pale reveal, a silver body between each of the lights, with arms outstretched on both sides, as though a swimmer seen underwater. The hum we have both heard accompanied the object's progress, a soothing noise similar to one that might be made getting a baby to sleep.

"He followed its progress through the sky as the shape became closer, became firmer. Then he realised that it was descending towards the land. His desire to discover the identity of the object exceeded his fear of it. He began to run towards the point where it seemed it might touch the ground. The hum became much louder as the object descended. He told me he remembered placing his hands over both ears. Finally it landed like a large bird on a wide expanse of land where it appeared scrub and rocks had been cleared, as though it was intended for that purpose. The object revealed wheels at the point of landing, and after a screech and a roll it came to a halt.

"Book described it as the largest object he had ever seen, standing several people high and numerous in width. He sat watching it for some time, unable to shake his gaze. The object did nothing. Then, just when Book was wondering what to do next, a door opened in the side and someone came out."

Dell paused for effect. It had been a while since she had told a good tale, and despite herself she was revelling in it.

"Book described this person as smaller than himself, probably my height. He had the usual number of appendages. His head was obscured by a hard plastic hat inset with a mirror. His clothes were all white. When the hat was removed Book could see the man's facial features were similar to his, yet whilst a lack of beard suggested he might be a child it was clear to all appearances that he was a man.

"He had reached out to Book, one hand extended. Book had been unsure what to do. So he smiled and the person smiled back. This sealed Book's understanding that the person was also some kind of traveller, albeit different to us. They began to speak to each other. Whilst the man's language faltered, and he often used words Book had no translation for, they sat and talked for the remainder of the day, exchanging information in the way that all travellers exchange information: tales for food."

Calvin interrupted Dell, speaking into the darkness as the fire had dimmed once again. "But this cannot be true, can it? Was Book making this all up?"

"I have no way of knowing. I can only repeat his story, just as we repeat our stories. Only the traveller telling the tale knows the truth of it."

"Please continue," said Moss. "I'm sure there is more to tell."

They heard Dell shift in position on her bedding. It couldn't be comfortable.

"The traveller had a name. The Orbitist. He spends most of his time in the sky. Observing us, so Book put it. He says he is from Heart's past, before the destruction of the cities; or, if he himself is not from the past, then he is descended from those who were, in a different way to us now. Neither Book nor I could properly understand this. Book said he wasn't sure if the Orbitist understood it himself. You must also understand that Book did not reveal the full extent of this conversation to me. He was reluctant to talk about it – although at the same time he burnt with the need to do so. If I hadn't witnessed his constant scanning of the skies he might never have revealed this knowledge to me. He could be secretive at times; protective is maybe a better word. Sometimes he felt that he had dreamt it.

"The Orbitist told Book stories about Heart that Book couldn't believe. He said that once everyone had two names: their usual name and a second name that linked families together. He said that time had erased the second name so that families would not remember their relations. He said this was necessary to preserve the integrity of the species. Book did not understand what this meant. I have a theory which I decided never to reveal." Dell paused for effect, for a question, but when none came she continued: "He told Book that whilst he was friendly that there were others in the skies who were less so. That one day the original population of Heart would return to enslave us. He said they would use ourselves against us – again, something Book could not understand. He said the original inhabitants of Heart called it Earth. Book had smiled at this notion, then leant down and picked up some soil, let it run through his fingers. 'This is earth,' he had said. Then he pointed to his chest: 'Heart is in here'."

"This is a fantasy," interrupted Calvin. "This cannot be true." He could feel the pull of life unravel within him, as though the soul he carried was also in disagreement with Dell's account, as though neither of them could accept this as a reality which might affect everything they understood and hung on to.

"You've seen the lights yourself," said Dell.

"Even so..." Calvin began. But then he knew he had also seen the silver shape. And if that was a truth, might not the rest of it be so?

He felt Moss squeeze his arm. "Maybe this isn't the right time for this story to be told," she said. "We have other concerns right now. Things that are more important to us."

Calvin leant forwards, towards Dell although it wouldn't have been obvious in the dark. He was trying to discern her expression. "Do you believe this?" he asked. "Do you believe what Book told you was true?"

Dell sighed. "I had a long relationship with Book. We travelled together for some time. You know that story. I believe he related what happened as truthfully as he could, without embellishment. In fact, I believe there was more he had forgotten than he knew. There were silences were there should have been words. He wasn't struggling to make things up, he was struggling to remember. He was sifting through what he felt able to tell me."

Calvin snorted. "Struggling to remember? Struggling to remember *this*? How could that be the case?" He couldn't keep some disdain out of his voice. His whole body felt as though it had turned sideways to lie along the blade of a knife.

"Calvin," Moss said, quietly.

But Calvin couldn't stop. He had it in himself to do so, he knew this, but a ball of rage had knotted inside him and was rolling and rolling through his body, ready to burst out of his chest or force its way out of his mouth.

"How *can* this be true, Dell? Don't you think others would have spoken of this before? And Heart has stability, happiness. *We* have that stability and happiness right now. We don't need to hear your spurious tales a few days before Moss is due to give birth. It just isn't right." He stood. His heart was pounding. Without any preamble he stumbled in the dark to the back of the shack and forced the door open into the night.

The stench of the sheep he had strung up earlier that day permeated the air, caught in his throat. He stifled a gag, then ran away from the shack towards the brook. The continual babbling of the water comforted him, but even so he coughed violently and brought up some of the meal he had enjoyed with Dell and Moss that evening, before everything had turned sour.

The chill in the air cooled his sensibilities. He wondered what Dell and Moss were talking about in his absence. Suddenly his outburst seemed foolish, unnecessary. Perhaps he could put it down to his impending fatherhood, a protective, perhaps illogical, streak infusing him with anger. But also he couldn't help but think that Dell's story detracted from what he knew of Book. Whilst he couldn't place exactly why that should be or how it made him uncomfortable, he knew that it was a factor in his sudden exit.

He sat down on the bank and looked up at the stars. They hadn't seen lights in the sky since they arrived at the shack. Maybe the facts of Book's tale were an irrelevance. Truth transmuted through altered circumstances might no longer remain a truth. Calvin knew he only had to look at the ruined cities to understand the truth of people's past lives were meaningless in the here and now. The Orbitist might exist or he might not. Either way, unless there was a return, unless there was some kind of happening, the fact of his existence would not matter.

A cool breeze ruffled his hair and beard, reminded him of Moss's caresses. But it was too soon to go back with his head hung low. As neither of them had come out to look for him he knew they were expecting him to return when he was ready. He decided to make the most of a few minutes quiet. Once the baby was born, their lives would be turned upside-down.

However much he tried to concentrate on the water in the brook, in the way it reflected moonlight, and echoed its own gushing, Calvin couldn't help but consider Dell's story. He *had* seen the object in the sky, so this part of it had to be true. He had never considered it might be an object for transportation, although thinking about it now he realised the metallic sheen no doubt resembled the skeletal frames with wheels which always were left discarded alongside the Snake. Yet to travel in the air, it seemed impossible. There was no doubt in his mind that if it were true then the Orbitist could not be a resident of Heart. Or if he was, then he came from an area of Heart utterly unlike anything Calvin had ever encountered. He considered himself to be an experienced traveller – to believe there was much more to Heart than he had already seen or had been related by Moss's own travels was unlikely.

Other than the main revelation, Calvin realised Dell's account didn't expand much. The fear of enslavement also seemed an empty threat. The people of Heart were not bodies who had no will or purpose. Unlike the soulless bodies, who, whatever his personal opinion and the empathy he had for them, Calvin knew could be manipulated for simple tasks, the idea that forced labour might be rolled out through each of Heart's settlements for all of the residents was incomprehensible. Again, he felt Book's – or was it simply Dell's – tale lacked substance or credibility. And if the Orbitist did exist, who could determine the truth of his outlandish statements with regards to Heart? Calvin found himself shaking his head. The whole tale needed to be forgotten, with the focus remaining on the birth of his child.

He knew this should be evident, but as he returned to the shack he still couldn't shake out concern that the Orbitist, Book, and Dell were all correct, and that at some point in the future the life that he knew might be rent asunder by forces never previously experienced.

The deserted cities and settlements scattered across the surface of Heart were an indication that the future Dell had intimated had already happened.

10

Morning saw a dry wind hugging the shack, rattling the branches that insulated the sides as though stimulating a hundred tapping fingers.

Calvin was the first to wake. Dell and Moss had been asleep when he had returned the previous evening. He had stepped over Dell, and slid into bed beside Moss, curling his arm just above the bump in her stomach, insulated through the layers of clothing. It wasn't long before sleep overtook him too, catapulted him into dreaming.

Calvin's dreams had intensified steadily throughout the pregnancy, as had Moss's. Dell had explained this was natural. The changes in both of their bodies would unsettle them at night, leading to disturbed sleep and increased dreams. Even so, the dreams were as complex as they were entertaining. Moss in particular had dreamt of a talking, walking baby, advanced beyond her years. But some of her dreams had also been dark: babies born with malformed limbs, sightless, malevolent. Often she would wake in tears and Calvin would have to comfort her before she slipped back into dream.

For Calvin, that night had also created a dream baby. He recalled holding it in his arms, cradled against bare skin. The child was perfect: large brown eyes gazing at him with a rainbow swirl of colour mixed in. Fair hair like a breath of air barely covered the scalp. The child gripped one of his fingers in a tight grasp, its mouth open in a toothless smile. Calvin was filled immediately with a love never before experienced. When he woke, the closeness of the vision to his reality made him reach out for Moss's belly again. With one hand tracing the jiffling limbs beneath her skin and his other hand running rings across his own stomach and sensing the soul's movement inside him he lay silent, as the dawn made its presence known through the slats of the shack and gradually illuminated the room.

Because he hadn't had closure from the previous evening, and as Dell and Moss were still sleeping, Calvin rose quietly and let himself out of the shack; holding tightly to the door so that the wind didn't slam it shut. He toileted nearby, then examined the dead sheep. He planned to divide the flesh into cuts later that day and prepare a stew for the evening. Until then, he decided to work in the garden and pull up the necessary vegetables to accompany the meal. He had it in mind to atone for yesterday, whilst at the same time remaining practical and not getting under Dell and Moss's feet.

He picked up the hoe he had fashioned from a tree branch , slipped on his sandals which he found more comfortable working in the soft soil, and headed out across the increasingly shabby moorland towards the vegetable garden.

The further he walked from the shack the closer the mist clung to the ground. The wind flashed it past him, like clouded eddies in the brook; moisture adopted his clothing, sparkled it despite the dull light. At the patch the ground had hardened. Calvin was grateful that any frost had held back. He stove the hoe repeatedly into the earth, loosening the soil around the vegetables he needed. By the time the mist had cleared and the sun had whitened a circle in the patch of cloud it was hiding behind, Calvin realised that the hunger he had thought was in his stomach was actually something more.

The soul felt like it was doing cartwheels.

Calvin paused; allowed himself to sense what was happening, to feel what was going on inside him that had been masked through the physicality of his work. There was no doubt about it. Something was hammering inside his chest with the intensity of a bird trapped in a cage. The soul wanted out. It wanted out right now. And that could only mean one thing. Their baby was on the way.

Calvin ran.

Stones kicked up by his sandals flipped arcs in his wake, as though mimicking the soul inside his body. His right palm sweated where he clutched the hoe, the need for him to hold something tangible kept it in his grip. The dry wind caught at his clothing, as though seeking to replace his body inside it. His heart pounded in time with the excitement sensed by the soul: but there was fear there, a terrifying premonition of loss.

The vegetable garden was too far from his shack. Calvin knew Moss would never forgive him. He crested a ridge and the shack came into view, the only man made object on the landscape. He saw the repaired sides, the wood stacked against the walls, the sheep swaying in the breeze where it was hung. It wasn't much, but it was all that they had: a home made for them and their baby.

His sandal slipped sideways under his foot on the wet moorland and his ankle twisted, fired pain. He limped on. Smoke drifted at the front of the property, gave the appearance of dishevelled clouds. He couldn't see Moss. Knew she must be inside. Hoped Dell was with her. Knew that she must be.

The pain in his ankle burnt hot the nearer the shack became, as though a warning for him to stay away. He slipped, cursed. The soul ran in circles inside him, trying to find the way out. It spurred him forward as it pushed against his chest, leading him towards Moss. He gasped with the effort, his breath forced from his lungs. He hoped the soul wouldn't exit with it.

Despite the pain he knew Moss was experiencing worse. He could hear her cries carried on the wind. There had been no indication today would be the day. Hadn't Dell said that the birth usually took some time; surely all was yet to be lost? He couldn't believe that everything that they had planned for might simply be snatched away.

The wind tormented him. It strove against him and however hard he tried he couldn't block Moss's cries from his ears. He developed a pain in his stomach, a dull ache which then became stronger. He had to keep going. There wasn't much distance now between them. He could make it, he knew he could. Yet suddenly he expanded, with both feet mid-air he floated; just for a single breath, but as his feet regained the ground he knew that it was over. Something exploded inside him, a wrenching suction of air. He dropped the hoe.

His distended stomach deflated, and simultaneously the wind carried the cry of the baby. His mouth was dry.

He paused a short distance from the door of the shack, his breathing heavy. Despair stuck inside him, hurting his sides, his throat. He couldn't face Moss. He should never have gone to the vegetable garden, he should have stayed and made his apologies. Apologies that would seem trite considering the one he now had to make.

The shack door swung open. Dell appeared, sweat running over her forehead. She clutched a bundle in her arms. The midwife glanced up at him, expressionless.

"You better go inside," she said. "You don't want to see this."

Calvin faced away. Emotions surged through him: shame, rage, incompetence. But more than hiding himself from Dell he didn't want to see the child; not even in a glimpse. The pain overwhelmed him.

He nodded. Shuffled into the shack. In the bedroom Moss lay on one side, facing the wall with her back to him. He opened his mouth but words weren't enough.

The shack door swung closed behind him. He could hear the baby's cries through the thin walls, but a sudden crack shook one side of the building and then there was silence. Bile rose in his throat. The faint residue of the soul inside him – the extra soul that had spent many sun-ups accompanying and learning from his own – sifted out of his pores like wisps of smoke; a smoke mirrored as Dell stoked the remains of the fire until its heat intensified to burning point.

Calvin fell to his knees and watched as the fleeting tendrils of the baby's soul dispersed into air. Cracks in the walls sucked them into daylight. His breath collapsed into a sob. Moss remained still, but Calvin was shaking. The distance between them brief yet impassable. He desperately wanted to hold her, to be held by her; but he knew it would be a long time coming, if it ever came again at all. Their world had gone to nothing in a moment.

11

Dell had followed her midwife's instincts explicitly. There was no body for Calvin and Moss to bury, the fire had consumed it and the ash was mixed with embers and wood. Still, they needed the formality of closure, so two sun-ups after the death they stood by the side of the brook and Moss emptied the plastic container filled with the residue of their child into the muddy depths.

Calvin watched as the ash flashed grey in the water, reminding him of excess sperm that was sometimes discharged in his urine. It was over in a moment. Moss hadn't spoken to him since it happened, and she said nothing to him now. She simply looked up at Dell with tears in her eyes and Dell nodded back, also saying nothing. The two of them had had whispered conversations over the past two days, and Dell had sometimes spoken gruffly with Calvin – although not about the baby. He felt completely excluded, understandably so, but the loss was still felt keenly by himself whether or not he was to blame for what had happened.

Meanwhile the sheep still hung from the tree.

Calvin reached for Moss's arm, but she pulled away. He turned back from the river and walked towards the shack. Once inside, he found himself packing what little he had into his bag. As he picked up each item he couldn't help but run his thoughts through the life he and Moss had so far shared together: moments of laughter, happiness, and affection. Tears collected in his eyes and once he felt them there they fell freely. He clutched his bag of belongings to his chest, the bag giving the sensation of a body, the contents feeling like bones. He cried harder, jerking out the tears in sobs of desolation, his entire world sucked into nothingness with the lost of both Moss and the child.

A shadow blocked the light in the doorway. Calvin didn't look up. It would either be Moss or Dell. He wasn't sure which of them he wanted it to be.

"These things happen."

Dell's voice was low. She had tried to soften the harsh tones but it still came out cracked.

"Moss will recover. Women always do. Maybe one day you can try again."

Calvin had so much to say: that it wasn't his fault, that he couldn't have expected the birth to happen so quickly, that he was hurting just as much as Moss – maybe doubly so because he had also let her down. Yet none of these thoughts translated into words to come out of his mouth, because they all felt like excuses and none of them could reverse what had happened.

"There's something Moss hasn't told you," Dell added. She sighed – a heavy breath. "Something she hadn't told me."

Calvin looked up. Dell was watery through his tears, but he didn't wipe them from his eyes. It had to be made clear that he was hurting too.

"I probably shouldn't tell you," Dell said. "I guess it makes no difference either way. What's happened has happened and that's all there is to it."

"I'm going to leave," said Calvin.

"You're going to abandon her."

Again, Calvin had no words.

"She's down by the brook," Dell said. "You need to talk to her. I've had a word. I think she's ready."

Calvin stood. He desperately needed to be held by someone, anyone. He dropped the bag at his feet and Dell stepped back as he approached the door. The outside seemed vast – the countryside swept away under the brush of the sky. Calvin suddenly felt very small, overburdened by everything that had happen. Down by the brook, Moss was sitting with her legs underneath her. From this distance she was little more than a dot. Calvin remembered sitting by the brook not more than a few evenings ago, after the disagreement with Dell. That argument had flittered into triviality. Yet in some ways it was the root cause of their distress. But how far was it necessary to go back to determine blame? From that argument, from being offered the shack, from finding the settlement, from finding Moss, by beginning his travels, from meeting Book, from Sky meeting Royce and him being born? Everything fed into everything else, and other things would feed out of this tragedy. Some of those things might even be improved.

This couldn't be how he would talk about it with Moss, but as he walked towards her Calvin realised he could accept responsibility for what had happened as a way to deflect Moss's anger. If he were strong enough to absorb it for both of them, then maybe it would light a way out of it for Moss. Not that this would happen quickly, without doubt he knew it would take time. But Dell was right, he couldn't abandon her.

He sat beside her, not speaking. The silence weighed heavy between them. The previous two nights they had lain side by side on the bed without touching. Moss had rebuked any contact.

Calvin understood, so he hadn't pushed it; but he needed to push it now, or it would never happen.

"I'm sorry," he said. "I couldn't have known you were about to give birth."

Moss kept her silence.

"Nothing I can say will make a difference about the baby," Calvin continued. "But I need you to need me. I'm hurting too."

Moss sighed. She didn't look up, but she extended her hand towards Calvin's. He took it, gingerly, her fingers were cold and slipped into his so naturally; they connected and it was as it should have been.

Moss started to rock, her body shaking with silent cries. Calvin pulled her into him, feeling her warmth, her desperation. They clung to each other, holding tight, the pain of the loss unbearable yet tempered shared. Calvin looked over her shoulder at the brook, at the water running through the gouge in the earth. Where the water began and finished was an unknown quantity, just as life itself on Heart. He wondered, then, whether Moss had told Dell to destroy the body or whether Dell did this of her own accord. For a moment he thought it had been Moss's idea, remembering Dell's words that Moss hadn't told him something; but then Dell had added that she hadn't been told also, so that couldn't have been what she meant. Moss hugged him harder, began a new wave of tears. Calvin realised that nothing else mattered other than comforting each other in this moment of grief. It would only be later that they could talk about it and see what there was of their relationship to salvage.

12

Later that day there was a second burial.

Calvin cut down the sheep. Flesh flies had already begun to feast on the carcass, and maggots wriggled under the skin giving the semblance of life. An accumulation of gases had distended the abdomen, giving the carcass a bloated appearance. The smell was unpleasant; even after washing in the brook Calvin could detect it in his nostrils. Frothy liquids seeped from the sheep's mouth, nose and anus. None of this would have occurred had Calvin properly butchered the sheep, separated the internal organs from the carcass, and properly stored it. The failure of the celebration was reflected in the state of the animal that he had ultimately killed to no purpose. This weighed heavy on him – that in addition to everything else he had taken and wasted a life.

There had always been a clear difference between bodies without souls and animals. Animals had a use: whether for milk, clothing, or food. They were respected within the settlements and treated fairly. Whilst there was no consideration of consciousness – even amongst those animals that seemed to have an affiliation for human company, such as dogs – they were sometimes afforded the luxury of companionship. Unlike bodies, animals could show affection, fear, a basic understanding of their surroundings. Whilst there was no evidence supporting the need for sired animals to be together at birth – and therefore it was questionable as to whether an animal had a soul – they did not appear to be hampered by this fact. Calvin had often thought that animals, in some respects, were more manageable and advanced than humans, because they could procreate and birth at will. The benefits in having a soul if you were a body-without-a-soul were obvious, but for an animal there seemed to be no need to have a soul. Calvin had often raised such questions with the elders in his settlement, but had been told they weren't relevant and to simply get on with his work.

The more Calvin travelled the more questions he realised were unanswered and probably never would be.

He untied the rope that attached the sheep to the tree and gently lowered it to the ground. The carcass ruptured as it hit the floor and the fluids quickly soaked into the earth, the smell inflaming his nostrils. Calvin hauled the animal away, the rope digging into his shoulder. He pulled it into the trees at the edge of their settlement where he had dug into the soft soil and made a grave. He knew he should burn the animal or turn it into compost, but the smell of roasted flesh wasn't something he wanted floating around the shack, and it was unlikely they would remain static now there was nothing to tether them. Having compost for the vegetable garden was no longer relevant.

Calvin tipped the sheep into the hole and covered it with the loose soil. The pain he felt for the child carried through to the body of the sheep. Dell had decided not to reveal the sex of their baby to them. 'There is no point', she had said. Calvin could understand this. The less they knew the better. The less they viewed the body as a person, the better. Yet this lack of knowledge left a gaping hole in his heart and as he stood over the sheep's tangible grave – as opposed to standing at the side of the ever-changing brook – he felt a tug inside him once again for the child he would never know.

The light was failing by the time Calvin returned to the shack. Leaves streamed from the trees in a brisk wind, layered the route that he took, and fell around him almost weightless as though nature's acknowledgement of his pain.

Moss looked up as he entered. "All done?"

Calvin nodded.

Dell was leant against one wall of the shack. She had told them she would stay for a few days to check on Moss's health, but Calvin also wondered if she had concerns over their relationship as a couple. She had invested her time with them over the previous two seasons, and whilst her connection to Moss was greater than that with Calvin, they all had a certain respect and understanding for each other. She attempted a smile as he came in, but it was half-hearted. Calvin had a feeling he had interrupted a strained conversation.

He removed his jacket and hung it on a nail. Then sat beside Moss who automatically linked her arm in his – he couldn't tell if this was pure habit or whether they had begun to rebuild the bridge between them that had fallen so spectacularly.

Dell looked from one to the other, eventually nodding her head at Moss. Calvin mirrored the action, confused. Moss squeezed his arm, hard.

"I've something to tell you. Something I should have told you before. And certainly something I should have told Dell."

Calvin raised his eyebrows, inviting her to continue.

"There was a reason the birth happened quicker than Dell thought it would." Moss faltered. Calvin could feel her leaning into him as though all the bones in her body had turned to nothing.

"It's ok," he said. "Whatever it is. It will be ok."

Moss looked across to Dell, her face stained with tears. "Can you...?" she began. She fell silent. Guilt and sorrow written all over her face.

"You shouldn't have any secrets from each other," Dell began, "but I understand some things are harder to say than others and now probably isn't the time to lay yourself bare. But it has to be said." She looked directly at Calvin. "Moss has previously given birth. Twice. With a first birth labour is usually longer, often over several days. When a birth has already occurred, the elasticity within the womb isn't so tight and the birth is quicker. Each time a woman gives birth the likelihood is that the next time the procedure will be faster. I should have noticed this when I examined her, but considering her young years and the fact she didn't provide this information I hadn't been expecting it. My own experience is limited, to some degree, of course. So when she went into labour and the baby was ready to be born everything happened so much quicker than any of us expected.

"What I'm saying is that it is no one's fault that the baby was born without a soul. Neither of you should blame the other. These things happen."

Calvin looked at Moss, who had turned her face away from him. He understood clearly what Dell was saying, yet it was obvious Moss's holding back of information had caused the birth to go horribly wrong and that his delay in getting back to the shack wasn't the main cause for the body being born without a soul. If Dell had had this knowledge there was a strong chance he wouldn't have ventured so far from the settlement. In the two days of guilt and blame that he had taken upon himself he had tore up inside, been consumed with feelings he couldn't express because Moss had shunned him. Now he knew the reason why. She had been protecting herself, shielding herself from her own guilt. But despite this he couldn't be angry with her. They were both culpable, and reducing his guilt by half and then absorbing Moss's pain went some way to making things better.

Even so, he had to bite back on deflecting his grief and imposing it on Moss, something that instinctually rather than intellectually his mind was encouraging him to do. Instead he held her tightly and stroked her hair. "It's alright," he found himself saying, "everything will be ok. I'm with you."

Calvin decided now wasn't the appropriate time to discover why or how Moss had had two children previously; although even as he dismissed the thought it began to eat away at him as the maggots had begun to attack the sheep. If he wasn't careful, it would destroy him completely.

FUTURE WAR

1

"There it is again," Moss said, pointing towards the horizon above the swell of water that rose and fell in a great expanse before them.

Calvin shielded his eyes against the sun. The bright blue sky bounced light off the water, blurring the edges where they met so it appeared both sky and sea were one.

"I can't see it."

"Not there, silly. Over there!"

Calvin looked again, squinting into the light. Moss was right. A long silver shape, similar to the one he had seen all that time ago, was flying pale in the far distance. It might be a wisp of cloud if the speed didn't betray it. The object was too far away for them to hear any humming noises.

"I wonder if that's the Orbitist," said Calvin, remembering Dell's story.

"Who knows," shrugged Moss. "I don't think we should place too much importance on that old tale. If anything was due to happen, surely it would have happened by now."

Calvin nodded, unsure. He stretched out his limbs, dug his toes into the yellow soil. The heat of it was enticing. He felt clean. Both himself and Moss were naked. They had bathed in the sea daily since their arrival, the warm sun drying their bodies as they lay on the sand drifting towards sleep.

He closed his eyes, sunlight filtering through his lids making them a soft orange. The sound of a child playing carried on the light breeze. He couldn't resist a smile.

"It's gone," Moss said. She snaked her arm around Calvin's waist. "Don't sleep too much. You should keep an eye on Acorn."

"She's fine."

Moss kissed his cheek. "I know she is."

Calvin opened his eyes. At the edge of the water Acorn – twelve seasons old – was jumping over the incoming waves. She laughed each time the water hit her – she either jumped too soon or too late. They had named her after his sister, and he was always glad that they had. She provided a link to his past, present, and future. She was funny and happy and carefree and never seemed to mind that they moved from place to place. It was in moments like these, when the sun was warm and the air full of laughter, that he treasured what they had; could turn his mind away from what might have been.

Moss pulled on his arm. She had moved to a kneeling position and he knew what she wanted. They stood together and ran towards the water, scooping up Acorn under her armpits and pretending to throw her into the sea. She squealed and wriggled, her lithe body twisting in their grip, before they placed her back down on the wet sand and watched as she tried to jump another wave.

Sand, sea, wave. These words were fairly new to their vocabulary. There was a settlement nearby where they had gained knowledge of the sea. It was a different area of Heart to that where Moss had first encountered such a large expanse of water. The land curved in around itself, more than a semi-circle, not quite a circle. The cliffs sheltered the land from the wind. They had made use of an abandoned shelter close to the beach – a stone building made of smooth flints, which was almost intact. Arriving at the start of spring they were now mid-summer, with the intention of moving on early autumn before the full harshness of winter struck. Remaining for one place for a season or so at a time was the agreement struck between the two of them to gain the best of their situation: they were constantly moving, but sufficiently static also.

By and large they were accepted by each settlement they encountered, although there were always instances of rebuttal; either through the size of their party or simply the sullen nature of some of the elders. If Moss's pregnant condition had facilitated hospitality in the past, so Acorn's presence almost guaranteed it now. They always approached new settlements as a family, without one of them having to hide. It was all or nothing. All or nothing at all.

A larger wave splashed Acorn up to her belly and she squealed again. Her tiny fingers in Calvin's grip dug into his skin. He loved her. He loved her more than he might possibly have imagined. He knew he would do anything for her – would sacrifice Moss or even himself if he had to. Acorn's existence was paramount. It had drawn them together and couldn't keep them apart.

The days had been dark following their previous attempt at child. As much as they were hurting, finding solace with each other was beset by arguments and recriminations. The onslaught of winter had bound them together. Early snowfall had almost buried the shack, and they were forced to spend time in each other's company where the absence of a child was a hollowness that drew from their empty insides into a space where the baby should have been. Dell's return to the settlement had sped forth bitter words, unrestrained without her presence. For each of them, the building of an argument, from a simple truth to escalating insults, was something to be desperately avoided, but nevertheless they couldn't staunch it all the same.

By the time winter segued into spring all the anger had been wrenched from the relationship. Moving on from the shack which was to have been the family home proved to be a catharsis in their existence. At the point where they might have separated they turned to each other, travelled together as one. The alternative of a life lived alone had proven too much to bear.

Calvin looked across to Moss, at the smile on her face. Dell had been wrong. They had been able to deliver a child all by themselves. In fact, the more he thought about it, the more he had convinced himself that it was Dell's fault they had lost the first child. They had relied on her presence, but they should have relied on themselves. Without Dell, Calvin would have ensured he hadn't left Moss's side. This was partly how they had come to reconcile their relationship, to deflect all the blame. Whether it was true or not hardly mattered. The repair was done. Their relationship was salvaged. And Acorn was proof of this.

Raising their arms they lifted Acorn above the waves, over and over again, until they were all tired and returned to the beach to eat and sleep.

2

In the afternoon Calvin left Moss and Acorn at the shack and walked inland where they had previously passed a small crop of pear trees. He wore some light clothing, but it was still uncomfortable walking, his bag hooked over his shoulders making his back sweat. Acorn had fallen asleep shortly after lunch, and Moss had begun peeling potatoes for their evening meal which they would have with some beef and bread they had been given at the previous settlement. Calvin planned on collecting the pears as a tasty dessert.

He hadn't been alone for some time. He enjoyed the quiet: the light breeze ruffling leaves on the trees, the call of an occasional seagull, the sound his footsteps made through the grass. Yet whilst it was quiet amongst the landscape, his head became crowded with thoughts. The isolation from his family and their constant distractions allowed his mind free reign.

He wondered about the silver object in the sky. They had seen it only occasionally over the past few seasons, and scarcely paid any attention to it. Since Acorn's birth Calvin found his thoughts were grounded in the everyday, and he didn't have time for speculation over things that were ephemeral. Now his thoughts had a moment to breathe he ran once again through the conversation they had with Dell, over Book's possible interaction with the Orbitist and the warning he had given them. Amidst the grass, trees, bright blue sky, and the contentment which came with Moss and Acorn, Calvin could easily dismiss it. If the Orbitist were but an aerial traveller then Calvin knew his knowledge would be limited to the places he had been: just like he, Dell, Book, Moss, and all the other travellers. It did not mean that every tale he told was truth, or without embellishment. Whilst the story had originally unnerved him within the emotional state of impending fatherhood, in the warm light of summer it was an entirely different matter.

Drawn back to the death of their first baby Calvin couldn't help but revisit the trauma he felt discovering Moss had had two previous pregnancies. Within the darkness of their old shack, with Dell sat on her bedding encouraging Moss to speak but simultaneously breaking the intimacy of the moment, Calvin's emotions had run ragged from pain to desperation to condolence. He could remember it all, almost word for word.

"Go on," Dell said. "You need to tell him. He needs to know."

Moss sighed. It wasn't a normal sigh. It carried with it the weight of years.

"In my original settlement I had been paired with a man named Subway. I told you our settlement was considered idyllic, with its relaxed lifestyle and plenty of supplies. Well, this was only partly the case. We were allowed no choice of birth partners. Our sexual arrangements were predetermined. The elders believed healthier children would result if they were in charge of who we coupled with. I see this in principle, but when the person chosen for yourself isn't the most pleasant – in either appearance or manners – then it's frankly unpalatable. Anyway, I acquiesced because there was nothing else to do. Subway was rough, evil smelling. I don't know what it was about him, but I've never met anyone I disliked more or since.

"Apart from finding me physically attractive, Subway didn't have a high opinion of me either. Once the seed was sown we didn't have much to do with each other. He was disinterested in the entire process of creation. In our settlement, unlike in many others I've seen, we grew hops and had drinks which addled the mind. Subway was frequently addled. When the time came for the birth he couldn't be found. I had our baby knowing that it wouldn't have a soul. I never saw what happened to it. Whenever I chanced upon Subway afterwards he turned his sorry head away from me. His reputation was crushed within the settlement too. One day they found him dead amongst the vegetables. His face was bloated. They never knew why."

Moss had spoken softly during her tale, her body pressed close to Calvin. He understood how his own absence during the birth had affected her, not only through the loss of their child, but the resurgence of past memories. Even so, if only she had told him before; he could have comforted her during the pregnancy and they might not have lost the child.

But he didn't say this. Instead he said: "And the other child?"

Moss sighed again. "I told you how I left our settlement. The circumstances of my departure. That I had a conversation with a traveller named Esquire and subsequently was forced to flee – my action determined by the elders who anticipated what I was thinking, even though I hadn't even made up my own mind."

"Yes," Calvin said, "I remember you telling me this. The mad charge towards the glass."

Moss allowed herself a smile. "That's right." She paused, ran a hand through her hair, "Well, there's more to the story that I didn't tell you. Once I'd left the settlement I happened to catch up with Esquire. It was purely by chance. We spent a couple of nights together, and in fact were a little careless. It was quite some time after we'd gone our separate ways that I realised I was pregnant again."

Calvin couldn't stop the gasp that came up out of his throat like a winter wind. Moss had travelled whilst pregnant before. All the talk they had had of being careful travelling together was rendered meaningless by her previous experience. There was so much she had held back from him. His naivety hit him hard. How could they regain that trust?

But again, with Dell sitting quietly opposite, and the burial of their child only that morning, all he felt he could say was: "What happened then?"

"I travelled whilst pregnant. I tried to disguise it as much as I was able. I bound my stomach with rope and wore ill-fitting clothing. I stockpiled as much food as I could and in the final two months I ate frugally from my supplies and off the land. Of course, I knew when the baby was born that it would have no soul. I had no choice, Calvin; I had no choice but to destroy it after its birth."

Moss cried bitter tears: for the one, two, three children she had lost. Calvin couldn't help but feel aggrieved that the grief for their child was heightened by that of the other two children, however much he tried to fight against it. Truth was, it wasn't fair on either of those babies to have been born without a chance in the world. Yet he couldn't understand Moss's attitude towards those bodies without souls they had seen. How she could have tormented one with stones, for example, knowing as she did the circumstances of their births.

This thought was left to fester over the coming season, through the hard winter. Even now Calvin wasn't convinced he had come to terms with it; yet there was little point mulling over the past. On Heart, all they had was the future: it stretched before them like the view to the horizon. Maintaining a day-to-day existence was much more important than running yourself into the ground over events which couldn't be altered.

There had been a final part to Moss's story, which, once it was finished, she assured him was all she had to tell. "It was shortly after the death of that second child, Calvin, that winter began to ascend and I met you. You will recall I had little provisions with me. In fact, I had determined to die. If you hadn't have found me, protected me, shown me such affection, I wouldn't be here now, loving you, despite the loss of our baby. I know it wasn't your fault, but you were easy to blame; easy to hide behind. Dell convinced me to tell you my truths and I know she was right. I only wish I'd done this before."

Calvin had hugged her close, for his benefit as well as hers; the complications of her story so vast that he couldn't pin down his emotions. Occasionally these sparked within him, revealed themselves in moments of disagreement; but once Moss had fallen pregnant for their second time – and her fourth – he had regained his feelings for her to the extent that her well-being and that of their child was paramount. Despite all that had happened, nothing would snatch a child away from either of them ever again.

He pulled back from recollection and found himself by the pear trees, his memory having erased the distance he needed to travel. Putting down his bag on the grass, he ran his fingers over the fruit. They were just beginning to ripen. He twitched his hand and one came free from the stalk. He bit into it, the hard surface giving way to a moist softness within; they would be perfect if he chose carefully. He began to fill his bag.

He made sure to choose those that hadn't softened too much – the combined weight in the bag would compress them. After a short time the bag was full – yet he had barely made an impression on the trees. He loved this time of year, when food supplies were bountiful and there was no need for hardship. Even so, he took only what was needed. Overstocking only led to waste and waste couldn't be justified.

Having completed his task sooner than he imagined Calvin decided to walk further from the beach to see if he could find anything else that might be useful. The sun had slid into the second half of the sky, but it was no cooler. Sweat ran over his brow. Inland from the beach the grass was long and thick, initially coarse, gradually getting softer closer to the trees. Yet on the other side of the trees the countryside was pockmarked with signs of earlier habitation. The Snake, which Dell had informed him was called a road, began just beyond the orchard. Its surface showed underneath the grass like a spine, buckling the ground, hunks of stone extending skywards as it ran and extended towards a city in the distance.

Calvin had yet to visit the city. The residents of the nearest settlement could view it from their location, but none of them had been there. When he had questioned it they raised superstition about a city of lost souls. Calvin hadn't dared query it further – the people had been good to them and he didn't want to negate their beliefs. Having been in many cities since he travelled he knew the only ghosts there were made of metal and brick; but he could see how these ancient buildings might instil wonder and speculation. When pale smoke rose from the city as they had been about to leave the settlement he imagined it was from a natural fire that might have started due to the weather conditions, however the residents were heard to mutter again about souls and warned him not to venture there.

Needless to say, Calvin was determined to take a look; although with it being at least a sun-up journey there and back he wasn't keen on leaving Moss and Acorn behind for an overnight stay. And Moss had expressed no desire to see it.

"I've seen enough abandoned buildings to last me a lifetime," she said, tickling Acorn on her tummy as she spoke. "There will be nothing there, only a handful of artefacts which you'll be able to salvage but never sell. I don't need to drag Acorn there for that. And the way is dangerous – the rocks pushed up on the road and the metal carcasses and so on. Really, what good could come of going there?"

"Just stimulating the sense of adventure," Calvin had said.

"We've been here only a handful of sun-ups and you were like a little kid when you saw the beach and the sea for the first time. Hasn't that sated your craving for travelling for a while?"

Calvin knew she was right. He had run down to the beach when they first saw it, surprised at how his tracks were stopped short by the softness of the sand. His appreciation of the sea took a little longer to harvest: whilst he had marvelled at its vastness, intensity and power, he had been less keen on immersing himself in it. The drag at his feet as the water threatened to pull him away from the land, and the way the sand sucked at his ankles had unnerved him. Yet wandering out a fair distance and having the water only rise to his chest, and seeing the extent of the wet sand under the sea when it receded, alleviated that concern. He was left with the awe at the sheer difference of it all, and a smile that he would never have seen it if he hadn't started travelling.

So Moss was right. His desire to see new things had been fed by the sand and the sea, but it would never be sated; even if it had been tempered by the necessary requirement to serve Acorn's needs.

So he walked a short way along the road that led to the city in the distance, towering metal structures evidently intact. Crumbling ruins flanked the road, marked in ways that he couldn't understand. Moving his head to one side, scanning the horizon, his vision was suddenly caught by white light; the sun reflected off a shiny surface. He shielded his gaze, looked again, but the glare was too intense. Moving his position he tried once more. This time he saw the object that had refracted the light. It was only visible as a shape hidden between two buildings, located on the right hand side of the city, but it was clear enough: a silver metallic object. Clearly similar to that which he had seen in the sky.

He took in a breath.

Reality peeled away from him. He envisaged the canopy of the sky falling, pulling the horizon down with it, the trees and the clouds being drawn inside like a collapsing cloth bag. Sounds became muffled, the air compressing around his head; a crackling noise dominated his thoughts, couldn't be shaken out. His limbs weakened, the bones slipping inside his body, dislocating. As the soft fold gathered he became aware of the darkness hiding behind everything, the weight of space enveloping all he took as fact.

The heat had got to him. He regained consciousness to find himself lying on the ground, his palms and elbows smeared with grass stains and dirt. He took one of the pears from the bag and ate it, the sweet stickiness running down the sides of his mouth and making his fingers tacky. After a while the queasiness he felt at waking disappeared, and he stood again, his legs fully sure of his body.

He looked across to the silver object for a second time. It remained in the same position, as though waiting for something to happen. Calvin kept his gaze on it a long time before deciding he needed to visit the city. It took him even longer to make up his mind to tell Moss.

3

The following morning the sun rose raw, the sky once again unfettered with cloud. Calvin was woken by Acorn pulling at his face, her tiny fingers grabbing at his lips and nose as she tried to remain quiet. He opened his eyes and smiled. Moss was already up, preparing some bread for breakfast. Calvin allowed his eyes to close a moment longer, remembered everything that had happened the previous day, and then sat up quickly, holding Acorn just under her armpits and whirling her around his head.

"Hey," said Moss.

"Hey," he replied.

He plopped Acorn back to the floor, stretched, felt the muscles in his back relax, and then got around to wondering how he was going to lie.

"Are you ok with Acorn today? I want to go into the city."

Lying wasn't his forte.

Moss laid the bread out on the table. "Perhaps we could all go."

"It's a long way for Acorn when she has the beach and sea right here in front of her."

"It's a long way for you. We've spoken about this before. There really isn't any need for you to go into the city."

Calvin knew she was correct. But he didn't want to tell her what he had seen. He considered the reason for this and found the answer was simple: if she knew about it, then she wouldn't want him to go.

They hadn't discussed the Orbitist frequently, but whenever they had their views were found to be conflicting. Calvin saw his apparent prophecies as a threat to their current existence – whether they were true or not, having them in his head unsettled him. Yet, given the chance, he wanted to talk to the Orbitist – if he in fact existed – to reassure himself. Moss was ambivalent about his existence; but if he did exist she didn't want any connection with him. She believed knowing the truth would be an obstacle to happiness. Whilst her thirst for travelling and new things was paramount, she also didn't want anything to change. For her, not knowing was better than knowing.

Yet for both of them, these ideals slipped in and outside of each other. Because the entire question of the Orbitist and what he might or might not know was arbitrary and there could only be conjecture. This was why Calvin needed to know. To pin it down as fact so he would know how to react.

But he didn't say this. Instead he said: "I'm just curious. We'll be here for another season and then we'll need to find shelter for winter. Maybe this city will be the best place for that. If I can take a quick look then we'll know for sure."

Moss bit into the bread. The crust had hardened and it was tough on her teeth. Calvin watched her tear it apart as though she were an animal.

"Go on," she said, afterwards. "You better start out now if you want to be back by evening."

Calvin picked up his bread and packed it into his bag for later. A couple of the pears went in there too.

"Get some more of those on the way back," Moss said. "Acorn likes them."

Calvin nodded. He kissed Moss on the cheek and Acorn on the forehead. Then he walked through the open door, went around the side of the shack and up through the dunes towards the pear trees.

As he walked he knew his plan would come to nothing if the silver object were no longer there. With each step he alternated from hoping it was to hoping it wasn't.

The day was already hot. As Calvin reached the pear trees he decided to eat one for its juice and to conserve his water. The taste was warm and sweet in his mouth. It was only once the pear was finished that Calvin looked towards the outlying buildings at the edge of the city. The silver object was still there, still gleaming in the light. He turned for a moment, looked back in the direction he had come, then made up his mind – though he knew it was already made up – and headed in the direction of the road.

The going was hard. The ground under the road had twisted and the stone that comprised it had broken up accordingly. Like every road he had ever walked he kept adjacent to it where the ground was flatter. He understood through experience that the road must once have been flat, a manmade object scything through the countryside allowing people to travel faster than walking over rough ground. But now the road itself was rough, a testament to the endurance of nature over man's effort to dominate it. He was glad that the people of Heart, as it now was, seemed to pay greater attention to the world around them than their forebears had done in the past. Even so, the ground itself wasn't without its divots and ups and downs. Calvin wanted to make good time, hoped to be back by evening, but knew in his heart that he wouldn't return 'til tomorrow.

This knowledge, that he had in some way deceived Moss,

weighed against him; tempered only by the increasing size of the silver object as he approached it.

When the sun was at its hottest Calvin stopped and ate his bread and another pear. Sweat ran off his head, dripping onto the grass, a salty drink for plant life. The bread mushed in his mouth, it wasn't as fresh as it could have been and he had to chew hard and take in water to soften it in order to swallow. The pear was enjoyable, but he had eaten a lot of pears in the past two sun-ups and he began to long for something different. When he directed his gaze at the object, he thought he saw a figure moving along its length, however the heat haze distorted his view and he couldn't be certain.

At this angle, it was clear that the buildings partly obscuring the object were some distance from the city. In fact, they were closer than he first imagined. He stood and walked steadily, convinced he would reach it soon. The nearer he got the greater the number of abandoned buildings lined the road, their open-mouthed facades gaping black, absorbing sunlight. As he became immersed in the outskirts of the city his perspective changed and he lost sight of the object amongst the amalgam of streets. Keeping his eye on the sun's position in the sky Calvin navigated by chance mixed with his innate sense of direction. After some time the buildings fell away again, and with the hulking bulk of the city on his left the land opened and the object could clearly be seen, spaced between those two large buildings that were door-less and open.

The size of the object became impressive the closer Calvin approached. He couldn't understand how such a thing could remain in the air. Its interior capacity was greater than the shack he currently called home. The arms extended widthways with cylindrical canisters below them. Underneath the main frame the structure balanced on a series of small wheels. This close, the colour was more white than silver. Calvin couldn't understand how it might rise.

He walked around it, twice. A door was set in the body of the object and a moveable staircase led up to it. The door was closed. Calvin looked from left to right. There was no one in sight. He considered going up the steps and trying the door, but was hit with a sense of foreboding that wove its way beneath his skin, into his internal organs, and hung there, mocking him, to the extent that he had to sit.

He took a breath. He had been displaced by the crushing certainty of his death.

His head felt like it was spinning, a whirligig of emotions.

Closing his eyes didn't help. He was transported to his birth – a birth he couldn't remember – and the infinity of nothingness that preceded it. There could be no understanding as to how he came into being – other than the physicality of it. Equally, he realised now – although he had known it for some time – there could be no understanding of how he would cease to be. What would be true was this:

The object he saw in front of him, the grass beneath his feet, the blue sky above, the sensation of heat from the sun, the relationship he had with Moss, the joy he experienced from Acorn, the sense of self that had rested inside him for as long as he could remember, the memories of the places he had seen and the places he had yet to journey to, the taste of beets in his mouth and a cool drink of water running down his throat, his dreams whilst he slept and the day dreams whilst he woke, each of the hairs on his arms that flickered in a breeze, and the way his feet hurt at the end of each day; this and everything else would be lost to him. Replaced by an unfathomable non-existence the oppressiveness of which was unbearable.

Calvin shook his head, as though to dodge these thoughts. They fragmented as they fell from his mind, shards broke away and dissipated, the sensation of gloom became absorbed into his psyche and forgotten. Yet there remained an unease that would accompany his every waking thought: that he was only here on Heart for a brief moment in time. And once he left, then all the realities that had adhered themselves to him would no longer exist. Regardless of whether he left Moss or Acorn behind, for him the knowledge of their existence would be permanently, terminally, erased.

The sun beat on. Calvin felt tears stream down his face. He couldn't place why this vision had come to him, whether it was linked to the object from the sky or whether there was another source, but it tore into his emotions and left them ragged. He caught his breath, steadied himself, yet happy images of Moss and Acorn flooded into his mind, made all the more caustic in the knowledge that one day they would be obliterated. He stood, again; glanced up at the perpetual sun and railed against the battle of life against death. He found he was shaking. Eventually, something calmed within him and his current reality reasserted itself. He took in the beauty of his surroundings, the colours, the vibrancy of it all, and gave thanks that he was there to appreciate it. The black mood had passed.

He wiped his sleeve against his face, dull marks streaked the material. Life was bigger than him, he realised; yet as an individual his world was *the* world. There was no escaping his fate unless he could change his world. He knew this to be impossible. Taking a few deep breaths, and a swig from the water bottle, he chose to ignore the darkness that still clustered in the back of his mind, and instead he gripped the handrail hard and lifted his foot to take the first step towards the door of the object.

"I wouldn't do that."

Calvin pulled his hand from the rail as though it were white-hot. The voice was clear, male, yet had a hollow ring to it. Calvin swung his head from left to right, but could see no one. He realised he was shaking again.

"One moment," said the voice.

Calvin backed away from the object. Could it possibly be sentient. Had it spoken to him?

As these thoughts crossed his mind he saw the door in the object bulge, then swing to one side in a fluid motion. A man came into view. He wore a one-piece costume which must have once been white, but now was smeared with black stains and looked ragged in places. A long beard obscured the lower half of his face. Calvin remembered Dell's description, of how Book had said the Orbitist had no facial hair. He wondered if this was indeed the man from that story, or just another traveller who had happened upon the object and decided to make it his home.

The man raised an arm, then began to descend the steps. Calvin stood his ground. Now that he saw the man was but a man he saw no need for fear or flight. Instead, his curiosity was further roused; the past few years fell away from him and he felt for his artefact in his pocket as a reminder that he had travelled for such questions that were posed in front of him to be answered.

When the man spoke there was no hollowness to his voice, yet it was the same tone he had heard before. Calvin wondered if it had been augmented somehow from within the object.

"Hello."

"Who are you?" Calvin blurted.

"I am known as The Orbitist," the man said. His voice held an accent Calvin had never heard before. He smiled. He reached the bottom of the steps and gestured for Calvin to sit down nearby. He squatted, facing him. "What is your name?"

"Calvin."

The Orbitist nodded. "A fine name. Do you know what it means?"

"Means?" Calvin had never attributed meaning to his name before. Names were traditional, handed down through a settlement's generation. It had never occurred to him that his name might hold a meaning.

"When Earth transformed into Heart," the Orbitist began, "much of what had been was lost. The information I hold is clear on this. Mankind's collective memory was wiped – ineffectually, as it happens. Once Heart fully engaged scraps of humanity returned to its population. You can't read, can you?"

"Read?" Calvin was getting lost.

The Orbitist smiled reassuringly. "You've seen a book, I take it. Those pages with symbols on them. Those on Heart used to be able to read them."

Calvin shook his head.

"As Heart was transformed the ability to read became non-essential. Eventually, over a great number of years, it was lost. But in the crux of the transformation there existed those who had some knowledge of the written word. They renamed the population from information that was available. Your name probably comes from an advertisement for a product, maybe one seen at a bus stop, or on a hoarding attached to a building, perhaps even on a label on clothing. This is where your name comes from: Calvin Klein."

"Its just Calvin," said Calvin; having understood almost nothing of what the Orbitist had said. He remembered Dell's words that Book had told her each person used to have two names. If that was the case, then he wondered if Klein would have been his second name. He gave an imperceptible shrug; it meant nothing to him. What he wanted to know was how the Orbitist's presence might affect the here and now.

The Orbitist appeared to have been distracted by Calvin's comment. His eyes roved about as though he were tracking the progress of a fly. "I've seen a lot," he muttered. "A lot I've seen." He scratched the side of his head, gently at first, then vigorously. "I had my own name once, but I've forgotten it."

"You're the Orbitist," Calvin said.

"We're all the Orbitists. Each and every one of us." He sighed. "It can be so lonely out there."

Calvin looked at the position of the sun in the sky. He could return now, his curiosity abated, and Moss would know nothing of it. But the answer to one question only raised myriad others. He couldn't keep coming back. Perhaps he could take the Orbitist with him.

"I'm living by the sea," Calvin began, "with my partner and child. Would you return there with me?"

The Orbitist's eyebrows hunched. "And why would I want to do that?"

Calvin shrugged. "You said you were lonely."

"My work is here. I cannot leave the ship."

Calvin looked at the large white object. He had no understanding of the word *ship*, but he assumed the Orbitist meant the object from the sky. For the first time he noticed the ground under the object was a stretch of unbroken road. He followed it into the distance. After some way, it stopped; yet it was fresh, undamaged. He realised that its construction must have been recent. The Orbitist was aware of his gaze.

"There are a few landing strips dotted about the country. We try to put them in out of the way places. We don't want to be conspicuous. Now that you've seen it I'll have to kill you." He laughed a shrill tone, a warbling frenetic frenzy that stopped just as suddenly as it started. "I'm joking, of course. We're not allowed to touch any of you."

Calvin couldn't see the joke. The piercing laugh had unnerved him. He had yet to meet anyone like the Orbitist. Perhaps he had expected some kinship as they were both travellers, but if anything was certain then it was that the Orbitist exhibited behaviour that was alien to him.

He wondered how to continue. He knew there were questions he should ask about subjects of which he had no knowledge. He didn't want to appear ignorant, yet he also didn't know what he wanted to know.

"How long are you here?" he said, finally.

The Orbitist smiled benignly. "For as long as it takes." He paused. "I'm sorry, I know I'm confusing you. In terms of staying here, it will be for a few days. I'm waiting for a gas drop. If you mean how long are we staying on Heart, then it will be forever."

"If you're not from Heart, then where are you from?" Calvin's eyes scanned the sky. He thought he knew the answer, however improbable it seemed.

This provoked another spate of laughter, followed by some coughing. "I'm from Earth," the Orbitist said. "Earth is both here and also the flipside of Heart."

"I don't understand."

"No one understands. Even those who believe that they do."

"Who are these others? Who are the *we* you keep mentioning?"

The Orbitist sighed. "All these questions. What does it matter to you, little man?"

Calvin could feel the muscles bristling under his shirt. "It matters because I want to know," he said, restraining the anger in his voice. "I am a fellow traveller."

"You fellow travellers." The Orbitist paused. "You're the only ones we're allowed to communicate with and yet you don't know anything. These conversations are supposed to supplement our stability and yet all we end up doing is playing with each other." He ran a hand over his face, flicking sweat down with it.

"I know more than you might think," braved Calvin. "I know that this Earth you say you are from was once Heart. I know that something went wrong here. I know…" he thought back to what Dell had said, such a long time ago, "…that one day the original inhabitants of Earth will return to Heart to enslave us. I'm not just the little man that you think I am. And I probably know things that you don't know."

The Orbitist sat back, rocked on his buttocks. "Have you spoken to an Orbitist before? You've not spoken to me, I don't think."

"Where I get my information from is none of your business," said Calvin. "But there are things I want to know, as facts, not fancies. Tell me how you came to be on Heart."

The Orbitist chewed the insides of his lips. Overhead, a soft white cloud spoiled the utter blueness of the sky. "Okay," he said, eventually, "I'll tell you what I know. Not that it will do either of us the slightest bit of good."

4

Calvin shared what provisions he had whilst the Orbitist spoke. In turn, the Orbitist entered the ship and brought back some fruit Calvin had never seen before: curved yellow substances with skin that peeled away like petals revealing a paler yellow interior. The flesh turned to mush in his mouth, a thick paste that he wasn't entirely comfortable with, although the taste made up for the texture.

"You ask me how I came to be on Heart. I respond that I asked to be here. A decision that I regret. I had a fondness, a nostalgia, for a world that I considered home but which I never knew. I had a calling, if you will – you will understand this as a traveller, I know you use the same terminology. Something deep inside me wanted more than what I had. Not that I had much. None of the exiles from Earth have anything at all. Except for the leaders, of course. The leaders have everything. Everything except Heart.

"Something happened. Way back in the past. So far back that no one can remember. Some call it The Flip. But even those are unsure whether it was the term that was ascribed at the time or one that has stuck since. No one really knows what happened. And no one ever will. What we do know is that some of the original population that lived here on Earth were aware that the catastrophe would take place. And they made provision for it. They created large underground stores in the deserts where equipment, gas, food products, clothing, and people were kept. They retained information on the workings of machines, social documents on the history of Earth, a wide spectrum of information which they thought would be useful once it was safe to return.

"And then these leaders, these government officials, with their wives and their children, left the surface of Earth to settlements created on the Moon. It was a long term plan. They were aware of the catastrophe many years before it happened and they knew they could only return many years after it concluded. As it happens, it turned out there were more years afterwards than any of them could have imagined. Those who remain on the Moon are generation after generation after generation after generation removed from those of the original inhabitants. They are like the surface of the Moon itself: grey and stale, lifeless, inhospitable. I'm using metaphors here, forgive me. I am also a child of the Moon, returned to Earth as a scout. The instructions for me to operate the ship were handed down by the equivalent of the elders in our settlement. Those few who have retained an ability to read. They are few and far between, but just enough to reassemble the vestiges of the civilisation that we once were but has since been forgotten.

"Many, many years ago the majority of the Moon's population returned to Earth to reclaim the objects that were hidden underground. We have our own stories to tell of the hardship that followed, of the endless searches for what had once been, for the luck that enabled us to find it. Those people have been living under what you would call Heart ever since. They've been biding their time, waiting to gain strength, to return to the surface and rule over the remaining population: those who somehow survived the catastrophe and rebuilt new lives for themselves on Heart. People like you, Calvin; people like you."

The Orbitist sighed again, and within that sigh Calvin detected the distance between Heart and the Moon, and all the dust that was held between them.

"So The Flip is the event that happened. And the flipside is the interior of Heart, where the true descendants of Earth now live."

"The *true descendants*?" Calvin had found it impossible to understand much of what the Orbitist had said, but he clung onto those parts of the story which might matter to him.

"This is what they call themselves," the Orbitist explained. "They don't see people such as yourself as the genuine inheritors of the world. They don't see how you could have survived, they resent the tranquillity you have found. So they dismiss you and everything you stand for."

"But you are one of them," began Calvin. "Don't you think the same?"

"I might have done, once; but there's an old saying which one of our elders told me has been handed down from generation to generation. Travel broadens the mind. Do you know what that means?"

Calvin considered it. He did know. He nodded.

"Right. So you've seen for yourself how narrow-minded people can be, how entrenched they are in their existence that they look for truths no further than their own noses. Whereas you and I, Mr Calvin Klein, know that there are no truths. There is only the present, to be embraced constantly; and the search, the search for everything else that is out there and ready to be absorbed."

Again, Calvin could only glimpse at the meaning behind the Orbitist's story. Yet he found that he didn't doubt it. There was a sincerity in the telling which bolstered the words. If Book had heard the same tale, Calvin could understand how it had troubled him. To have that knowledge and yet be unable to do anything with it was a burden that Calvin now realised he was going to have to share.

"These people," he said, choosing his words carefully to make it appear he understood more than he actually did, "who reside underground. Do you really think they are ready to enslave us?"

The Orbitist shook his head. "They will never be ready. They are too few in number, too dislocated in intention. However that is not the point. For the fact is that they *believe* they are ready. And that belief will be enough to carry them through with their task; even if they no longer have an understanding of what it is they will do."

"They can't just live like us, harmoniously?" Calvin could almost feel his hope drain away, like rain into the dry earth.

"You must understand that those who made the plans to leave Earth, those who were determined to perpetuate their existence amongst the stars until they were ready to return, these people were never ordinary people. They were the powerful, the ruthless, the privileged. Ever since their expulsion they have desired only one thing: to return to Earth to reclaim the power they consider their birthright. This is why they wish to enslave; to re-establish their inheritance. But they are blinkered, inconsiderate. The Earth has changed. *Heart* has changed. But this fact only enrages them. You cannot reason with such people, you can only hope that they will find the truth for themselves."

"And the truth is?"

"That Heart is for everybody. That there is space enough here for us all to dwell without impinging on anybody else. That there is no benefit to enslavement. If there's anything I've learnt from my time in the sky then it is this: there is nothing to be had in abundance to make fighting for it worthwhile."

Calvin felt a bud of pride for Heart. In the same way as Heart itself seemed to have pushed out of the soil of Earth, so his admiration for the land that he walked poured out of his body. It was clear there was more to what the Orbitist said than Calvin could understand, yet he had faith in the peoples of Heart and the landscape they lived with. Should the old inhabitants of Earth try to take this away from them he had no doubt they would be met with resistance.

"Where are these places," Calvin asked, "where they live under the ground?"

The Orbitist considered for a moment, as though he were

wondering if the information was free to be told. Then he said: "In places whose names no longer exist. The Atacama desert in Chile, the Gobi desert in Northern China, Death Valley in the United States of America."

Calvin shook his head. "I have never heard of these places." Yet even as he said this he realised settlements were never named.

"And you never would have done. You would never have travelled there. They are all on the other side of the sea, some almost an entire sun-up away, even when travelling in my ship."

"Do you go there often?"

"I no longer go there. I came from the underground facility in Death Valley. I have been back once. There is no reason to return. My job is to observe and report. When I need it, food and petrol are dropped for me to refuel and continue. I'm no longer certain what I'm reporting or how the information is used. But I know they are still out there because of the communications I receive."

Calvin's understanding was still only a fraction of what the Orbitist was saying. He was aware that the extent of Heart must be greater than the areas he had already traversed, but he had never considered if there was land beyond the sea. He understood now why the Orbitist had to travel in the sky – even if he had no conception of how that might be done. Even so, the knowledge he was being given was so vast that it transcended the limits of his understanding. He wondered if he would ever understand it, or if indeed he would ever need to.

The Orbitist had disappeared into his memories. Calvin realised he had gone, in a sense, from the glazed expression on his face. He decided to wait until he resurfaced. He understood, clearly, that the Orbitist being a traveller such as himself was open to periods of reflection and introspection. Calvin knew that if he hadn't had Moss accompany him then his own life would have been filled with unanswerable questions which might consume him and drive him into whorls of confusion. The Orbitist seemed to need a moment to recover his thoughts. Calvin imagined his was a tale often rehearsed, but rarely told.

"The underground chambers," the Orbitist continued, after a jolt that seemed to shake his entire body, "had remained intact after the catastrophe. We know that the equipment, the storages of food, the books, the infrastructure; these were all present. But the people, those who had been stored there, had been reduced to bone and ash. The leaders from the Moon had to populate their kind again. And – after a period of inhabiting the underground – this was when they realised the fundamental change that had occurred between themselves and the new population of Heart. You see," he turned to Calvin, "they have no souls."

Calvin must have looked puzzled, because the Orbitist continued:

"At least, they have no separate soul. Whether it was because of the catastrophe or whether it is something the new peoples of Heart have evolved is unclear, but the original inhabitants of Earth did not have the female carrying the body and the male carrying the soul. The female carried both – or, perhaps more specifically, she carried the body and the soul developed independently within that body. Our records show there has often been confusion between the nature of the soul and the consciousness developed by the brain for hundreds of thousands of years. Entire religions have been created because of this; but the main aspect to focus on here is that the new peoples of Heart are unique. If the father wasn't present at the birth of a baby on Earth, it made no difference at all to the child's development. This is the fundamental change between you and me, between yours and mine."

Calvin considered carefully what the Orbitist was saying. From his perspective it made no sense, but Calvin knew from his travels that he shouldn't expect the expected, and if something sounded impossible that didn't mean it was so. If he had tried to describe the sea, for example, to Sky or to Royce or to any of the elders from his place of birth they would not have believed it. But it didn't mean to say it didn't exist, and now he had seen it with his own eyes. So he couldn't dismiss what the Orbitist had told him, he could only absorb it. An assimilation of information at the point where worlds collide.

Assuming he took the Orbitist's words as truth Calvin couldn't help but impose them on his existing knowledge. He thought of all the babies born on Heart – his own included – who would not have died needlessly because of the father's absence at the time of birth. He thought of the bodies he had encountered, those who hadn't been killed, but who were subject to abuse and ridicule, who would not have had to suffer under the ancient birth methods on Heart. It was impossible to peel away the benefits or the bond from having both parents at the birth, he couldn't strip away his own experiences or the knowledge of how things were which was entrenched within him, but he could speculate at the freedom the birth process on Earth must have provided. And of the numbers of babies that might have been born to live rather than born to die.

"So what happens," he finally asked, "at the point of birth? Is the soul glimpsed?"

"We do not have that luxury," said the Orbitist. "In fact, it is only through the evolution that has occurred on Heart that the semi-physical nature of the soul has been proven. This is another reason why our peoples are jealous of yours, and they have also considered it should be reason for your undoing."

Again, Calvin was not convinced he understood all of what the Orbitist said. *Evolution* was not a word that was known to him and he didn't want to prove his ignorance by asking. He was being assailed with information, he needed to pick and choose the essentials, but also he had to work around the unknown words and fumble their meaning. The only thing that was clear from the Orbitist's last words was that the original inhabitants of Heart saw the body and soul divide not as a strength, but as a weakness.

"How do you mean, undoing?"

The Orbitist linked his fingers together, circulated his thumbs. "What better way to enslave a population than by utilising a method of enslavement that they hold within themselves?"

Calvin was confused. "Our souls?"

The Orbitist shook his head. "Your bodies. Your bodies, that is, without your souls."

"Without our souls?"

"The clue is in the question," the Orbitist said. When Calvin shook his head further, he added, "What are your bodies without their souls? I'll tell you. They are nothing. At best they can be trained to perform simple tasks. What if simple tasks were all that were required of them? Then their status would suffice. Do you understand what I'm saying?"

Calvin shook his head. He had an idea, but decided in this instance that to appear ignorant might yield further information.

The Orbitist sighed. "If the original inhabitants of Earth were to forcibly separate the women from the men in your settlements it would take but a couple of generations to create a slave workforce and to annihilate your existing culture. Do you see how easy that would be? Frightening, isn't it?"

Calvin nodded, slowly. The truth in the words was evident. Whether it could be practically achieved was another matter.

"How likely is it that this would happen?"

The Orbitist shook his head. "Who knows? This has been their plan since they returned to Earth and discovered your circumstances. Are there enough of them to do this? Possibly. Are your settlements spread out and unprepared for such a challenge? Yes. The Earth has a history of improbable wars, we know this from books. I would have been an advocate myself had I not been selected for travelling and properly understood the nature of life here on Heart."

"And what would that understanding be?"

"That it would be better to work together to establish a more interconnected life instead of working against each other."

"Yet you continue to work for them. Spying on us. Reporting back what you've seen."

"Just as you are doing with your kind. You do so in exchange for food, shelter, the necessity for some company. You and I are no different in that respect."

Calvin was about to summarise their differences but his mouth remained open without speaking. The Orbitist was right. In a sense they were both outcasts who needed their past as much as they looked forward to their future. He glanced at the sun's slow descent to the horizon. There was still plenty of time to return to Moss and Acorn. His offer for the Orbitist to join them remained.

He voiced it, but the Orbitist shook his head. "I have to remain contactable at all times. If I were to leave my ship, who knows what might happen."

Calvin nodded. He glanced up at the dark interior.

"Did you want to take a look inside?" The Orbitist stood, held out his hand. "Come."

Calvin refused the hand and helped himself to his feet. He followed the Orbitist up the metal steps into the object. Inside, there was a connecting door that was open which led to the front. Calvin glanced in the other direction and saw a large space with a few seats. Boxes with symbols written on them were stacked low to the floor. A pungent, acrid smell which he couldn't identify lay claim to his nostrils. The Orbitist gestured to the open door. "This is where I fly this thing."

Calvin couldn't help but detect an element of pride in those words. He wasn't surprised. The interior of the small compartment was bedecked with a confusing array of buttons and switches. How these could interact to lift the object from the ground Calvin had no comprehension. There were two seats adjacent to each other, both had handles facing them. For a brief moment a thrill ran through Calvin's body that he might also be able to journey through the air.

The Orbitist seemed to sense this. "Impressive, isn't it. Old technology. You should see what they used to get us back from the Moon."

Calvin nodded, without much understanding.

"You're wondering if I could take you up in this." A smile played around the Orbitist's lips.

Calvin forced a shrug.

"In theory, I could. In practice, it wouldn't be appreciated if it was discovered I took a resident of Heart on a joy ride. Fuel is precious. Perhaps another time, once the differences between our peoples are resolved and we can all be friends."

Calvin detected the irony beneath the Orbitist's words, tinged with regret. Again he felt a cold dread that life as he understood it was on the verge of being ripped asunder. He could feel everything falling away from him.

"I have to get back."

The Orbitist nodded. "You can come again, if you wish. I should be here for another couple of days."

Calvin said nothing. He made his way down the steps, picked up his backpack, and began the journey back to Moss and Acorn and the world that he knew.

5

They had a day at the beach. Moss had raised a few questions about the city when Calvin had returned, but in truth she wasn't interested. She saw such journeys now as fripperies, with the daily care of Acorn at the forefront of her mind. Calvin had refrained from telling her about the Orbitist. Instead he said the city was much like all the others, appeasing Moss with the thought that she had been right and it had been a wasted journey. Calvin didn't consider his withholding of information to be a lie. He would tell her when the time was right – just as she had eventually told him about her previous pregnancies. Whilst he didn't believe it as such, a part of him considered it a trade off.

It had rained the previous evening, bringing down the temperature awhile, but whilst the sand was wet underneath the top had already dried. Calvin remembered apple cakes baked by Sky in his original settlement – the pastry crumbling on top with the moist filling below. He formed sand cakes with Acorn, pressed his hands atop hers to shape the cakes together. Moss lay asleep, catching what respite she could from Acorn who was getting more boisterous by the day. The sun peeled skin from Calvin's back, curled it. Despite the heat he found that by the time the sun was directly overhead he needed to wear a shirt.

Whilst his focus was with Acorn, who delighted in his attention, the back of his mind was crowded with everything the Orbitist had told him. On reflection, he saw no need to doubt any of it, yet he still wasn't convinced that the nature of his reality was about to change. From what the Orbitist had said, this enslavement of Heart had been scheduled over many sun-ups without anything having happened. Additionally, all those peoples underground were a very long way from Calvin. Quite possibly there were an almost infinite number of small settlements spread across the surface of Heart that he now realised was much larger than he could possibly have imagined. What sense did it make for those people to journey over the sea to here, when they might equally be able to enslave those closer to home?

And yet, the Orbitist was here. And one of many, it appeared. Maybe those underground regions were bereft of people. Maybe it was only here, in Calvin's small corner of Heart, where people flourished. The more he thought about it, the more questions it raised. Knowing the Orbitist would soon be leaving, he realised that once again he would need an excuse to journey to the city;

unless, of course, it was time to tell Moss what he knew.

He considered this, as the tide rolled over their sand cakes and consumed them.

His time with Moss had made an indelible impression, yet sometimes he considered they were bound more by circumstance rather than affection. The birth of Acorn had woven a connection deeper than he could ever have imagined, yet simultaneously it undermined everything they had previously had. The transition from two to three was a double-edged sword – it protected them as much as it cut them. Despite the security he found in their relationship and their unequivocal bond with Acorn, Calvin couldn't help but feel that their happiness was precarious, and anything could take them to the tipping point.

Moss would not be happy that he had spoken with the Orbitist, despite her thirst for knowledge. Calvin knew she would find the threat against them to be personal rather than universal, that she would fold herself around Acorn in protection. If the threat was non-existent in fact, it still would breed within her mind and become all-consuming. For Calvin to discuss it with her he knew he would be seeding that threat. Perhaps it was better to leave Moss in the dark, but it pulled against Calvin's conscience. He knew that an absence of discussion would only lead to later remorse; and above all he needed Moss to trust him. To know that he was reliable.

So, he could either tell her and risk her anger or he could not tell her and do the same. Or he could simply forget about the Orbitist and the perceived threat and his thirst for knowledge. In some respects, this would be for the best. For what could further knowledge do than raise further questions? And Calvin had no intention or indeed the means of somehow opposing the threat, should it even exist. To see the Orbitist once more was a selfish, pointless thing to do. It would also involve lying to Moss once again.

He picked up Acorn and carried her into the sea, revelled in her squeals as they leapt the waves together. The salt left raised grains on their legs which the water added to as it cleared. The sand under his feet shifted and curved with the water, each jump returned him to a changed ground. Like the sand, Calvin understood the surface of Heart was mutable. That what was now, once wasn't; and might well not be again.

That night, once Acorn was fast asleep, Calvin and Moss sat outside looking up at the stars. Moss's gaze was spurious, as it might be on any night, whereas Calvin kept his eyes open for the tell-tale red or white lights: either those of the Orbitist leaving, or of another ship planning to drop food and whatever else the gas was that the Orbitist had said was required. Calvin was tense, his muscles taut, his teeth pushed together as he gritted his jaw. As night had fallen he couldn't dispose of the ghosts of the day so readily.

Moss leant into him, her face tucked between his chest and his shoulder. She smelt salty fresh. They both appreciated the sea and its power to clean. He could detect her soft body odour under the salt, and repeatedly kissed her limbs gaining the coolness of her skin and sweetness of her scent simultaneously. Moss was somewhat different from the filthy being he had first encountered. For Calvin himself, he imagined Moss saw him differently too.

Dirt was engrained as a traveller, part of the role. Here by the sea the story was different. He knew they would both be sad when they had to move on.

"What's up?" Moss asked, her voice almost lost to sleep.

"Hmmm?"

"You're all tense. Is something worrying you?"

Now was the time. Calvin thought through his options. Then he said: "I think I should go back to the settlement, the one nearest to here. We're running low on meat; they might provide us with some."

Moss moved her head back, tilted it, looked him in the eyes. "It doesn't usually work like that."

"I know, but they were friendly enough when we visited them. They know we have a child with us. I think it's worth a try."

Moss sighed, half-heartedly. "It's at least a sun-up from here. Still, it would be useful to stock up on supplies."

Calvin knew she would agree to it. She was too tired to argue, too comfortable to be suspicious. It gnawed at him that he was lying, but he reasoned it was for the best. Her mood might be different when he returned empty handed, but he knew that could be explained away. No doubt it was the warm weather that soothed her. Sometimes she could be quite abrasive.

"Some bread too," she said, drifting further into sleep. "We could always do with more bread."

Calvin murmured an assent. When Moss was fully asleep he disengaged their limbs, carried her into their shack and rested her on their bed. He fell asleep besides her shortly afterwards.

Come morning Moss's mood hadn't changed. She handed Acorn a pear and then got a few supplies together for another day on the beach. Calvin noticed their skin had darkened under the sun. It suited them and was much better than the deathly pallor associated with winter.

In farming, the seasons were essential; yet as a traveller Calvin was more aware of the dangers and hardships the colder months brought with them than he was of their benefits. During the summer it seemed impossible that the warm, dry landscape and hot air might sometime change to snow and ice. That the few layers of clothing they wore would need to replaced by much hardier material. That going barefoot would no longer be an option.

In fact, he thought, as he waved goodbye to Moss and Acorn and began a circular journey which would take him in the direction of the settlement before he needed to curve back towards the city once he was out of sight, the transition of the seasons was not unlike the transition Earth had made to Heart. From a cold, inhospitable people there had come the warmth and hospitality of almost everyone that he knew. He shuddered, despite the sun, at the thought of Heart entering a period of winter again: both climatically and politically.

After taking a detour Calvin headed in the direction of the city, relieved to see the now familiar ship wedged between the buildings in perspective. He picked up his pace, wanted to spend as much time as possible with the Orbitist before returning to Moss and Acorn. He knew it would be the final time he saw him, unless he confessed to Moss; although doing so now would only expose his earlier deception and he imagined that unless the situation dictated it that he would forever remain quiet.

The Orbitist was not in sight. Calvin approached the ship warily, expecting to hear the distorted voice telling him to keep away. He shielded his eyes against the sun, tried to look through the panes of glass that flanked the ship, but could see no movement. The metal stairway was in place and he tentatively grasped the rail, began to ascend. The door was sealed into the side of the ship and he fumbled with it, couldn't see how it might open. He tried knocking instead. Nothing happened. He looked back at the ground from the height of the steps, and saw the Orbitist on the other side of the large open buildings. From where he stood it was impossible to see what the Orbitist was doing.

Calvin descended the steps and walked around towards him. A strong smell hit him. The smell he had detected within the ship itself on his last visit. The Orbitist was crouched on the ground, on the road, bent over a large white plastic canister with some fabric attached. He was muttering under his breath, soaking a rag into the foul-smelling liquid that had spilled, and then wringing it out into another plastic container. The air over the liquid rippled, distorting the view beyond.

The Orbitist seemed to have sensed Calvin's presence. He looked up, without any surprise. "We seem to have had a little accident."

"Oh?"

"The drop came last night. Several large tanks of gas and food. Most of them landed ok. They parachute them in, as though they wish to reduce the amount of contact. But this one fell too rapidly, something up with the chute I guess. And of course it doesn't hit the soft ground, does it? Whole thing split open. I need this fuel."

Calvin took a closer look. Whilst he had understood barely a word of what the Orbitist had said, he could see how the plastic container had split as it fell from the sky, and the contents that the Orbitist deemed so precious had run across the road. The stench burnt his nostrils, and he couldn't help but gag.

"What it is?"

"Gas. Fuel. This is what makes the ship go."

Calvin had no conception of how the liquid might power the ship, so he remained standing, watching the Orbitist attempt to salvage the last few drops as it evaporated skywards in the blistering heat.

After a while the Orbitist said: "There's only a finite amount of this stuff left. We don't have the means nor the knowledge to make any more. Maybe you'll be lucky, Mr Calvin Klein, and it'll run out before the Earthmen get here."

Calvin nodded, slowly.

"I see you came back," the Orbitist spoke again. "I had a feeling you would."

"There are so many questions..." began Calvin.

"And so many answers," finished the Orbitist. He squeezed the rag one last time and stood. He picked up the smaller plastic container, which must have been a quarter of the size of the one that had burst. It wasn't even half-full. "Come on, let's go over to the ship and we can talk properly. I'm leaving this evening at nightfall. Raises fewer questions that way."

They walked around the large buildings, which were open-ended on both sides. "These used to store similar ships," said the Orbitist. "I've seen pictures of these in books."

Calvin nodded. "Do you have any books with you?"

"Oh no. They don't allow us to take anything out of the underground." The Orbitist smiled. "We have a very rigid society. Yours is rigid too, by necessity. But ours is rigid by design."

They reached the ship and the Orbitist carried the plastic container up the steps and opened the door. After a few moments he returned.

"So, what's been troubling you?"

Calvin ran a hand through his hair. "Everything that you've said."

"You see why they don't like us interacting with the locals," the Orbitist laughed. "Our arrival here just causes confusion."

"The problem is, I'm not sure what I should do with your information." Calvin sat, sweat pouring down his back from where his pack rested against his shirt. A pack that was empty and within which Moss was expecting him to return full of meat. "I realise that there isn't anything I can do with it at all, and yet at the same time I feel compelled to do something. Also, I both want and don't want what you've said to happen. I'm intrigued by it, as a traveller I want to meet these original inhabitants; yet any change repels me. But I *want* to see it come into force. I don't want to continue my travels whilst constantly watching the skies in expectation. I *need* it to happen before my death. Anything less than that would be disappointing." Calvin paused. "I'm not making much sense."

"It makes perfect sense," the Orbitist said, "in an imperfect world."

"I don't understand."

"Neither do I." The Orbitist sat on the grass, leant back, his hands under his head looking up at the sky. "I get the feeling that a very long time ago, before the catastrophe which befell Earth, things were both a lot simpler yet also much more complicated. There was a duality to existence. Not that experienced with your body/soul divide, but more of a spiritual/technological thing. Technology improved life to the extent that people couldn't do without it. It made travel faster, communication faster, brought all the disparate corners of the Earth together; yet in doing so it undid the spiritual links between people. It made communication transitory, meaningless. It gave the appearance of removing confusion, but in the alternative it created it. I've travelled a lot since I left the underground, much of which has been solitary. My conclusion is this: everything happens simultaneously and everything is true at once. It just comes down to perspective."

"I still don't understand."

"You understand perfectly, yet you understand nothing at all. It's a philosophical question that you're posing, not an actual question. Until you understand the level at which you're posing your question you won't begin to understand the answer." The Orbitist closed his eyes. "Although I cannot see you, I believe that you're still there. This is how the universe operates; by belief."

Calvin wondered if the fumes from the liquid had somehow addled the Orbitist's head. Maybe his thinking would have gone the same way, if he had spent so much time alone, flying through the air making reports to people he could never see, turning questions and information over and over in his mind like trying to plough a field that hadn't been allowed to lie fallow and regenerate itself. But then if he doubted the Orbitist's sanity, then he also had to doubt everything he had said, which made his own attempts to understand it futile.

Yet there were certainties. Whether he closed his eyes or not, the Orbitist was with him, the ship was a physical presence, the unbroken road a surety of outside interference. How much of this information might be hung as truth, how much as false? Returning only made Calvin's head spin all the more.

"What do you mean by technology," he said, eventually, to break a silence that had descended and which made him wonder if the Orbitist had fallen into sleep.

The Orbitist sat up again. "That ship," he said, "is technology. Myself, that's spirituality. At some point in Earth/Heart history the equilibrium between the two tipped. I think that people lost their spirituality and that's why there was a catastrophe. Imagine that ship as a body with myself as the soul. If we relied on the body more than the soul, that disparity wouldn't work, would it? You've seen the results yourself, I'm sure. A body without a soul is little more than a zombie."

"A zombie?"

"That's how my leaders describe a body without a soul. Our books indicate that zombies were animated corpses resurrected through scientific means. They served no function other than to become slaves. That's the traditional explanation. Folklore also has it that they consumed the living, but I believe that's been debunked."

Calvin remembered the stories he had heard about bodies without souls. Most of which he felt he could now discount through his own experience. But slavery – enforced labour – made perfect sense. If you were to have a body without a soul then you needed it to work. Without it working, it was utterly useless. He thought again of the Orbitist's claim that the original inhabitants from Earth intended to enslave the population of Heart. This made him consider what happened to the soul. He had seen his child's evaporate as it poured out of his body with the baby they had lost, and he had seen it infiltrate Acorn's body as it was birthed. But where all those lost souls might be he had no idea. Maybe the Orbitist had an opinion.

"The spirituality, the soul," Calvin said, "where do you think that goes if there is no body to contain it."

The Orbitist didn't pause: "Ghosts. Have you ever heard of ghosts?"

Calvin shook his head.

"It doesn't surprise me," the Orbitist continued. "I've spoken with a handful of travellers over time and none of them are aware of the concept. It sometimes surprises me how much of Earth's thinking was lost when the planet converted to Heart. Ghosts were considered to be souls that remained on Earth after the body's death. Souls that were trapped here, that couldn't ascend to a higher plane. The previous inhabitants of Earth had complex religious ideas – none of which appear to have been transmuted to the people of Heart. In fact, you are a happy Godless society."

"God?"

"A concept that you really don't need to worry about." The Orbitist sighed. "Some of my leaders have suggested that the absence of God led to an abuse of technology, but the past seems to indicate that atrocities were committed in both names hand in hand. This is an irrelevance here. But ghosts, souls with nowhere to go, these are how we would describe what you are talking about."

"So," Calvin questioned, "if the body is enslaved, as your leaders are suggesting, then the soul remains trapped on Heart."

"As such. In the past it was believed the soul or ghost could manifest itself. I have seen no such evidence here, other than the ethereal wisps that emanate when a child is born. Wisps, you should know, which do not occur when a child is born to an original inhabitant from Heart."

More questions crowded Calvin's mind: "What you've been telling me is that the population of Earth split at the point of the catastrophe. That some people went skywards and some people remained. That for the people who remained, the birthing process was altered, but for those who left it stayed the same. So, for those people who returned to Earth and who now live underground, they do not have the split between body and soul, they do not need the father present at the birth, that their children develop properly, just as you and I."

"Indeed. Although from my experience, from my own personal experience, I would say the people of Heart have more soul. In many respects."

"But not in others?"

"Well, perhaps not now. But certainly in the past. Our records indicate that we had a much greater sympathy for those born with disabilities."

"Disabilities?"

"Genetic defects. Although, to be fair, it seems that it is only when a body is born without a soul on Heart that it is subject to maltreatment. In Earth's past, such people would have been protected."

"But you said people were not born without souls in Earth's past."

"And I am correct. But sometimes people were born with other abnormalities. Deformed limbs, brain disorders, enlarged body parts, twins joined at the hip..."

"Twins?"

"Two children born simultaneously. It doesn't happen on Heart. Not so far as I know."

Calvin nodded. He had never heard of it. Except in the animal kingdom.

The Orbitist continued: "It appears there were many people born with various physical abnormalities. These people were encouraged to live normal lives on Earth. On Heart, they would be destroyed."

They allowed the significance of this to sink like a stone thrown into a muddy bog.

"Food is scarce," Calvin finally said, defending his people.

"So is humanity," the Orbitist replied.

The sun was at its highest point in the sky. Calvin couldn't help but notice how vivid Heart became. The grass was a brilliant green, even areas burnt to a patchy brown were enlivened by the sun's rays so that their colours seemed super-real. The ship hurt his eyes to look at it – the reflective surface channelling the sun's light with a whitened glow. The sky, open as far as the eye could see, was a deep resonant blue. Even the heat itself seemed flammable: a burn that hurt as much as it caressed.

Calvin closed his eyes, lay back; the sun making orange shades of his eye-lids. Immersed in the heat he felt satisfied. The Orbitist had answered all his questions, and whether or not he understood the answers – whether or not he believed in them – the physical world was unchanged. What he needed to ensure was that the world inside him, his perception of how things were and should always be, was not transformed. If he held onto his sense of self he believed he could do his part in keeping things as they were. It might be a false expectation, but it was all that he had.

After a while he opened his eyes to find the Orbitist asleep. Calvin walked quietly towards the steps leading up to the ship, and made great care to ensure his shoes didn't clang against the metal. The Orbitist had left the door open. Calvin ducked his head inside and then followed it with his whole body. He made his way into the dark interior, in the opposite direction to the front seats, and began to examine the contents in the rear.

The ship wasn't in any way full, but it was much more compacted than it had been when he viewed it a few days ago, leading credence to the Orbitist's assertion that supplies had been dropped from the sky. Calvin hadn't really understood the process which led to a safe drop, although he wondered if the material that had been attached to the plastic container that had split created a drag through the air like a sycamore falling from a tree.

Several of those large containers were now stored within the ship. Most of these were empty. Calvin assumed the liquid must somehow be inserted into the machine for it to work, but gave no further thought to how that might occur. It was a dead end to understanding. Other containers were fashioned out of wood. Small slivers of metal secured the lids, but Calvin found these easy to push upwards. Inside were circular metal containers with symbols on the side and occasionally pictures of food. He examined these curiously then dug further into the boxes.

Encased within sealed clear plastic envelopes were strange yellow twisted shapes which were hard when he pressed his fingers against them, other softer packets contained white grains similar to wheat but much smaller. Other packets contained dried leaves. Still others, dried fish. Calvin looked at each item afresh, further evidence supporting the Orbitist's claim that he was not like everyone else on Heart.

He carefully resealed the containers as he made his way further back into the darkness, listening out for the Orbitist stirring in his sleep. Finally, at the rear of the ship, he hefted open the lid of a large metal container, expelling a sudden waft of cold air. Here he found similar clear plastic packages containing meat. The packaging was sealed tight, but he could determine what appeared to be different cuts. Grabbing three of these packs from the container he placed them in his pack and then slowly returned through the length of the ship, descended the metal steps, and sat once again on the same patch of grass beside the Orbitist.

The meat would validate his journey to the settlement and if it were missed the Orbitist would be long gone before the discovery were made. Calvin felt no regrets about taking it. It was a necessary evil.

A short while passed before the Orbitist opened his eyes. Calvin checked the position of the sun in the sky. He knew he should be going, but he didn't care to move. The Orbitist had given him more knowledge and information than he might care to know, and he couldn't do anything with it. Even so, losing that stream of knowledge was a wrench. Calvin knew that once the Orbitist left he would feel displaced within Heart, in much the same way as when he first left his original settlement. Even the company of Moss and Acorn wouldn't fully reverse that sensation.

"Apologies," the Orbitist said, "it had been a long night, and it will be a long night again. Like yourself most of my travelling is done during darkness."

"Where are you headed to?"

"Each of the Orbitist's – none of whom I have ever seen – are assigned a different area on Heart. Not every area; only those which are populated. Most of these populated places cover an area of Earth once known as Europe. This evening I have to travel due North, make my usual reports, it's just routine."

"Make reports of what?"

"The number of settlements and where they can be found."

"For what purpose?"

"For enslavement, should it ever happen. My leaders have a thirst for knowledge that I'm sure exceeds their capabilities. Do not worry Mr Klein, I'm sure this will never happen in our lifetimes."

Calvin ignored the Orbitist's repeated insistence in calling him by an incorrect name. He wondered, however, if the Orbitist's assertion of the tradition of name calling was correct. If so, from what did Royce, Levi, Moss and Acorn originally derive? Did Sky come from *sky*? He deliberated over asking, but decided not to know the answer. Calvin wasn't happy that what he considered to be a tradition might come from a source never known to him.

Instead he said: "Would it be possible for me to stay to watch you leave?"

The Orbitist sucked in his bottom lip. He rose to his feet, scratched absentmindedly at his chest through his shirt. "Yes."

Calvin let out a long breath. It would mean his return to Moss and Acorn would be delayed, but for the moment that didn't matter. He wanted to see the ship return to the sky.

6

Night had taken charge of the sky by the time the Orbitist had made all his checks and was ready to leave the surface of Heart.

Calvin had considered taking the ride, but hadn't raised this with the Orbitist. It was a flight of fancy, nothing more. He knew his responsibilities were towards Moss and Acorn and, perhaps even more importantly, the peoples of Heart. Nevertheless, the thought of travelling through the air was as exciting as it was terrifying.

The two buildings assumed a menacing air as darkness fell, their open mouths like gap-toothed behemoths, with a hot dry wind channelled through them as stale as breath. Inside the ship the Orbitist had light. Calvin couldn't establish where it originated, but it didn't flicker and was sufficient for the Orbitist to see what he needed to do. Under the circumstances, strange light was simply another aspect of the Orbitist's world that Calvin didn't need to trouble himself to understand. If the ship could rise in the air then any other miracles were peripheral.

Calvin had two reasons for the spectacle. Firstly, he knew watching the ship depart would finally validate all the Orbitist's claims. Whilst he felt he no longer had reason to doubt him, there was still a matter of seeing is believing. Secondly, Calvin simply wanted to view it as spectacle itself. He couldn't imagine being subject to anything like this ever again.

Once the Orbitist seemed ready to leave he descended the steps one final time and held out a hand. Calvin looked at it, unsure what was required. The Orbitist clasped Calvin's hand and raised it up and down. "This is how we depart on Earth."

Calvin nodded. He raised his own hand high. "Our greeting on Heart. As I'm sure you're aware."

The Orbitist mimicked his nod. "Some of our customs are not so much removed. Well, goodbye; no doubt I won't see you again."

He ascended the steps. At the top he turned. "Actually, Mr Klein, it would be of great use if you could wheel these steps over to the side. Makes departure much less tricky. And, once you've done that, I'd suggest moving to the other side of that building. There can be a substantial amount of heat and noise."

Calvin pushed the wheeled steps to one side then did as the Orbitist had suggested. The door in the side of the ship sealed shut and he saw the Orbitist take position through the small window at the front of the craft. Without warning the two large oval objects that were formed into the under-surface of the ship began to hum, and Calvin could see something turning slowly inside them. There was a sudden popping sound and smoke began to pulse out into the night, merging with the dark.

A whining noise began to dominate Calvin's ears. A sound longer and louder than he had ever heard before. The backdraft from the wind shook the walls of the building he had edged behind. Once the noise was at such a pitch that even with his hands over his ears he could no longer bear it, Calvin saw the wheels on the ship begin to turn and gradually it moved forwards. He watched as the object made its way slowly but surely along the road, 'til it reached the end, turned, and halted. Calvin held his breath. Perhaps it hadn't worked. Perhaps the ship would not make it into the air. But then the noise increased intensity again, and once more the craft moved, this time with increasing rapidity, until, in fact, it was going so fast that Calvin could not comprehend its movement considering its size.

The roar also intensified and the ship surged forwards, getting faster and faster. Calvin knew it couldn't stop. He envisaged it reaching the end of the road and then ploughing into the field, smashing and spinning, bursting and popping; but then, miraculously, the tip of the craft rose skywards and the body followed, the wheels left the ground and the entire contraption pulled upwards, the noise diminishing the further it travelled until it was but a speck in the sky and the hum reduced to a sound recognisable from Calvin's previous experience. For the second time that day he let out a long breath.

He had seen the Orbitist lift a hand as the ship had soared past him. A hand that was now way up in the sky. The immensity of that sight was beyond his belief. Now, in the quiet of the field, it regained some mystery, it lost its reality, and he knew if he were ever to relay it to Moss it would appear as no more than a fantasy.

Hefting his back pack from where he had rested it on the ground, Calvin carried the spoils of the day back to the beach.

7

"What's this?"

Acorn had been rummaging through Calvin's coat whilst he tended the fire. He had his back to her. Moss was outside, trudging through the snow to the small pen where they kept their chickens. Calvin was hoping she would return with enough eggs to make a hearty breakfast. His stomach was knotted with hunger, he had been subconsciously clenching it all night. They weren't on the brink of starvation, but he had been conserving supplies for Moss and Acorn. Acorn's appetite had increased remarkably over the past eight seasons. Her curiosity was insatiable too.

"What's what?"

Calvin turned his head to see Acorn had found his shell.

He knew the name of his artefact now. Those eight seasons ago when he had spoken to the Orbitist and they had lived on the beach, the inhabitants of the nearby settlement had named the sand, the sea, the dunes, and the shells. Calvin had even picked up some of these objects to find living animals inside. Perhaps it was because of his association of the shell as an artefact that he always carefully replaced them where he found them: in pools or water, or on the sand, or back in the sea. Acorn had also delighted in them at the time, but it had been a while since they lived seawards and he wondered if she had forgotten what they were.

"Oh," he said, "that's my shell."

"I know what it is, silly. Why do you have it?"

Calvin smiled. Acorn was starting to ask questions that were open to complicated answers rather than simple *whys* and *hows*. He loved the input he had in her development, the single responsibility he and Moss had over her. If she had been born in a settlement then she would effectively have become the property of the settlement, with all of the elders involved in her upbringing. He knew how effective that was – he was a product of the system himself of course – yet having had the close bond with Acorn that he had, he knew their relationship was very special indeed.

"It was given to me a long while ago," he said, "by a traveller named Book. It was him who started me on my journey."

"Is he why I don't play with other children?"

Calvin's smile wavered. "Why do you say that?"

"I never get to play with other children unless we're visiting. If we never left those places I'd always have children to play with."

"We play with you," Calvin countered.

Acorn nodded her head, vigorously. Calvin let out a sigh.

"If Book hadn't encouraged me to travel," he continued, "then I would have never met Moss and you wouldn't have been born."

But Acorn seemed to have become disinterested. She pushed her finger into the whorl of the shell, then removed it and put it up to her eye. "Why do you keep it?"

Calvin wanted to say that he still wondered if it had magical properties. He wanted to believe it, although now he knew this wasn't true.

"Sometimes we keep things to remind us of other times. You've seen the artefacts Moss and I collect. I know you have a few yourself. After a while you might find you gain an attachment to one of them. There's no particular reason for keeping it, but you do."

Acorn developed a mischievous look in her eye. "So, you could throw this away if you wanted to."

Calvin nodded, slowly.

"Shall I throw it away for you? Or can I keep it?"

Calvin moved away from the fire and prised the shell from Acorn's slim fingers. "I'd rather keep it with me, if you don't mind."

"But why?"

Calvin pushed the shell deep into his trouser pocket, felt the familiar smooth and rough sides with his fingers and was comforted by its return. "Because I like it," he said. "We can find something special for you, if you like."

Acorn shook her head. "I want the shell."

Calvin found he shook his own head. "It's mine," he said.

Acorn's bottom lip quivered and then she seemed to reassert herself. She dropped Calvin's coat and moved away to the rear of the shack, turning her back on him. It was a quiet protest that strangled Calvin's gut, but he didn't push it and he returned to the flame.

Possessions were few and far between on Heart. In truth, there was no reason for them. But the shell connected Calvin to more than Book, it also reminded him of Sky and Royce and the Acorn who was his sister rather than his daughter. It reminded him of Levi and his lack of common sense, and the somewhat bullish Citroen. The shell was a conduit to past, present and future, and whilst it might be nonsensical to hold onto it, to bestow it with such importance, he knew full well that under no circumstances would he ever consider parting with it.

The door to the shack opened and Moss hurried through, followed by a twisting flurry of snow. The flakes spun upwards then fell and melted on the floor, creating brief stains which dissipated slowly, leaving misshapen residues in their wake. Moss was panting. Calvin glanced up and saw she was empty handed. The chickens couldn't have lain.

"You have to see this," she said. "Something's very wrong."

"What is it?" Acorn's interest was piqued at the rear of the shack.

"Nothing for you, Acorn." Calvin was surprised at the directness in Moss's voice. "It's just something I have to show Calvin. You wait here."

Moss hopped from one foot to another as Calvin pulled on his boots and coat. When he opened the door the white glare hurt his eyes and he blinked rapidly until he became accustomed to the light. A strong wind was blowing the snow directly towards them. As they walked out, fat flakes fell on his eyelids and then melted, water obscuring his vision. He wiped them away like ice-cold tears.

"What's up?"

"You'll see."

They forced their feet through the snow at ankle-height, the bottoms of Calvin's trousers soaking quickly, and his boots not much better. He had had them replaced four seasons ago at a settlement atop a hillside, but wear and tear had damaged them almost beyond repair. Despite the snow, the air felt warm, but the compacted ice water got between his toes and soon he was stamping his feet as he walked, trying to shake the cold out of them.

He wondered what had spooked Moss. Since his chat with the Orbitist he had seen little to concern him. Nothing the Orbitist had hinted might happen had happened. There had only been a few instances where they had glimpsed lights in the sky, and never the white object, *the ship*, during the daytime. Because of this, Calvin had never felt obliged to tell Moss of what he knew. Other than a little suspicion she had raised about the quality of the meat he had returned with from 'the settlement', his forays into the city had been forgotten. But now, seeing the anxiety on Moss's face, he wondered if this bubble of serenity might be about to collapse.

The snow stretched as far as he could see. They had camped for the winter in a solitary shack in a valley with a river running through it. Moss had delighted in the way that the trees leant over the riverbank, dragging thin tendrils of branches through the water. Calvin had pointed out that the scene wouldn't be so pretty come winter, but they both knew they had found somewhere interesting and were tired of hitting the cities every time there was snowfall. The shack that they chose had a well-maintained vegetable garden, and Calvin wondered if a traveller had used it before. A handful of chickens had made the shack their home, and Calvin had shooed them out and cobbled together a run for them, from which – so far – they had had a reasonable supply of eggs.

Yet the harsh realities of winter had unbalanced a decision so easily made during the warmer months. And whereas the vegetables had yielded a reasonable crop they were proving insufficient for the three of them. Perhaps this was the first indication that travelling with a child was not the best idea – yet the urge to continue ran through them like a blade.

They forced their way uphill through the snow, the expanse only spoiled by the dips created through Moss's footprints on her previous journey, there and back again. The snow had deepened overnight and was continuing to stack. Calvin could hear Moss panting beside him as they crested the ridge, but when they reached the top his own breath stopped.

The solid white view had been bisected by a black road.

The length of the road mirrored that he had seen when he had met the Orbitist. In Calvin's mind there was no question that it was designed for the same purpose. He couldn't remember having come this way before, but even if the road was not new it looked new. And the absence of snow was a startling discovery. He could see now why Moss had been spooked.

"I don't understand it," she said. "What is it doing here?"

"I'm surprised we haven't seen it before."

"We don't come this way. The snow has confused you. The chickens are over that way." She gesticulated to her right and Calvin saw the pen clearly. He couldn't understand how he had become disorientated.

Moss continued: "I came this way because I thought I saw something. Turns out I was right."

"What did you see?"

"A black shape, against the horizon." She scanned the whiteness. "See!"

Calvin looked where she pointed. Moss's footprints clearly led up to the ridge where they stopped. But thereafter another set of prints led down to the road.

"I don't understand," Calvin said. "If you saw someone. Where did they go?"

Moss pointed again. "You see that crop of trees? It's the only hiding place."

Calvin mused. There was not much sense to be had. "What should we do?"

"I think we should go down there."

"What about Acorn?"

Moss glanced back at the shack. Irritably, Calvin thought.

"She'll be ok. We'll only be gone a few minutes."

"Perhaps I should go alone."

Moss hesitated. "Perhaps *I* should go alone."

Calvin knew there was no arguing. "Ok, let's both go, but quickly."

They began to scramble down the soft snow on the other side of the crest. The going was deeper here, the wind was blowing against this side of the ridge and therefore had stockpiled snow in greater abundance than on their side. Several times Calvin sank to his thighs and he knew it would be more than a few minutes before they returned to the shack. Nevertheless, Acorn would be fine. She wouldn't venture out alone and he couldn't conceive of any danger here.

As they descended their perspective of the strip of road narrowed until it was lost due to the bank of snow. Its location remained clear, however; a heat haze rose off the surface. Calvin saw it glimmer in the air, giving the whiteness beyond it a silvery sheen. None of it made any sense, but when dealing with the Orbitist and his kind Calvin knew that this was usual. It was better to expect the unknown in order to be able to deal with it.

They kept as close as they could to the tracks, yet as they left the ridge and the snow was less deep, so the new flurries began to obliterate them. And once they reached the road, quite naturally the tracks disappeared completely.

Moss knelt and touched the surface. She turned to Calvin, wide eyed. "It's warm!"

Calvin also knelt. Moss was correct. The surface of the road was indeed warm to the touch. That explained why there was no snowfall on it. But it didn't explain *how* it was warmed.

"What is it?" Moss asked, for the second time.

Calvin shrugged. "I can't begin to guess." He dismissed the idea of another ship having landed there. He was sure they would have heard it. The night had been quiet, sounds suffocated by the falling snow. Whilst it was obviously intended for that purpose, that hadn't been its use recently. Which didn't explain the heat or the footprints.

He ventured onto the road. Although his shoes were compacted with snow and melted very slowly he could immediately feel the heat through the surface.

It hit him, then. Should a ship need to land it needed a road. The Orbitist had explained that the ship had to remain in the air through the liquid substance that had been delivered. If that was used up then presumably the ship would fall. And presumably it could fall at any time. So the road had to be clear of obstacles to enable a safe landing. That was why the road was warm, and therefore unobstructed by snow, although how it was warm was another matter.

Calvin remembered that the day he had met the Orbitist had been in the height of summer. There would have been no need for the road to be kept warm at that time. So was the surface somehow temperature dependent? Was it actually possible that the road could warm itself dependent on the weather?

However much Calvin tried to dismiss the idea the certainty of it assailed him. Yet he didn't voice this to Moss. He couldn't do, unless he made his knowledge of the Orbitist known.

"Well," he said, finally, "the figure you saw obviously isn't on the road, so he must have left it. I'll look this side, you look the other side. Let's see if we can see his prints."

Moss nodded. She moved directly over to the side where the group of trees were closest, her expectation being that was the only place he might have gone.

Calvin walked slowly, looking at both the surface of the road and the snow beside it. Wondering if there was any way *under* the surface that the figure might have disappeared into. It seemed impossible, but no more so than any other explanation.

Moss called to him. "Nothing here." He could sense the disappointment in her voice. The figure had not headed towards the trees. He continued to search. The snow was lessening slightly, the flakes growing smaller and smaller as though they were melting as they fell, even so the covering was increasing. He wondered what would happen if they didn't find the figure? Would it make them wary? Was it an Orbitist, another traveller? The unknown tantalised.

At the far end of the road he picked up the trail.

He paused; breathing heavily. The exhalations puffing in the air like soul clouds. Something started hammering in his chest, not dissimilar to the feelings he had experienced at birth; a sense of excitement fused with expectation. With protection. That was it.

The feeling was linked to protection; with the protection of his baby. Of Acorn.

He looked again, scanned the tracks in the direction they ran. They curved back from the end of the road and over the ridge they had just came.

The tracks headed back in the direction of their daughter.

8

Calvin couldn't protect Moss from everything. He shouted loudly and pointed, but then he began to run.

This time the snow really seemed against him. Going up the ridge was much harder than descending. The white stuff slipped under his feet, creating holes that fell in on themselves like mini-landslides. The hammering in his chest intensified, although he couldn't quite identify the fear. The source was obvious, the outcome unsure. He remembered running across the moor, terrified that his baby would be born without a soul, and knowing that he was failing. These memories assailed him as he ran now, the elements fighting against him, whereas the surety of the footprints in the snow identified what had already happened and intimated what might already *be* happening.

And this time – under his heavy fogging breath – he couldn't help but curse Moss and her curiosity and her occasionally ambivalent connection to Acorn; however tenuous his internal assertion might be.

He crested the ridge. The first thing he noticed was that the chicken run was open. The cockerel was strutting atop the structure, but the hens were stick-knee deep in snow. Not all of them. A dark stain was clearly visible, a deep red smear on the white. Blood pumped out of the neck of a still twitching body. Calvin felt bile rise in his throat and his eyes roved to the shack. The door was open and it was unearthly quiet. A twist of smoke rose from the fire through a hole in the roof.

He glanced back at Moss. She was still only halfway up the ridge. Words caught in his throat. She didn't need to know this, yet. He began to run down the other side of the ridge, through the escaped chickens, towards the open door of the shack. Just before he reached it he slowed down, stilled his breathing. He needed to be ready, to expect anything. He didn't want to rush into the shack and find his daughter gone.

A sob almost escaped from his mouth as he heard her voice.

"Like this."

Calvin saw the fire flare for a moment. Smoke billowed out of the roof and the open door, obscuring the insides. He knew what she had done. Some of the wood they had stored was still damp. When thrown onto the fire it split from the heat and dispersed steam. Acorn always laughed when this happened. And she laughed now, accompanied by a deep grunt.

Calvin held his breath. He moved so he could see through the door without being seen. Looking back at the ridge he saw Moss crest it. She saw the dead chicken and then she saw him. He put a finger to his lips, waved his hand in a downwards motion, then turned back to the door.

What initially appeared to be darkness turned out to be the bulk of a man. Calvin's eyes adjusted to the dark, the fire in the foreground playing with his vision, twisting what he saw into barely definable shapes. He saw Acorn touch the man's hand, place some of the wood into it. There was something not quite right with the scene. The man looked at the wood, then threw it towards the fire. His aim wasn't so good, and it almost fell short, but then the end caught and it crackled and Acorn laughed and that same deep grunt resonated through the shack.

Calvin made no move. He felt he needed to ascertain the danger before entering. Something about the man's demeanour reminded him of someone, but he couldn't quite place it. Moss had held back. Waiting, stamping her feet. He could see the frustration building in her, but seeing Acorn appeared to be safe tempered his action.

Acorn reached around for another stick. It seemed to be the last one. Again, she threw it into the fire and it split and the smoke billowed outwards. The man's grunt became staccato. Calvin now understood it as laughter.

Acorn said. "All gone. Last one."

The man stood. His movements were jerky, ill-defined. He appeared to be looking around the shack. Then he bent and picked up Acorn in his arms. She laughed, but there were nerves threading through it. The man bent his arms and legs slightly, then threw Acorn into the fire.

She screamed as she fell. Calvin rushed into the shack and pulled her out of the dying flames and heaved her outside. The impact had deadened the fire rather than caught her alight, but nevertheless he rolled her in the snow and after checking she was ok sent her to Moss.

Then he entered the shack.

The extinguished fire actually improved visibility without the flames highlighting the dark. Calvin could see that the man appeared distressed, was looking around as if to find an alternate way out. But there was something else he realised as soon as he had entered the shack. The man was not quite a man. It was a body.

"Hey," he said, much quieter than he thought he would. "It's ok."

The man swung around at the sound of his voice. Calvin could see there was no danger there. He realised Acorn had been thrown without any understanding.

"Sit, please."

Calvin reached out for his arm, pressed down on it and the man sank to the floor. Light darkened within the room. Calvin turned and saw Moss standing there with Acorn in her arms.

"What's going on?"

There was an edge to her voice. Calvin remembered her prejudices, didn't need them right now.

"It's ok. He's just a body. He doesn't mean any harm."

Moss choked back anger, clutched Acorn tight. "He threw her onto the fire."

"He didn't know what he was doing."

"He thought I was a stick," said Acorn.

"That's right," said Calvin, "I saw it. He thought she was a stick."

Moss clenched her teeth. "It doesn't matter. Get him out of our shack." She dropped Acorn to her feet and started to advance into the room. Then, realising she would have to touch the body to physically drag him out, she stalled and sighed. "Forget it. I'm taking Acorn for a walk. Just be sure he's gone by the time we're back."

"But it's freezing out there."

Moss left, pulling Acorn with her. Not knowing if Calvin's response related to them or to the body.

Calvin closed the door behind them. Then sat on the ground opposite the body. He regarded his face. He looked like an ordinary man but there was nothing inside his head. He sat quietly, comfortably; at peace now the ordeal was over. Calvin knew they couldn't keep him – their food supplies wouldn't allow it and he had already killed one of their best layers – yet turning him out into the snow would almost certainly mean death. He wondered where he had come from, if there was any link to the strip of snow-bare road.

"Can you speak?" Calvin asked.

The body turned sorrowful eyes towards Calvin. Something registered there, and the familiar low grunt came out of his mouth; yet it was inconceivable that Calvin might understand it.

"Where have you come from?"

No response.

"Do you have a name?"

No response.

"I want to try and help you." Calvin looked around the shack. He wanted to take something Moss wouldn't miss. Reaching forwards he removed a strip of dried mutton from a line tied across the ceiling. He passed it to the body who took it, sniffed it, and began to eat slowly.

It was a last meal. Something caught in Calvin's stomach.

Where had he come from?

He asked him. But of course there was no response.

But there had been some understanding there. He had played with Acorn. He had watched her throw sticks into the fire and he had copied her. Yet when the sticks were gone he had no comprehension that Acorn wouldn't want to be thrown into the fire. So there was some understanding or learnt behaviour but no conception of danger or consequence. Calvin thought back to the dead hen and shuddered. In retrospect Moss was right. Acorn could easily have been that dead hen.

But then, could she? Had the body been hungry and recognised the hen as a source of food? The Orbitist had suggested that the previous inhabitants of Heart might want to enslave the population as bodies; yet what was the sense in that if they couldn't be coerced to perform simple tasks? Maybe they had a means of doing that which ran against everything Calvin had seen so far. As he watched the body finish the strip of mutton and then slacken its body and fall quiet, without even glancing at the remaining strips hanging from the ceiling, he wondered if that were remotely possible. The bodies were just shells, nothing more. If they were animated it was through natural chemical stimulation rather than consciousness. Yet regardless if they could be used for work – and possibly even worse than that – Calvin could see that, should it be possible, deliberately preventing souls from bodies would in but two generations pervert the tranquillity which prevailed on Heart.

Who knows if that wouldn't happen in Acorn's life time. Would he witness her pregnant and then have her birth a body without a soul. He knew what that felt like. He couldn't bear the heartbreak.

He reached out for the body, intimated it should stand. They couldn't feed it. Calvin had to protect those he loved before extending charity to others. He led the body out into the snow.

Blinking at the white he saw the clouds had lifted. Melted snow dripped off the side of the shack. Moss and Acorn's footprints led away around the back of the property, in the opposite direction to the road. He saw the dead hen. Knew they would be eating well this evening. Again, he felt a twitch of empathy for the body. Surely it couldn't have travelled far without food? There must be a settlement nearby from where it had come. Calvin wondered if they could retrace its tracks, but knew the combination of more snow followed by melting snow would have obliterated the trail. Instead, he led the body up the ridge, progress faster than earlier, until he could view the road from the top.

It remained unchanged: a black strip of unreality set against the white background of snow.

Calvin pushed the body towards it. One foot sank deep into the softer mound on top of the ridge, and the body unbalanced. It rolled over and over down the other side, its clothing picking up snow as it went, like the transition of a stoat's fur from brown to white during winter.

At the bottom of the ridge it lay still for a while. Calvin wondered if he had killed it. If so, it was unintentional, he hadn't intended the roll – only a good shove to indicate direction. Then he wondered if it were better dead. Or at least, better from a quick death rather than through starvation. Then he thought better of himself and willed the body to rise, which it did, eventually, before standing still for some time and then gradually moving away towards the horizon without once looking back.

Calvin sat, uncaring about the wet snow seeping into his trousers. He watched as the body made slow progress out of sight. Despair fought inside him, embroiled against other emotions. He almost wished the Earth people might arrive out of the sky there and then, and put an end to the uncertainty he carried like a stone in his heart.

Hunger made him rise. He returned to the shack, picking up the dead hen and a handful of eggs on the way. Kicking open the door he saw Moss and Acorn had already returned.

Moss looked up, calm now; satisfied that Calvin was alone.

"See, that didn't hurt, did it?"

But it did hurt. Her indifference cut through Calvin as surely as a blade.

9

Winter segued into spring. The division between the seasons mirrored that growing between Calvin and Moss. A slow divide that could only be appreciated once the transformation was complete, with each interstice altering by slow degrees until before they knew it, they were more individual than couple, with Acorn the only bridge between them.

They had eked out enough supplies to survive but Calvin didn't want to endure another winter like it. He escalated their lives through his mind. What would happen when he and Moss were too old to travel? At some point they had to find a settlement that would take them. And what of Acorn, would she remain with them, surrounded by the extended family that they had previously denied her, or would she leave them and continue to travel solely, so that he might never know what became of her.

In those moments, reflected upon in the depth of night when Moss and Acorn were asleep, Calvin saw how selfish his own actions had been leaving Sky and Royce behind. He wondered how often they thought of him, realised it must be everyday. Even if he wanted to return, he had no idea of which direction. It struck him that in an attempt to find himself he had become lost. That sadness seeped into the spring, further distanced him from Moss, yet brought him even closer to Acorn with promises that he would never leave her alone.

Before they left their shack to begin another season of travelling Calvin popped over the ridge to the road. Both of them, but especially Calvin, had kept an ear to the sky since the discovery, but also an eye to the road. For a while Moss was convinced the body would return, and Calvin was content to divert her attention to that as a problem. But for him, the knowledge that a ship might arrive close by at any moment was a worry. If it were the same Orbitist, then Moss might discover the information he hid from her. And if it were something more sinister, then as a family they were too close for comfort.

Nothing had happened, however; other than the slipping away of relations between Calvin and Moss. No longer did they wait for Acorn to sleep before cementing their feelings for each other. Sometimes, in fact, they were asleep before Acorn.

Calvin reached the road, placed his hand on the ground. The snow had long gone, and the road surface was cool to the touch, and dry. He knew something must initiate the heat, but he couldn't fathom what that might be. Rather like the ship itself, which he had no conception of how it might rise into the sky. Who was to say there wasn't something that could regulate temperature under the ground. However unlikely it might be, it had to be possible.

Calvin sat on the surface. Then lay on his back, shielding his eyes from the sun. He closed his eyes. Spring was happening all around him. Birds, which had made a more increasing appearance of late driven inland from the sea, made noises above him; insects hummed like the distant memory of the Orbitist's ship, flowers budded and released their odours reliving memories of previous times.

Calvin knew his position in the world.

He made his way back to the shack. Moss and Acorn were waiting.

"Where have you been?"

"Just checking out the road. It's no longer hot."

Moss nodded. The road had ceased to be of interest to her. "Let's get going."

"Can I say goodbye to the shack?" Acorn's voice was small and light. Calvin knew she hated moving on; the only benefit she saw was being with other people.

"Of course."

Acorn ran back inside. Calvin took the moment to check his shell was in his pocket. He looked across to Moss. A sadness lay behind her eyes, he knew what she was thinking. They were together, inevitably, despite their change in feelings. Within the freedom of their travelling lifestyle they were trapped.

"Which way are we headed?"

Moss jerked her thumb behind her. "We came in that way, we go out that way." Her thumb moved from south to north.

"Couldn't you be more disinterested?"

"Pardon?"

"Nothing."

"Come on. Out with it."

Calvin sighed. "No, it's nothing. I'm tired. We're at the start of a new journey. I wonder if this life is right for us."

Moss attempted a half-smile. "We made this decision a long while ago."

"It's just with Acorn..."

Moss put a hand on his arm. "Calvin. We made this decision a long while ago. That's all there is to say."

The feel of her fingers on his skin enlivened him. In so simple a touch all their interconnectedness came flooding back. He became filled with air, the essence of spring itself; the passages of his heart fluttered in expectation of happiness.

"We can't escape this life, Calvin," Moss sighed. "However much we might want to. Acorn comes first."

Calvin opened his mouth, but Acorn came running out of the shack and launched herself into his arms. The pressure and Moss's words deflated him. He swung Acorn above his head but the pleasure in doing so was diminished. However they continued, he knew it would always be tainted by necessity rather than desire.

Acorn was old enough to carry her own backpack. As they were about to leave she tugged on his sleeve.

"I have my own artefact," she said.

Calvin looked down. She pulled out a piece of wood. It was small and fitted into her hand. "Fire crackle wood," she said, and smiled.

Calvin remembered the body, rolling down in the snow, shambling off into the distance.

"Good," he said. "Keep it. It's a good memory to have."

10

They had been travelling for less than four sun-ups when the sky became heavy with noise and white shapes separated from the clouds and shot overhead, the sound reverberating into the ground, their heads, and their bones.

As one, they ducked; although the ships had been high in the sky. White trails plumed from their rears, as though they were creating the clouds. Calvin's body shook. The ships had gone in the direction they had come. They were of such a height that he imagined they must be heading for the road. Moss gave him a worried look, saw it reflected on his own face however he tried to hide it. Acorn, uncharacteristically, burst into tears.

He pulled her close. "Come on, it's nothing."

"We can't tell her that." Moss bent to her knees, head height to Acorn. "We don't know what it is, but it's going in the opposite direction. We're safe."

Calvin thought *we can't tell her that*, but he held that thought as close as he held Acorn. She recovered fairly quickly, he realised it was probably the noise and the suddenness of the ships which had scared her. It was quickly replaced by curiosity.

"What was it?"

Calvin bit back on what he knew. "We're not sure, Moss just told you that. You see, Acorn, the joy in travelling is discovering new things. We've sometimes seen these things in the sky before, but not for a long time. Chances are we won't see them again for another long time." He released his hug, took her hand instead and continued to walk. "Now, let's get on. We've got a lot of ground to cover before dusk."

He strode ahead with Acorn, Moss at the rear. Calvin knew she was looking back. He wished they could talk, but Acorn was a barrier between them; even if he wasn't sure what he was protecting her from. They should have no secrets, yet he had secrets. He wasn't sure if his knowledge hampered or hindered.

They continued for the entirety of the morning without anything eventful happening. After a while, Acorn let go of his hand and ran ahead. When they sat for a brief meal, Acorn finished hers before them and went off to explore. Calvin could see the worry in Moss's eyes, wondered if it were reflected in his.

"What's going on?"

"How am I supposed to know?"

"I'm worried, Calvin."

"We've seen them before. Further away, I know, but..." his voiced trailed off. He knew he was tempering the situation, but had no reason to.

Moss saw the change in his expression.

"You know something?"

"Know? How could I?"

"I don't know." Moss replaced her unfinished bread into the plastic container. "I feel sick." She gazed across to Acorn, jumping for the lower branches of a tree. "If anything should happen to her..."

Calvin sighed. "We have no reason to suspect there's any danger. This is Heart."

Moss shrugged. "Sometimes I don't understand you." She stood. "Let's get going."

The afternoon segued into the evening and the pattern repeated over the next few sun-ups. Calvin braced himself for the sound of the ships, the roar that preceded their appearance, but none came. The absence of happening lulled security. He pushed it as far as he could to the back of his mind, in the place where his conversations with the Orbitist, and now also Dell and Book were locked.

Their supplies were at a minimum by the time they reached the settlement. Calvin was more than glad to see it. From their vantage point on a hill the shacks were spread out box-like before them; the paths straight. It reminded Calvin of a vegetable patch, with neat lines carefully tended. If the ground view was well-ordered then the sky above it was opposite. Storm clouds pressed dark blue shapes on the horizon, folded in on each other, like a bundle of blankets. Wind whipped the first lashes of rain against their faces; fat drops with promises to come. They hunched their shoulders forwards, into the breeze. As they spoke, their words were caught and carried by the wind.

"All three together?"

Moss nodded.

It had been that way for a while, although during the summer they sometimes alternated. The colder seasons had necessitated shelter for all of them, especially since Acorn's arrival. So far they hadn't been turned away.

They advanced before the settlement, the multitudinous shacks morphing into three as their perspective became closer to the ground, the others lined up behind them and hidden.

A low stone wall enclosed some animals. Chickens, sheep and goats. The cloud had accentuated the dusk, shadows roiled on the ground. Some elders emerged from the shacks, three of them, mirroring the travellers. Calvin had the sensation that they were approaching themselves in a large mirror, slightly distorted, yet somehow them.

One of the elders raised a hand.

"Welcome."

Calvin raised his own hand, trying to hide a smile as Acorn did the same. They had taught her this.

"We are travellers come to tell our tales, may we find food and shelter for the night?"

"You are three?"

"That's right. My partner and our daughter, Acorn."

The elders spoke amongst themselves. Calvin couldn't catch the words.

"This is most unusual."

"We understand. But we have been travelling for over four sun-ups and are cold, hungry and tired. We have stories, one apiece, from the girl too. We will entertain you heartily for food."

Again, the elders conferred. Another one spoke, stepping in front of the group.

"We will take her," he said, pointing to Acorn.

His expression was clearly one of suspicion.

Calvin gripped Acorn's hand tighter. "We can't do that."

Moss nudged him.

Calvin glanced at her, puzzled.

But she wasn't suggesting Acorn should be left; instead he followed the low line of her gaze and saw they were in the process of being circled by other members of the settlement appearing out of the shadows. They held tools, pieces of wood; he was reminded of the elders in his birth settlement approaching the body that they subsequently killed.

There were no options. They might back away, there was still time for that, but they needed the supplies. Going back was just as difficult as going forwards.

"We mean no harm," he said.

The elder in charge didn't believe him.

It happened quickly. Calvin and Moss found their arms pinned by their sides, Acorn was picked up and carried into the settlement.

Moss screamed. In that moment Calvin heard all the anguish and love that she felt for Acorn, and any doubts he sometimes harboured were stripped away. He struggled against his captors but was held hard.

Acorn disappeared into one of the shacks.

The elder who had ordered the assault was grinning, black teeth speckled with yellow that could barely be seen in the decreasing light. Yet Calvin saw quickly that all the elders were not in agreement with what had happened. The first of those who had spoken to them stepped forwards now, edging to the front of the group.

"We don't mean you any harm," he said, echoing Calvin's own words but a few moments ago. "But you can understand our suspicion. These are strange times on Heart and a family of travellers is not usual. We have to be sure who you are."

The elder's discomfort was evident, his confusion also. What had happened, Calvin wondered, to spook them? This wasn't something they did often, he was sure of it.

"My name is Calvin, this is my partner, Moss. Our child, who you have taken into your settlement, is Acorn. We have been travelling together for many seasons, before Acorn was born. Originally we were two separate travellers, but fate drew us together and kept us there. We have never had any difficulties at other settlements we have visited. We have the usual amount of stories and information to share, and we won't over burden you with our requirement for food and shelter. We can be on our way by tomorrow morning, but really need sustenance this evening." Calvin paused, reluctant to add a condition. "If nothing else, please feed our daughter."

The elder nodded. "My name is Greggs. This is Campbell," he gesticulated to the man Calvin was taking an increasing dislike to. "We would like to check the contents of your bags." His voice wavered, clearly not happy in his role.

Calvin glanced at Moss. "Certainly."

The grip on their arms relaxed so that their back packs could be removed. Their contents were spread on the ground. The light had almost completely failed, and Calvin saw no use in their task, other than to wet their belongings in the driving rain. He watched as they ran their fingers through a traveller's usual collection of artefacts and necessities. As they did so his initial anger dissipated. Surely they would see there was no cause for alarm? His stomach started growling in anticipation of food.

But the elders didn't finish there. Calvin felt the pockets of his coat sag and realised hands had pushed inside. As one withdrew he saw a brief flash of white as his shell was removed. Irritation coursed up his spine.

"Have you finished?"

Greggs nodded, apologetically. "It's just that..."

Campbell finished it for him. "I think you should be on your way."

Calvin looked directly at Greggs. "We've given you what you wanted. There can be no fit purpose served in denying us entry."

Greggs glanced downwards, away from Campbell. Tradition indicated that as he was the eldest he had the right of say, but it was evident there was a power struggle happening. Calvin racked his brains for a solution.

"Something's happened," he said, eventually. "Hasn't it?" He looked around the group. "Tell us what has happened."

Greggs opened his mouth but it was Campbell who spoke. "As if you didn't know."

"We don't know..." began Calvin, then tried to duck as Campbell's fist aimed for the side of his head. The blow glanced off his hair. Calvin shook – more from surprise than fear. He looked down at their belongings on the ground, watched the rainwater run rivulets around the artefacts. He tried to still his breathing.

When he looked up he saw Campbell had been pulled back by the other elders. They stood in a group, muttering to each other, Campbell glowering at the rear.

Greggs stepped forwards again. "We apologise for the aggression," he said. "This has gone too far. Please pick up your belongings and follow us. We assure you the child has not been hurt."

Calvin felt the grip around him lessen. He turned and held out a hand. His shell was returned to his palm. He bent down and replaced everything in his back pack, noticed Moss do the same. She had remained silent throughout the altercation, but he knew inside she would be wondering and plotting. He was trying not to think ahead, was taking each new circumstance as it came.

Once they were ready they followed Greggs and the other elders into the shack. Acorn was sat at a table, and looked at them curiously. She was eating hot soup from a bowl. Calvin could almost taste it in the air. His stomach growled again and was pleased when places were offered them at the table and full bowls placed under their noses.

Both himself and Moss broke bread into the soup and began to eat greedily. It was lamb, spiced with rosemary. Potatoes, carrots and celery bobbed alongside the fatty meat in the bowl. It was delicious.

They didn't eat alone. The elders had crammed into the shack, again with Campbell muttering at the back. Around the edges of the door Calvin could make out the faces of children. Candlelight flickered around the room, simultaneously making it seem bigger then smaller than it actually was. Calvin continued to dig in until his bowl was empty. Considering the difficulty they had entering the settlement he wanted to entertain them with a story before trying to figure out what was going on. Even though his hospitality was strained.

Aware that most of the settlement were gawping at the travellers Greggs made a decision after glancing around at his fellow elders, but studiously ignoring the gaze of Campbell.

"Come closer, come closer. We have three stories to hear. Children at the front, elders at the rear."

Calvin wiped his mouth with the back of his sleeve. Moss had finished eating and Acorn had long ago. He stood, wanting to tell his story first. A hush descended in the room. When he spoke, he spun the tale of how he had left his settlement, met Moss, and had Acorn – missing out the death of their first child, but emphasising their history together; wanting to make it apparent that whilst they were unusual, probably unique, they came from the same backgrounds as those who listened to them now. The children yawned frequently during his story, but Calvin was pleased to see some of the elders nodding and their women smiling at Moss. He seemed to have broken through the barrier of suspicion.

Moss spoke next. She told her usual tale of finding the sea for the first time: the immense stretch of water, the noise, the texture of the sand. For these people who lived inland, with only a river as a water source, this story always beguiled. And the youngsters became entranced by her descriptions of the animals that lived in shells, and the spiral indentations made by worms on the beach.

Acorn stood next. She was used to telling stories. Calvin was always impressed by the lack of nervousness in her demeanour and her voice. Usually she spoke of things she had found. What was natural to her was always unusual to others; she didn't necessarily know she was informing them of strange things, but she had a knack of selecting topics that were of interest. Children in particular always paid her the greatest attention. He sometimes considered her as an ambassador for travel.

"My story," Acorn began, "is about something that happened this morning. Four large *things* came out of the sky! They passed over us like birds. It was so noisy, but scary and exciting at the same time. I didn't cry though."

Despite Calvin's horror at the tale Acorn had chosen he couldn't help but smile at her non-admission of her tears. He glanced at Moss and knew she wanted Acorn to stop, but he briefly shook his head. To end the story now would seem suspicious, and for the first time he wondered if the elders' strange behaviour was due to them also seeing the ships. In retrospect, it explained everything.

"Calvin and Moss told me not to worry," Acorn continued. "They said it was nothing. That they had seen these things before. But for me it was the first time! I wanted to see them again!"

She waited, as usual, for the applause which always culminated the end of her stories. The children were enthusiastic, if a little hesitant; whilst the elders only joined in at the end, again confirming Calvin's suspicions.

Greggs dispersed the children and the less important members of the settlement, until standing before them remained the group that had confronted them at their arrival.

Acorn yawned. Greggs glanced at Calvin and a mutual understanding passed between them. Greggs stuck his head out of the shack and called one of the women back to take Acorn off to bed. Moss stood, head down; she had also picked up on the inference in Acorn's tale and didn't insist on accompanying her. From her demeanour Calvin realised that whilst she suspected they were safe, she needed to play the situation calmly.

He wanted to reach out for her hand, for the soft touch of her fingers. Instead he looked directly at Greggs, focussing on their understanding, aware that out of everyone in the room it was himself that knew the most.

The door to the shack closed. Calvin and Moss had stood when Acorn left, now they were beckoned to sit. Three of the elders, with Greggs in the middle, sat opposite them at the table. The others flanked the rear.

"That was an interesting story your daughter told," began Greggs. "It both answered and raised some questions."

Calvin chose his words carefully: "It surprised us," he said.

"But there is truth in it?"

"It was all true," broke in Moss; aware the elders were male and the conversation was directed at Calvin. "Why should she lie? She is just a child."

Greggs turned his palms outwards. "We understand," he said. "In fact, from her forthrightness we now believe that you have nothing to do with the objects in the sky, other than as observers; just as we are. She did raise an interesting question, however. The fact that you have seen these before."

"Have you?" broke in Calvin.

Greggs shook his head. "Our experience this morning was the first."

"We haven't seen them at close range before," Moss said. "Over the past several seasons, even before Acorn's birth, there have been occasional lights in the sky and a couple of times we've seen these objects at a distance, but nothing like what we saw this morning. We have no more understanding than yourself."

"They're lying," shouted Campbell from the back of the shack. "They wouldn't tell us the truth even if they knew it."

Greggs turned to face him. "Whether they know more or not isn't relevant. What we said we would consider is if they were a threat. They are obviously not a threat."

"What if they came from the objects?"

"I think the child's story indicated otherwise."

Calvin noticed the other elders nodding in agreement.

"If they can travel through the air then who knows what else they are capable of. I say we either contain them here or cast them out. No good will come of it otherwise."

"You're in the minority, Campbell," Greggs said. "It is clear they mean us no harm. We will treat them as we do all travellers, as we have done. They have been fed, they have told their stories. They will be allowed to rest for a while and then sent off with a few provisions. You may consider that *casting out* if you wish, the effect is the same."

Campbell opened his mouth, then closed it again. He muttered something under his breath that Calvin couldn't hear.

"May I ask," said Calvin, "exactly what you saw today?"

Greggs leant back in his chair. "Four white objects in the sky. They came low over the settlement. Objects on our shelves rattled and our livestock skittered. Before we knew it, they were gone."

Calvin nodded. "I can see how that made you suspicious of us. Even a solitary traveller arriving after such an event might be given the same scrutiny. I admit that the three of us are unusual."

"Indeed." Greggs steepled his fingers, Calvin could see the control oozing back into him. "Do you have any idea what these objects are?"

"None," interjected Moss. Calvin was glad she stepped in. It was getting late and they needed sleep before they journeyed again. Whilst he had no intention of telling these elders what he knew – especially in front of Moss – he had been unsure if his pretence would hold under the gaze of so many elders.

"We've only seen them at a distance," continued Moss. "Apart from today. We know no more than you. Now, we would like to go to sleep before we have to depart. We appreciate your hospitality and we trust you appreciated our stories, however that exchange is now complete. Unless there is anything else...?"

But her question was closed, her observation final. Greggs looked at the other elders, and besides Campbell who remained unhappy and no doubt ever would, the consensus was that they were done.

Calvin and Moss were escorted to the room where Acorn was sleeping, her face rosy in the candlelight, a thumb halfway out of her mouth. Provisions had been laid out on the floor beside her: a plentiful supply of meat – both fresh and dried – vegetables and spices. A figure of a person, carved out of wood, lay within Acorn's reach. It seemed the women of the settlement had already decided their innocence before the conclusion of the conversation with the male elders and had gone some way to make up for their initial treatment.

Before long, the three of them were sleeping.

They were woken by Greggs whilst it was still dark.

"Time to move on," he whispered.

Calvin stirred himself quickly, used to rising at speed. Moss rubbed sleep from her eyes and gathered their bags together, packing the provisions left for them. It seemed Greggs was the only elder awake; the settlement around them exuded the silence of sleep, a kerfuffle of soft slumber.

Calvin picked up Acorn and rested her head on his shoulder, his arm underneath her legs. Carrying her like this they left the shack, her breath warm against his neck.

Outside dawn was breaking on the horizon – a strip of pale yellow set against the black landscape of the night. The morning was cool, but with a promise of heat to come. Greggs had accompanied them outside. Some of the goats bleated at his presence.

"I trust you slept well."

Calvin nodded, as did Moss. "Thank you for your hospitality."

"You must excuse Campbell. Unlike me he saw those objects yesterday. I can't imagine how it affected him."

"What's done is done," said Calvin.

"Understood."

Greggs raised his hand in farewell, and Calvin, Moss, and the still sleeping Acorn headed in the opposite direction to that which they had travelled the previous day.

The sun was still less than half-emerged from the surface of Heart when they stopped at the noise, and turned back to look at the settlement they had just left.

Initially Calvin thought the glow emanating from the buildings was from the sun's morning caress, but then he realised the noise they had turned at was crackling wood. The settlement was on fire. Small black shadows ran around the outskirts of the shacks. At first appearance Calvin assumed they were addressing the flames, but then it became obvious they were corralling the people, ensuring they remained within the boundaries of the settlement. Moss gripped his arm. He was thankful Acorn was still asleep. They watched – unable to look away – as the flames took hold and the ring of shadows strengthened. Cries flew up like embers, lost in the air around them. At the height of the flames a channel opened in the wall of shadows and the residents of the settlement were forced through it. The shadows had weaponry. Blows rained on the heads of those who passed but it was evident this was preferable to remaining in the flames.

Moss was shaking. "What's happening?"

Words almost stuck in Calvin's throat. "I don't know."

"Could it be Campbell?"

"Unlikely, surely?"

"We should go back." But Moss's words held no conviction. Instead, she added: "Thank goodness Acorn is still sleeping."

Calvin didn't want to look any longer. He had no desire to see what happened to the settlement nor to view the faces of their assailants as the sun continued its inexorable rise. It had started. That thought echoed repeatedly in his head. Everything the Orbitist had told him was the truth and it was coming into action. There could be no doubt about it. The number of the ships, the burning of the settlement, the enslaving of the populace. Upon the entire surface of Heart there might be no escape. Despite the Orbitist's dismissal of their abilities and numbers the happening was occurring in front of Calvin's eyes. He had to make his suspicions known to Moss; but not now. Instead, he turned her away and they moved swiftly forwards, over the next ridge, and out of sight.

"We have to keep going," he said. "Just keep going."

*

Despite the tumult that was behind them, the next few sun-ups were only conspicuous through being uneventful.

Calvin and Moss travelled as though nothing had happened, bearing witness to what they had seen only through their imaginations. They couldn't discuss it whilst Acorn was awake; whilst she slept and dark began to encroach on their surroundings, they found speaking of it abhorrent. Much of this was due to the certainty that they could have no influence. They simply had to press forwards, away from what was alien to them; yet knowing however far they travelled the speed of the objects might overtake them in a moment. To remain unseen was paramount, but this impacted on how they might approach the next settlement they found. Should they assume it to be friendly, might it already have been taken over, or – worse – would they find it razed to the ground. Their supplies couldn't last forever.

If Acorn picked up on the deafening silence she didn't show it. She ran ahead, invigorated by the coming of Spring. White petal flowers with yellow circular spots pushed out of the ground, turning their heads towards sunlight. Trees budded, their branch-tips splitting at the ends like fingertips poking through gloves. In the evening, rabbits were prevalent, their dusky bodies jerking and skittering in the twilight. Calvin didn't have the heart to trap them whilst they had food in their bags. Acorn chased the animals around in circles, and whilst both Calvin and Moss wanted to temper her behaviour they were reticent in doing so against the danger that might be coming. Acorn should have her time to play.

If all this was a burden, then Calvin's knowledge over Moss tripled it. He couldn't imagine what Moss was thinking, how she was assimilating the information. All she had was what Dell had told them: the prophecy of enslavement. Yet whilst Calvin knew so much more, he still didn't know enough to alter anything. The dichotomy of placing his burden on Moss to alleviate his own distress was countered by the knowledge it would increase hers. It was a dilemma he didn't want to deal with.

They camped one evening on a hillside, protected from a light rain by a hollow in the ground, with the wind direction favourably on the other side of the mound. Calvin had already scouted ahead, and seen a settlement apparently intact less than one sun-up's travelling ahead of them. With Acorn asleep, the words they hadn't voiced over the preceding days reached a peak and began to fall out of them, tumbling over themselves in their willingness to be spoken.

"What are we going to do?" Moss said.

Calvin shook his head, gently. "I don't know."

"I mean, we have supplies. We could go on."

"But how long for? We never know how far the next settlement will be."

"Those things." Moss shuddered. "I imagine they can see everything from the air. They can pick out a settlement just as easily as we can identify an ant nest. Just the three of us might not be worth bothering about, but if we become part of a settlement, however briefly, we make ourselves a target."

Calvin realised he was withholding information about the ship's necessity for a flat strip of road upon which to land. Those had to be few and far between, judging from the very small number he had seen. Instead, he tried to play down Moss' fears, knowing it was only part of conversation, the to-ing and fro-ing of words, rather than out of any certainty.

"They came from this direction, didn't they? And that settlement appears intact. We can't make assumptions about stuff we don't know."

Moss reached out and held his arm. "What's going to happen to us?"

Calvin saw the beginnings of tears emerge at the corners of Moss' eyes.

"I'm serious Calvin. What's going to happen to us, to Acorn, to everything? What if Dell was right? What if Book had spoken to this Orbitist and his foreshadowing of life that we know on Heart was correct? How can we fight against that. How can we do anything? They burned the settlement, Calvin. They've forced those people to become travellers, or worse. Maybe they've taken them up in their objects, taken them away from Heart. What might they do to us?"

Calvin pulled her closer, wrapped her in the first hug they had shared for some time. Her body warmth enlivened him, sent love coursing round his body. The simple touch imbued them romantically, and as Calvin wiped her tears away from her cheeks with his thumbs he found himself bending forwards, touching her lips with his, further instilling the history they had between them with the application of a solitary kiss.

Moss held him tighter, buried her face in his shoulder. "I can't lose this," she said.

"I know."

They kissed again, repeatedly; the urgency of their passion revived through the possibility of separation, distortion, even death. Calvin remembered the feeling he had when he had approached the Orbitist: the certainty of his demise. This sensation enveloped him again, now, and substantiated and cemented his desire for Moss. Whatever it was they might have lost over the winter months had come back with a force. They worked their bodies together, searched beneath their clothes, until fingers and mouths connected and accepted and they finally fell apart, satisfied, adrenalin-fuelled, and momentarily happy.

Even so, the black cloud of the future descended over them again, and lying in each others arms, Moss' head resting on Calvin's chest, their conversation turned back to the impending threat; imagined or otherwise.

"Maybe this is our role," Calvin said, "as travellers. To forewarn the others. We have to learn to protect ourselves. To defend what we want as ours."

"Maybe," said Moss. She ran her fingers through the hairs on his chest. "But there's not enough of us, is there? How can we convince these settlements to combine when we have no evidence of what is happening, when we don't even *know* what is happening?"

"Maybe there's not enough of *them* either," Calvin said. "Maybe these incidents will be isolated, will fizzle out. Maybe we should just keep going."

"Maybe. Maybe. Maybe."

"I know. We just have to take each day as it comes."

"And her..." Moss nodded towards the sleeping Acorn. "What does she know of anything. She's so beautiful and innocent. She doesn't deserve this future, Calvin."

"We don't even know what this future will hold. Please don't be negative, Moss. We have to hold onto what we've got."

But already he could tell that the resolution they had found within themselves was wavering. If the past was the land, then the future was the sea. All the certainties that had been assured were behind them, all the uncertainties were ahead. The sea was a shape-shifter of unknowable dimensions and depths. It was foolish to throw themselves into the sea expecting to fall onto the land.

Come sun-up Moss had shifted away from him, either through the vagaries of sleep or with intentional purpose Calvin wasn't sure. But with Acorn also awake, conversation dried like evaporated water. A tacit agreement that they should approach the settlement ballooned between them, and after packing up camp they set off, over the top of the ridge and down the other side, the settlement's visibility decreasing as they reached ground level but the surety of its placement on the landscape embedded in Moss and Calvin's memories.

The day swung by without event. A cool morning gave way to a pleasant afternoon. Again, Acorn skipped ahead, through air flooded with pollen particles and distorted sunlight refracted through dragonfly wings. This exterior sheen belied Calvin's feelings that were once again just below the surface. He tried to shuffle them out, almost succeeded, yet as the settlement began to loom ever closer he realised they would need to be confronted depending on what they found there. And their role of travellers had been subsumed by the need to warn. The stories they now had to tell had to carry more weight and substance than ever before.

Skirting around the issues was no longer an option.

As the blue sky was strained thin and the horizon coloured its edges red, they reached the outer wall of the settlement.

The buildings had been adapted from an existing domicile, that much was clear. Unlike many places that were wood-built, here stone predominated. A handful were two-storey, resembling a mini-city, although the dimensions of the settlement belied that. Nevertheless it was larger than all of the places they had seen since the last time they were in a city, and the scale of it gave Calvin some hope that any defence they might have against those originally from Heart might be sufficient.

As usual, they were met by a few of the elders before they were fully inside.

Their reception, however, surprised them.

"Good evening," one of them raised a hand, "you must be Calvin."

Before Calvin's jaw could hit the floor the elder added, "And you must be Moss."

They had been excused storytelling duties despite the number in the settlement who had crowded around them, obviously eager for a tale. The elder, Nike, led them through some interconnected buildings to one of several small rooms off a kitchen, where the tantalising odour of lamb casserole hungered their stomachs. They ate greedily, the lamb almost melting in their mouths alongside carrots, potatoes, green beans, and swede. Acorn ran her finger around the bowl when she had finished and sucked it into her mouth. Everyone laughed. Calvin realised it had been a long time since he had heard the laughter of others.

Once Acorn was sound asleep, Nike gathered them into another room where a handful of elders sat on soft rugs. Calvin realised this settlement was rich in both foodstuffs and comfort. They must have been lucky to have such a range of gardeners and artisans in their midst. From experience, it seemed some settlements fared better than others, and as they had been formed where they stood and were not populated by travellers then that mix could be fortuitous or calamitous; without much ability for change.

Nike had held back on answering the questions that bubbled from their lips when they were first welcomed. Instead, he had asked for an introduction to Acorn, the only member of their party he was unaware of. He had gathered her up in his arms and then held her aloft, accompanied by much squealing from Acorn and smiles from the other residents. Whilst Calvin thought it strange he allowed it to happen. What was clear was that their reputation had preceded them, and because of this any usual formalities could be foregone.

Now, however, sitting on the soft rugs with a warm fire spiralling smoke through a tube that led through the roof to the outside, it was clear their questions would be answered.

"I expect you're still wondering how we know your names," said Nike. "I've heard of no other travellers together as a couple, so it's nothing magical that you are who I thought you are."

"Understood," said Calvin, "but the presumption is someone *told* you our names."

"Of course." Nike sat forwards, resting his elbows on his knees. "Do you remember a traveller by the name of Book?"

Calvin's heart beat a little faster. His perception of Book had been romanticised over the seasons, and whilst he had tried to force him out of his mind with the belief their paths would never cross, he had found it difficult to totally dismiss the enigmatic traveller who had been instrumental in him starting his own journey.

"Yes," he said, trying to slow his breathing. "I know of Book."

"Book was here," Nike said, "only three seasons back. He advised me if you were ever to attend here that I was to give you this." He reached over and handed a roll of paper to Calvin. It appeared it had once come from a book. One side was torn and symbols adorned the page.

"I don't understand this."

Nike gestured for the page to be turned. On the other side were more symbols, this time handwritten, with lines between them.

"I still don't understand," Calvin said.

"I do," said Moss, looking across. "It's a map."

Calvin looked at her, puzzled.

"My settlement used maps," Moss said, "to pinpoint the extent of our domain. They were useless, really, a hangover from days when presumably they were important. They show you where things are."

"But what does it mean?"

"Book is trying to direct you here," Moss pointed, "from here," she pointed again. "Which I assume is where we are now."

"But why?"

Moss looked to Nike.

"I'm afraid I don't know," he said. "But he did stress the importance. And I hope this doesn't disappoint, but the request is not specific to yourselves. I'm advised to give this *map* to any traveller who passes through. However, it was just with yourselves that Book provided a name."

"He's getting all the travellers together," realised Calvin. "He wants us all in one place?"

"But why?" This time it was Moss with the question.

"I think we can guess why," Calvin said. They exchanged a look.

Nike was about to open his mouth and speak, however Moss suddenly said: "Wait. How does he know my name?"

More confused glances. They looked to Nike.

"I'm afraid this is something else I don't know," Nike said. "All I can add is that Book said he would be very happy if you had a child with you. I was to welcome you both with open arms."

Calvin mused: "Book has been crisscrossing us. He must have been."

"But why?"

"*Why* seems to be the question of the moment," said Calvin. "We won't know why until we find him."

He turned to Nike. "Have you seen any objects in the sky?"

Nike's cheerful expression faltered for a moment and he looked at the other elders for guidance. One of them said, "Not recently. But the lights come and go. We don't know what they mean."

"Did Book mention them?"

Nike shook his head. "We don't discuss them with travellers. We considered it bad luck."

Calvin understood. Sometimes voicing a fear gave weight to it. He held himself in that camp.

"We come with a warning," said Moss, who was less reluctant to face harsh truths. "A few sun-ups ago four of those objects were clearly seen by us passing overhead. We believe they came to land. A settlement we recently left was attacked. Our assumption is that there are people in those objects whose express purpose is to destroy what we hold dear on Heart. Book had proffered a rumour about this many seasons ago, and it appears to be holding true. We have no other information and cannot even confirm what we have told you, but we can find no logical alternative. Our message to you is to be wary of the skies, be vigilant on the ground. The threat is real and shouldn't be ignored or dismissed."

Calvin nodded slowly as Moss spoke. She was right. They couldn't withhold the information they had. This made it harder for him to withhold his own information. Yet he still did so, for now. When they encountered Book he would take him to one side and expand on what they knew.

For it was certain, in his mind and he was sure evident in Moss', that Book was getting as many travellers together as possible in order to share their knowledge. The settlements were isolated, but travellers were gatherers. If there was indeed a threat and if it could be defeated then the travellers might hold the key. For the first time since Dell had spoken of Book's meeting with the Orbitist Calvin felt genuine hope that a disaster might be averted. He could bury the threat all he liked, but what they needed to do was unearth it and kill it.

"Is this true?" Nike was looking at Calvin for confirmation. By the absence of female elders Calvin assumed they were a patriarchal settlement. He disliked the necessity to speak for Moss, but nodded and confirmed the details.

Their conversation continued sporadically – the usual question and answer session between travellers and settlements. Calvin was eager to begin the search for Book, but was persuaded that instead of leaving in darkness they might stay a full night, be breakfasted come morning, and then given the opportunity to tell their stories before they left. It was a fair exchange for the information they had been given, but they both slept fitfully with the anticipation that what had been intimated for so many seasons might finally be coming to a head.

Morning broke like an egg across a landscape painting. Moss rubbed her eyes, confronted the sun that burnt a yellow square through a window and illuminated their bed. Calvin was already awake, sitting on the side with his legs dangling off the edge.

"Where's Acorn?"

"She's having breakfast," Calvin said. "What did you think of yesterday evening?"

Moss yawned. They had gone to sleep quickly, exhausted by the travelling and conversation. "I think we need to find Book and get some answers," she said.

Calvin nodded. He began to pack away the few things they had pulled out of their packs the previous night. He automatically checked his pocket for his artefact, his shell, his eternal link to Book, and was pleased to feel it there. Moss dressed slowly, sleep falling away from her as though she were emerging from water. Shortly they joined Acorn in the food hall who was making friends with other children and telling them impromptu stories. After Calvin and Moss had eaten, they also regaled the settlement with stories. They had quite an audience, perhaps the largest they had ever seen. They wisely stayed away from scaremongering – their information could be disseminated by the elders once they were gone – and instead told of strange landscapes and wasted cities.

As they were about to depart Moss pulled out the map and they studied it as best they could. The directions were clear enough. Book was decamped a few sun-ups away. The line between the camps was marked with drawings of three suns. The direction was clear. Trees indicated the line they should take from the property, and thereafter it appeared they would follow the direction of the sun.

Acorn expressed a reluctance to leave. There was an embarrassing moment where Calvin almost had to pull her away from a hug with another child. She didn't cry, but her face crumpled downwards and she stamped her feet. These instances were increasing, depending on the friendliness of each settlement. Calvin had begun to wonder how wise it was to take a child on the road; yet knew they had no alternative.

The three sun-ups passed without event: no lights in the sky, no sudden noises. They ate well and walked easily in the pleasant weather. The coming of spring, however, still foreshadowed winter.

Each plant that blossomed held the seed of its future demise. Calvin was aware as they walked that despite the outward signs of nature, their destination would lead to a change in the season on Heart, a further foreshadowing of what might well come.

It was the end of the afternoon on the third day that the settlement that they had been heading towards came into view. Calvin was surprised: it was a city. A large, devastated settlement of stone buildings and strewn debris. As they approached they saw a network of roads submerged under vegetation. The city itself seemed overrun by greenery. Trees shrouded the buildings, ivy smothered the brick. The grass was higher here than Calvin had seen it elsewhere. It was almost as if the city were deliberately hidden, although he knew this to be nonsense. Rather it must have been chosen as a centre for the travellers because of this, not the other way around.

Calvin realised his heart was pummelling his chest as they neared what he considered might be an entrance.

As the city sprawled, it was difficult to know where they might be welcomed. Unlike smaller settlements, with clearly defined borders and fewer exits, they had never encountered a city that might be considered populated. Other than the suggestion from the map there was no sign of habitation; yet from experience they knew that within the myriad interior walkways might lead into a multitude of buildings. They might wander for hours without someone seeing them.

He mentioned this to Moss.

"I've been looking," she said; then pointed. Calvin followed the line of her finger. She was indicating one of the tall, tapered buildings that remained standing where some of the other cleaner-brick buildings had fallen. It was similar to the one Calvin had ascended in the first city he had found. As his eyes followed the structure to the top something glinted three-quarters of the way up. He squinted but they weren't close enough for anything to be discerned.

"That's happened a few times," said Moss. "I think there's someone up there. A lookout."

Calvin nodded. It made sense. They continued towards a section of the city that seemed to act as a gateway to the interior. As they neared, the flickering appeared to intensify. Acorn spotted it too, and together they counted the number of times it happened each instance.

There was a sense of anticipation that rolled through the three of them, surging like a wave seen on the beach long ago.

Book folded his hands in his lap. "There you have it," he said. "My story is told."

Calvin nodded. He looked around at the other travellers in the room. There were twenty-six in all. Some of them had been together for many seasons, others were recent additions. Book had assumed the role of leader but had also continued travelling, making sweeps of increasing distance and duration, picking up a few travellers along the way. In one corner of the room Moss was smiling as Dell tickled Acorn's stomach. Calvin was surprised to see Universal had accompanied her. It made sense now that Book had heard of Moss. He had found Dell once again and she had given him that information. Other than Dell and Universal – who strictly wasn't a traveller – Moss and Calvin were the only couple in the room. And Moss, Dell, and Acorn were the only females.

Their reunion had been tearful. Dell had clasped Moss as though she were her own daughter, and then she had hugged a surprised Acorn to her breast as though she were the child delivered that day in the shack. Acorn was pleased with the attention; she made a point of asking each of the travellers their names and beguiling them to tell stories. After Calvin and Moss had been met just inside the city boundary and had given their names, they had been walked quickly through seemingly labyrinthine walkways to the pointed building where they were now ensconced. Moss had been right, their presence had been detected long before they had seen the flickering light.

Book's face was grave when Calvin told him about the settlement that had been attacked.

"It has started then," he said. "When I first heard the Orbitist's warning I didn't know whether to accept it or dismiss it. After all, what could I do? So for a while I did nothing. And then, close to here, a few settlements away from where you met Nike, I ran into Colegate..." he gesticulated to one of the other travellers, but Calvin wasn't sure who he meant "...who had also been approached by the Orbitist. Although whether it was the same one or another who can tell. I increasingly get the impression they go by a generic name."

Calvin nodded, and in hushed tones he told of his experience, whilst Moss was preoccupied with catching up with Dell.

"You know more than most of us," Book said, when Calvin had finished. "So, the likelihood is that Heart will come under attack. Possibly not with some force or with any great numbers, but we are scattered enough as it is and over the course of time should they be successful then I can clearly see how they might rend what little society we have apart. This isn't good news. Let me pass this new information on to the others."

"I don't want Moss to know it came from me," Calvin whispered. "I shielded her from the worst of it."

Book half-smiled. "I understand."

He rose and selected a few of the travellers to disseminate the information Calvin had given him. Moss hadn't appeared to have paid attention to their conversation. Even so, despite discretion, Calvin knew that she would work out those details came from him. How that might affect their relationship was unknown, yet so was the future. For example: what were they to do now?

The entire concept of travelling, of exploring Heart, of encountering new stories and relating them, seemed undermined both by the potential attacks from the original inhabitants of Earth but also by Book's commune. It was evident from conversation that Book expected them to join him permanently, to consolidate the forces that he had, to make regular forays to the surrounding settlements to warn them of the danger, and to create some kind of plan to rout the invaders. Calvin wasn't sure he wanted any of that. And even if he did, did Moss? And what about Acorn? Should they proceed with her best interests in mind, or those of Heart as a whole.

A headache pulsed under his skin around the peripheries of his skull. There were too many unknowns. Calvin realised that despite his love of travelling, of winkling out such unknowns, what he enjoyed were sureties. Even if those sureties were imbued with the unknowns which travelling provided. Through repetition, travelling itself was a surety despite its inherent unknowns. Whereas the big unknowns now presented to him were outside that comfort of travelling.

This wasn't doing his headache any good.

He stood and walked over to Moss and Dell. Acorn smiled at him, the innocence of facial recognition unhampered by the turmoil present in his mind.

"How's it going?"

Dell smiled. "Good. You have a lovely child Calvin."

He returned her smile. "Thank you."

"Dell's been telling me how Book came to collect her," said Moss. "He's been mapping all the settlements since he spoke to the Orbitist, but only recently decided he had to act rather than observe."

"I know," said Calvin. "Listen, what are we going to do?"

"Right now?" Moss yawned. "Get Acorn to sleep and then follow her. We don't have to make any quick decisions, Calvin."

"But should we stay or should we go?"

"I just said we needn't make any decisions." Moss couldn't quite keep impatience out of her voice. Calvin knew it was edged with tiredness. "Let's discuss it another day." She rose, took Acorn's hand in hers, and left with Dell to the section of the building allocated to them when they arrived. Calvin watched her go. His feelings were mixed, as they had been over the past two seasons. Sometimes he wondered if he would be better off without her, without both of them, despite the love that they brought.

And yet other times he knew he would defend them to the death.

Might that not be what he had to do? If he left them, it would be like leaving his birth settlement all over again. And to what purpose? To travel with the shadow of a fight hanging over him. To be unaware of their fate? Even if they returned to travelling as a threesome the future of Heart would follow them. Shouldn't they be prepared, to group together, just as Book intended?

He pushed all the questions out of his mind and joined a group of men that Book had been briefing about his experiences.

Book smiled as he arrived. "Here he is. Our prophet," he said.

Calvin's brow furrowed at the word. The men raised their hands and smiled.

"We've been wondering how best to handle this threat," said Book.

"Until recently I wasn't sure there was one," Calvin replied. He felt compelled to choose his words carefully amongst this group of strangers. The atmosphere was different than those of the settlements where he was viewed as an outsider. Being somewhere where he was considered kin would take some getting used to.

"You said your Orbitist suggested the Earthmen would try to part our bodies from our souls," said one man, older than Calvin but younger than Book.

"Not *our* souls," Calvin said, "those yet unborn. I don't think there's a way to part souls from bodies already inhabited, is there?"

The man shook his head. "Who knows? The more we know the less we know."

Book laughed. "Colegate considers himself a philosopher. Those I have met who felt themselves to be the same always seem to believe in less than the common man."

Colegate shrugged. "All knowledge is theft."

"And," Book continued with a smile in his voice, "they present us with pithy epithets which sound intriguing but which are ultimately meaningless." He gave Colegate a good-hearted shrug. "However, this much is true. We have to assume that we know nothing about these men from Earth. That anything is possible. We have seen their flying machines, after all. But if the Orbitist is to be believed they are here to enslave us, not kill us. Perhaps this is something to be welcomed, and worked with. Calvin, what was your impression when that settlement was attacked? What did you think of their intentions?"

Calvin thought, hard. What happened was they had fled without looking back. He had already told Book this. Was Book trying to embarrass him?

"We didn't tarry," he said, "once it was evident what was happening. Our child, of course..." his voice tailed away.

"Naturally," said Colegate. "No one expects you to fight the unknown single-handed. We would just like to gain an understanding of what we might be up against."

"They had encircled the settlement," said Calvin, "and set fire to it, driving the occupants outside. They were attacked with sticks. That's all we know."

"No other weapons?"

Calvin was puzzled. "They had sticks," he repeated.

"Nothing that actually shot fire?"

Now Calvin was beyond confused. "We didn't see how they set fire to the settlement. I'm not sure what you're suggesting."

"Neither is Colegate, entirely," said Book. "Over the next few sun-ups we'll sit you with each traveller who has had contact with an Orbitist and they will inform you of what they know. If we piece enough together we might find we have one picture. This is how we have been assembling information, all of which has been gleaned from Orbitists, little of which from direct experience. We are in the dark, with sacks over our heads, fighting an unseen enemy. If some of the questions we ask seem puzzling or vague, that is because sometimes we are unaware of the nature of our own questions or even the relevance of our answers. We ask you simply to bear with us, until such time as enough travellers who have met enough Orbitists can tell us all we need to know. If, of course, such a day ever happens.

"What is important, though, is that we get as much information as we can before further attacks occur. Otherwise we remain in the dark whilst fires burn all around."

Calvin nodded. Again, the extent of his knowledge did not prepare him for this. Again, he wondered how much of Earth was lost when Heart was transformed on the Flipside. Again, he realised that it was Book's intention – or expectation – that he would remain in the city with them. Yet he saw that all they might do for the remainder of his days were to seek answers to questions never known.

"Come," Book said, "let me show you something."

He led Calvin away from the group and out of the room, past where Moss and Acorn were now sleeping, and through dark corridors that seemed to fold back in on themselves. When they had been led here Calvin wondered if the building had been specifically chosen for defence. The constantly bending corridors would limit an attack, and the building itself seemed to be in the middle of the city whose layout seemed to mimic its interior. He could imagine becoming confused and lost within the city for days, should he lose track of Book's bustling figure.

Eventually they left the confines of the building and crossed a pathway, skirting hunks of skeletal metal, before entering a similar building with a similar set of corridors. Book's breathing was heavy in the quiet and Calvin wondered about his health. They didn't speak. The darkness and the apparent subterfuge seemed to cushion the need.

"Here," Book said, finally. He gestured towards a room lit with candles around the edges, in sharp contrast to the dark corridors they had been negotiating.

Calvin entered.

He almost recoiled. The room was filled with bodies.

Calvin stepped inside.

He estimated there were at least two dozen bodies in the room; certainly a greater number than the travellers in the building he had just left. They flanked the walls, ropes led from their ankles to poles that fitted from floor to ceiling. Other than being tethered, they seemed to be in good repair. They were clothed, they were silent, and from the bowls and leftovers amassed on a table in the middle of the room they appeared to be well-fed. Having light in the room also indicated the travellers meant them no harm. Even so, the place seemed more of a storage facility than a hospitality area. He turned to face Book, more questions than ever formulating in his brain.

"Just what is this place?"

"I thought you would be interested. These are bodies we've managed to salvage from our recent travels. They had been ejected from their home settlements and left to fend for themselves."

Calvin noted all the bodies were of an average age. None were children, for example. He mentioned this to Book.

"Our assumption is that if a body without a soul isn't killed at birth then until it reaches a certain age it is unable to survive by itself. These must have been held by their birth settlements for some time before being released. For what purpose, we can only guess."

Calvin nodded. He remembered the mistreatment of bodies he had seen. He could only assume some of them had once been held for sport. He thought of the two bodies he had seen wandering and how he had wanted to help them. It seemed that here, with his fellow travellers, he had found kindred spirits.

"You've taken pity on them," he said.

Book's expression was difficult to read in the candlelight.

"We have to ensure they don't get into the wrong hands," he said. "If your Orbitist is correct – and your account tallies with other information we have been given – the Earthmen intend to use bodies as some kind of workforce. Futile it may be, but giving them a head start or allowing them to experiment with an existing supply isn't a good idea. We corral them here and they can't fall into the wrong hands."

"But you haven't killed them," Calvin realised how direct that must sound, but it was true. The travellers had exhibited some humanity towards the bodies that he had found rare on Heart.

A smile flitted across Book's face. "Why would we kill them? It may turn out they are useful to us. Either way, they are *us*. And the more of us there are then the greater chance we have of defeating them."

They turned away from the room and began to walk back to the main building. "Who knows," continued Book, "if the Earthmen attempt to separate souls from bodies at birth maybe there is a way to put them back. We might need these… *receptacles*."

Calvin grabbed Book's arm. "Put souls back?" The idea seemed incredible.

"It's just a theory, of course. But where do you think the soul goes when there is no body to house it? We know what happens to the body – it exists, ineffectually. But the soul is ephemeral. We see them dissipate, but that doesn't mean they cease to exist. Maybe they are just looking for a home."

Calvin thought it through. The logic was there, but it was embedded in fantasy.

"Put it this way," continued Book. "We have all known people who can remember their births. I'm sure you must have discovered that, during your travels; from stories you have heard."

Calvin remembered Levi and Citroen, who in turn had recalled their births, the amalgamation of their bodies and souls, as an explosion of light with a sound like two metal pans being banged together. He had always assumed they had collaborated in their description – how could one remember noise, when querying anything that happened to them subsequently for their first few seasons always solicited vague responses. Yet it was true stories abounded that added to their veracity. If this was the case, then it was clear the soul had consciousness at the point of birth. And if it had it *then*, maybe it had it before then. Maybe it always had it. Maybe it retained it, when the body wasn't there to receive it.

He imagined them restocking old bodies with new souls just as quickly as the Earthmen tried to separate them at birth. But again, wasn't that just a fantasy, speculation?

The burning of the settlement reminded him of fact.

"You're thinking it through," said Book, as they left the building housing the bodies and re-entered the other. "It's plausible, isn't it? If nothing else, it's something to consider when we enter into this war."

War.

Calvin had heard the word before, but he hadn't been able to put it into context. He realised it must have come from a traveller's story, from such a long while ago that he could no longer remember it. But it was there: *war*. And it was coming: *war*. He knew for a fact – suddenly, a blinding realisation – that it was war that had destroyed Earth and created Heart.

Might it not be the case that war might now destroy Heart and create Earth? Flipping them over, like turning a clod of green grass in the earth and finding the underside redolent with worms and bugs. He remembered the Orbitist mentioning The Flip.

"Have any of the other travellers heard of The Flip or the Flipside?"

Book sighed. "It's an explanation given for what no one seems to have an answer for: how Heart came to be. We can see the extent of the previous civilisation all around us; but how it disintegrated is unknown. A couple of the travellers have mentioned their Orbitists talking about The Flip. But it's a useless term for something we will never know for a fact. We could call it anything, and our understanding would remain the same. Like everything, it comes down to what we know and what we don't know. We have to work with what we know."

Calvin nodded. He touched the shell in his pocket. He was glad he had been reunited with Book. And he was proud of the information he had gathered; whether they decided to remain in the city or not.

*

Next morning all three of them awoke refreshed. They breakfasted with the other travellers. A simple meal of bread and milk, prepared by Dell in a room set aside for a kitchen. The mood was good. Calvin realised that a part of him had ached for the familiarity and family to be found within a settlement. If he wasn't careful, he might find himself staying here permanently.

Should the war allow that to happen.

Moss smiled at him frequently between bites. Calvin realised she also craved some stability outside of her tough exterior. Acorn had gulped her food down and was running around the room, asking questions of each traveller in turn. He realised they were providing her with mini-stories. When he overheard Colegate mentioning he remembered his birth as a flash of light he realised it added credence to everything Book had told him the previous evening. Yet there was also another reaction that couldn't have been anticipated. Acorn stood stunned, with her mouth hanging open.

"That's exactly how it happened to me," she said, "the second time. The first time there was nothing but darkness."

Calvin stood bolt upright, as though a metal rod had been passed through his clothing from trouser leg to shirt collar. Conversation had stilled.

"What did you say?"

"I said," Acorn repeated, emphatically, "that that was how it felt to me, exactly, the second time I was born. But the first time there was nothing but darkness."

Moss beckoned Acorn over and sat her between her legs. Acorn's joy at being the centre of attention had wavered now it seemed she was actually at the centre of something important. "You're a special child," she said; choosing her words carefully, her voice low. "None of us here have experienced what you've experienced. Can you tell us again, exactly, what you felt that first time."

Acorn sighed. She was a child of the moment. No sooner had she one thought than it was replaced by another. She wriggled as she sat, suddenly uncomfortable. Calvin knelt down beside her. "Please," he said. "It might be the greatest story ever told."

EPILOGUE

Acorn ran.

The ground under her feet was fleeting, as though she were flying through the air. She could feel her heart pounding in her chest, a fluttering slab of meat opening and closing, pumping blood around her body, giving her the strength to catch the soul. Her breath was fluid, regulated. She had long since learnt the best way to hunt and her body worked in harmony. She was a skilled, capable young woman, and she revelled in her role as one of the custodians of Heart.

The soul – never much more than a glimmer in the air, like a heat haze or the space where a dragonfly's wings had once been – flitted back and forth; darting horizontally, vertically, diagonally, almost without purpose to the casual observer, but for Acorn the movements were defined and easily tracked. She held her soulcatcher aloft – a handmade artefact created from a piece of fire crackle wood bound with sheep's wool, the fibres plucked at the end so they stood proud of the stick, like an old woman's hair that you could see the light through.

Acorn's movements resembled a dance. For those who couldn't see the soul – and these were many – she appeared manic, a leaf battered by conflicting winds, a will o' the wisp, a dust ball. But like the soul her movements were pre-determined. It was less of a hunt than a courtship, and once the soul became entranced and then ensnared by her soulcatcher she would gather it up and jar it and return it to the city where she would select a body for it and its true purpose would be returned.

Her followers watched in a circle, knowing they had to keep their distance and not distract her, yet also needing to be close enough for assistance and within shouting distance should any Earthmen appear by land or sky.

As one, they held admiration for this girl of sixty seasons. Some of the men in the group coveted her, hoped that one day she would choose them to bear her own children; although they knew that for the moment she was content to consider each rejoined body and soul as her brethren and she had no need for closer comfort. Nevertheless, they admired her slender limbs, golden hair, and determination to do the right thing.

The soul twisted a final time against the whirl of the artefact, knotting itself and dropping into the swirl of the wool. Acorn immediately drew the artefact close to her face, breathed a few words of assurance – although there was no proof the soul understood she liked this part of the task – and then she plunged the wool-end into the open jar suddenly provided to her by one of her followers and clamped on the lid.

"There you go," she said. "Another one for the cause."

She remembered the vagueness that had accompanied her own soul's journey between one body and another, the invisible thread that had tethered her to Calvin and bobbed her alongside him, ensuring that when Moss had become pregnant again she had been drawn back into his body and given the nourishment to develop. She would do the same for this soul. And in doing so, the peoples of Heart would increase and the army she was creating to oppose the original inhabitants of Earth would become stronger and more knowledgeable and would win.

She threw back her head, her hair whipping away from her face, and revelled in the life that she led. She had inherited her parents desire for travel; her father's morals, her mother's obstinacy. She knew she was a force to be reckoned with.

And she knew that she had to be.

It was her destiny. Book had once called her father a prophet. But that was only half the story. The rest was yet to be told.

The soul rested quietly in the jar.

Elsewhen Press

delivering outstanding new talents in speculative fiction

Visit the Elsewhen Press website at elsewhen.press for the latest information on all of our titles, authors and events; to read our blog; find out where to buy our books and ebooks; or to place an order.

Sign up for the Elsewhen Press InFlight Newsletter at elsewhen.press/newsletter

The Sundering Chronicles by Mark Iles
I: Gardens of Earth

Imagine an alien life force that knows your deepest fear, and can use that against you.

Corporate greed supported by incompetent surveyors leads to the colonisation of a distant world, ominously dubbed 'Halloween', that turns out not to be uninhabited after all. The aliens, soon called Spooks by military units deployed to protect the colonists, can adopt the physical form of an opponent's deepest fear and then use it to kill them. The colony is massacred and as retaliation the orbiting human navy nuke the planet. In revenge, the Spooks invade Earth.

In a last-minute attempt to avert the war, Seethan Bodell, a marine combat pilot sent home from the front with PTSD, is given a top-secret research spacecraft, and a mission to travel into the past along with his co-pilot and secret lover Rose, to prevent the original landing on Halloween and stop the war from ever happening. But the mission goes wrong, causing a tragedy later known as The Sundering, decimating the world and tearing reality, while Seethan's ship is flung into the future. The Spooks win the war and claim ownership of Earth. He wakes, alone, in his ejector seat with no sign of either Rose or his vessel. When he realises that his technology no longer works, his desperation to find Rose becomes all the more urgent – her android body won't survive long in this new Earth.

ISBN: 9781911409953 (epub, kindle) / 9781911409854 (264pp paperback)

Visit bit.ly/GardensOfEarth

II: A Voice in the Darkness

A gateway and a changeling on a colony world, prompt a return to Earth to confront the aliens.

When children on the colony of Semillion go missing they return changed, the parents even claim they are not their offspring. Sherrif Andrews soon finds himself investigating the bizarre situation. What he discovers leads to him being recalled by the military and sent back to Earth, a place now quarantined and where colonial humans are forbidden to venture. The intention is to recruit ex-commando Seethan Bodell, who's living with the survivors of The Sundering and the mythological creatures that now inhabit the world.

Earth is still ruled with an iron fist by the alien Spooks, but there is something else going on behind the scenes, a new and deadly threat. To succeed, Andrews and Bodell need to call on that grand tapestry of inhabitants: the shapeshifters, elves, the ravening pack of werewolves that Seethan now belongs to, and even the dead; in the hope that it will be enough to prevent an escalating situation that could so easily lead to war.

ISBN: 9781915304575 (epub, kindle) / 9781915304476 (192pp paperback)

Visit bit.ly/AVoiceInTheDarkness

ABOUT ANDREW HOOK

Andrew Hook has had over a hundred and seventy short stories published, with several novels, novellas and collections also in print. Being a multi-genre writer, his stories have appeared in magazines ranging from *Ambit* to *Interzone*. Recent books include a collection of literary short stories, *Candescent Blooms* (Salt Publishing); *Commercial Book* (Psychofon Records): a collection of forty stories of exactly one thousand words in length inspired by the songs from the 1980 record "Commercial Album" by The Residents; and *Secondhand Daylight*, an SF time-travel novel co-written with Eugen Bacon.